"Let me make sure I understand...."

Victoria could barely keep from gaping at Noel. "You don't like me. You don't trust me. You suspect me of being, at best, a St. Clare spy, at worst of being the traitor I'm supposed to help you find. You don't think I'm qualified for the job. And yet you are prepared to take me into your confidence regarding the most sensitive matter the company has faced in decades?"

"I didn't say that. I said I would work with you, Victoria."

She swallowed back a hot retort. "Do you mind if I ask exactly what you expect me to do?"

Noel returned with no hesitation whatsoever, "Whatever I tell you to."

Rebecca Flanders has written over seventy books under a variety of pseudonyms. She lives in the mountains of north Georgia with a collie, a golden retriever and three cats. In her spare time she enjoys painting, hiking, dog training and catching up on the latest bestsellers.

REBECCA FLANDERS

WOLF IN WAITING

Silhouette Books

Published by Silhouette Books
America's Publisher of Contemporary Romance

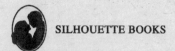

SILHOUETTE BOOKS

ISBN 0-373-51212-0

WOLF IN WAITING

Copyright © 1995 by Donna Ball.

This edition published by arrangement with Harlequin Books S.A.

Visit Silhouette at www.eHarlequin.com

Printed in U.S.A.

CHAPTER ONE

Victoria

My name is Victoria St. Clare, and I am a werewolf. Now that we have that out of the way, let me be quick to point out that you would never know I'm a werewolf if you saw me on the street—or anywhere else for that matter. If you were a man, in fact, you'd probably ask me out; quite a few human men do.

They tell me I'm quite striking looking. I'm tall, five feet nine inches, and slender—one advantage to being a werewolf is that we never have to worry about our figures, what you see is what you get—with long black hair and gray eyes. My ivory complexion is due to the northern climes from which I hail, although I've always suspected a few weeks in St. Tropez would do wonders for my coloring, and I have the high cheekbones, patrician nose and full lips which are St. Clare-family characteristics. Many people—humans, that is—tell me I look like a ballet dancer, which I find enormously flattering. I think human ballerinas are some of the most beautiful creatures on earth, and I sometimes try to play up the resemblance by wearing tights and gauze skirts and pulling my hair back in a chignon.

But I don't want you to think I'm vain. I am, of course—all werewolves are; we're an exceptionally good-looking species and proud of it, but that's not the only reason I told you all this. It's important that you understand that many preconceptions you might have about werewolves are wrong.

For one thing, we don't have hair all over our bodies or have long teeth and claws. For another, we don't eat humans. Most of us, in fact, don't even like the smell of humans—no offense intended, but our noses are exceptionally sensitive. We don't go mad during the full moon. And you can't become a werewolf by being bitten by one; you have to be fortunate enough to be born that way.

What is true about us will probably surprise you even more than what is false. For example, we're listed on the New York Stock Exchange. Oh yes, several of our companies are Fortune 500. You see, the same cunning, skills and extraordinarily adaptive senses that enabled us to survive, indeed to thrive, for thousands of years in a wild and essentially hostile environment have evolved over time to make us kings in a very different kind of jungle: the world of human big business and corporate finance.

Our parent company, the St. Clare Corporation, is the umbrella under which we manufacture and merchandise everything from computer chips to perfumes. We are completely pack-owned and operated, although of course we employ quite a few humans and even sell stocks to them. We're not averse to taking your money or using your skills when necessary, but make no mistake about it: The company belongs to werewolves; it is run by werewolves; it exists solely for the livelihood, ambition and perpetuation of werewolves.

We collect art; we go to the opera; we sun ourselves on the Côte d'Azur. We do business with you; we share cabs with you; we dine with you every day and you would never guess that we're not one of you. Life is simpler that way, trust me.

As for me...I'm in advertising, a junior account executive in the marketing division of Clare de Lune, a very small cog in a very big wheel. Clare de Lune is a perfume company, and it is the foundation on which the St. Clare fortune was built. This shouldn't surprise you. The werewolf sense of smell is approximately five hundred times greater than that of humans. What more appropriate business for us to be in than perfumery? You've probably worn some of our fragrances: Honesty, Ice, Ambition for Men? I know you've seen our television commercials. The one with the man getting out of bed and putting on his clothes in the morning—Wear Ambition or Nothing At All—was my idea, by the way, although no one will ever know it except you, me and the account exec who stole it.

I am twenty-six years old, and I've never had a date. This isn't particularly surprising when you consider that I am a werewolf and most of my friends are humans. Werewolves don't find me attractive for reasons I'd rather not go into right now, and I don't find humans attractive for reasons that should be obvious. Actually, I *do* find humans entertaining, articulate and a great deal kinder than many of my own species, but to *date* one in the classic sense of the word—wherein one puts on sexy lingerie and enticing perfumes and puts clean sheets on the bed and engages in all kinds of other arcane rituals that humans, ever-hopeful, endure for the sake of finding a mate—well, the entire concept baffles me.

As for why I don't attract members of my own species…well, allow me to get clinical for a moment. An essential part of our nature—some might even say *the* essential part of our nature—is the ability to change from human to wolf form and back again. The Change occurs at will, or can be triggered by strong emotion or sexual arousal. We mate only in the wolf form.

Most wolflings are born with the ability to change; all of them achieve it by the time they reach puberty. All except a few genetically disadvantaged anthromorphs, like me. I can't change. In all other ways I am a perfect representation of our species, but for this one little defect I am considered a freak, a pathetic imitation of a real werewolf, an object of pity and scorn.

I learned to accept who I am and live with the antipathy—indeed, the rejection—of my own kind long ago. I'm not embarrassed to talk about it. I can't erase my nature, and I see no point in trying. It is, however, sometimes a lonely existence.

So really, I can't be faulted for finding Jason Robesieur's dinner invitation flattering and for feeling, at this point in my life, just self-indulgent enough to accept. True, Jason is only a human, but he is very pleasant to look at, and among his kind considered a powerful and successful man. In fact, his company had given Clare de Lune reason to be alert over the past few years, and that was no small accomplishment.

Jason is a senior partner in the Gauge Group, one of the top Madison Avenue advertising agencies whose accounts include Sanibel Cosmetics, here in Montreal. I met him at a seminar in New York last year and was surprised and gratified that he knew some of my work. I found him pleasant and interesting to talk to, and since that time we have occasionally met for lunch when he was in town.

Dinner, of course, was an entirely different matter.

We were having lunch then, at an elegant little café that had become a favorite of ours. When he asked me to dinner, I hesitated so long that the moment became uncomfortable, and he laughed a little to cover the awkwardness.

''Say, I didn't mean to cause a life crisis here. It's just

that I'm going to be in town for a few days and I thought..." He shrugged. "I'm not sure what I thought."

I said quickly, "No, it's just that...what I mean to say is, I don't want you to think I'm...that is, I was just surprised."

He gave me one of those very charming smiles. "No one's ever asked you to dinner before?"

I knew better than to admit the truth. So I gave him one of my very coy, very secretive smiles.

"It's okay," he said. "I understand. It wouldn't look good for you to be seen with me. After all, I represent— even if it *is* several times removed—your biggest competitor. And I've heard Clare de Lune is a real stickler about such liaisons."

"The company is more like a family than an employer," I agreed carefully.

That was an understatement. Loyalty to Clare de Lune—to the St. Clare Corporation—is practically a genetic trait. In this one way, perhaps more than any other, we have the advantage over human business. We stick together. We defend our own.

This of course made what happened later all the more difficult to understand. But I'm getting ahead of myself.

I didn't care what other werewolves thought of me, as I'd demonstrated on more than one occasion. But Jason didn't know that, and I found I was glad that he had given me an excuse to decline his invitation. He was diverting enough for an occasional lunch, but what would I do with him for an entire evening? Suppose he wanted to get romantic. *That* would be bizarre. How could I ever explain that I simply wasn't interested without hurting his feelings? No, better to simply avoid the problem in the first place.

Jason nodded. "The Japanese management technique.

Well, there's no denying it works. But Victoria…'' And
now his expression grew grave. ''I've got to tell you,
Clare de Lune might be your family, but they're treating
you like an ugly stepsister.''

I stiffened. ''I really don't see—''

''It's true,'' he insisted. ''And if you don't see, you're
the only one who doesn't.''

I'd been about to say, ''I really don't see that it's any
of your business.'' But, being human, he wouldn't have
understood that his pointing out to me that I was being
badly treated was a worse insult than being badly treated
in the first place.

I sighed. My instincts had been right from the start:
relationships with humans were far more complex than
they were worth.

''Victoria, listen,'' Jason said earnestly. ''I'm a senior
partner with one of the most prestigious firms on Madison
Avenue. I pay more in taxes every quarter than most people make in a year, and I didn't get where I am today by
ignoring the obvious. The fact is that you're one of the
most talented people Clare de Lune has. You've been
working there for what, five years?''

''Six,'' I corrected.

''And you haven't had a single promotion. In all that
time, you haven't played a decision-making role in even
one campaign. That's not the way we handle our talent at
the Gauge Group, I'll tell you that, and you've got to
know this is not the way a bright, ambitious young woman
handles her career, either.''

I smiled and sipped my coffee, sorry our lunch was
almost at an end. Jason might not have much potential as
a social companion, but I did so enjoy these little debates.
''And how does a bright, ambitious young woman handle
her career?'' I inquired.

"She comes to work for me," Jason replied seriously. For once, he left me speechless.

"I mean it, Victoria. I've spoken to Hammond Gauge about you, and he's ready to bring you aboard. Of course you'd start out as a junior, but within a year you'd be managing your own accounts. And we'll put that in writing. In the meantime, you'd be working under my direct supervision, and I personally promise you hands-on decision-making input in every account you work on."

I put down my coffee cup slowly. "Why?" I asked.

He laughed. "I just offered you the chance of a lifetime, the best deal anybody's got since Cinderella went to the ball, and that's all you have to say? Why?"

"Well, thank you, of course," I amended, "but if someone offered *you* the chance of a lifetime—and we haven't agreed that's what it is, yet—wouldn't you be curious?"

"Not if I were you," he replied frankly. "You're good, you know that. You're being wasted at Clare de Lune, you know that, too. You can bring an awful lot to us, and we know how to show our appreciation. What could be simpler?"

I caught the eye of a passing waitress across the room and signaled for the check. "You forget one thing," I said. "I already have a job. And I'm very loyal to my employer."

"You can't be telling me you're happy there."

I hesitated. "I didn't say that. But I am loyal."

The waitress set the check between us. Jason reached for it, but I lifted a staying hand. "My turn. Besides—" I smiled at him sweetly "—we have an account here."

His expression was dry. "Fringe benefit?"

"One of many," I assured him.

We walked to the vestibule together and I waited with

him for his car to be brought around. Jason helped me slip on my long, hooded silver fox coat. Yes, I wear fur. I get cold, okay? It's fake fur, of course. It would be politically incorrect to wear anything else, even in Montreal, and even for a werewolf.

He drew the front of the coat closed beneath my chin, a charmingly affectionate gesture that made me smile. I wondered if he was in love with me, and then dismissed the notion immediately. But that *would* be interesting, and nothing interesting had happened to me in a long, long time.

"I'm in town for the rest of the week if you change your mind," he said.

"About the job?"

"Or about going out with me."

I smiled. "Goodbye, Jason. I had a lovely lunch." I pulled open the door and hurried out into the blustery day.

I stuffed my hands into my pockets and walked the block to the Metro entrance, my head held high and my shoulders back, enjoying the taste of the wind. I wondered what had gotten into Jason. Not, of course, that anything he'd said about my employment was untrue. I was badly used and underappreciated, and I certainly would have a far better future in almost any human company than with Clare de Lune. But Jason and I had been friends for almost a year, and he surely knew me well enough by now to realize I would never leave Clare de Lune.

Would I?

The truth was, it was a fascinating possibility. To live in the human world, as one of them…this was hardly the first time the fantasy had crossed my mind. Even as a child, when all the other wolflings would tease and torment me to tears, I vowed to get even with them. I would show them all. I would run away to live with humans, which was the worst, most denigrating threat I could think of. Today, I practically *did* live with humans, and it wasn't so bad, particularly considering the fact that humans were, in general, a great deal nicer to me than my own kind had ever been.

In fact, the more I thought about it, the more appeal the idea had. All my friends were humans. Jason was right: I had gone as far as I would ever go with Clare de Lune, which was nowhere. And I had *so* much more to offer. But if I worked for a human company...with my natural cunning and imagination, with my enhanced senses and with all I had learned about being the best in the business from the best in the business...why, within five years I could be running any human company that let me get a foot in the door.

And of course, such a thing was not entirely without precedent. Michael St. Clare, heir apparent to the entire St. Clare empire and future leader to us all, had only last year walked away from his family and his fortune to go and live with humans. He had even married one of them. As a group, we were still reeling with shock from that one. And I suppose that knowing how much distress Michael had caused everyone did take some of the appeal from the prospect of striking out on my own.

Still, it was a pleasant fantasy, and I smiled over it during the brief subway ride to the office. Unlike the subways in most major cities, the Montreal Metro is clean, safe and relatively enjoyable. The train took me back to the main business and shopping district, and I did not even have to go outside to reach my office. I followed the underground brick sidewalk past bright store windows filled with colorful displays, then hurried through the revolving door that leads to the elevators for Clare de Lune.

The offices that house the marketing division of Clare

de Lune are like any other in the city, perhaps a little
more expensive, a little more elegantly decorated. We use
only the best, and the company has a great deal of money
to spend. No one would ever know, upon entering, that it
was an office managed by werewolves.

First of all, as I've mentioned, werewolves are not dis-
tinguishable from humans by appearance, except, of
course, that they are a little more handsome, a little more
beautiful and possess, I am told, a noticeably higher level
of sex appeal than the average human. Second, in the
Montreal office, we employ a much higher percentage of
humans than anywhere else in the company. The fact of
the matter is that, although werewolves are superior in
many ways—again, no offense intended—when it comes
to marketing our products to the human world, we are
smart enough to rely heavily on humans.

The support staff and quite a large percentage of the
junior account executives are human. All of the management and senior account executives are werewolves. But
as I said, it looks like any other advertising office for any
other company in any other city in the world.

Before I got off the elevator I heard voices, scraps of
conversation that humans would have no idea I could
overhear even if they had thought to conceal their voices
from me. Did I mention the werewolf sense of hearing is
also several hundred times more acute than humans'? And
mine, without meaning to brag, is in the high range of
normal even for a werewolf.

"Must be something big—"

"You can tell he's important just by the way he
walks."

"Yeah, and that eighty-thousand-dollar limo doesn't
hurt any, either."

"But why was he asking about her? Of all people—"

"Well, he's waiting for her now and he didn't look any too—"

"Trouble's happening, you mark my word. Don't you have any idea—"

"I'm just a secretary, I don't—"

"You might be a secretary looking for a job before this day is over. You know what they say…"

By the time I was halfway down the hall, all the conversations—the interesting ones, anyway—had faded. The werewolves, who would have heard me coming from almost as far away as I could hear them, continued with business as usual, but I did not miss one or two furtive looks from them as I passed. The humans were far less adept at concealing their emotions. Their body language practically radiated danger. Something had happened to upset them, and I had a cold tight feeling in the pit of my stomach that it had something to do with me.

But there was no point in expecting anyone to enlighten me. The looks that followed me from desk to desk, from cubicle to cubicle as I passed made me wonder if I had food on my face, or something equally as embarrassing, and I even managed a quick sidelong glance at my reflection in a glass door—dark hair, fur coat, neat lipstick, no food. The wary looks followed me.

The human secretary who served me and three other people was conveniently not at her desk, so there was no hope there. Fighting trepidation, I rounded the corner into my own cubicle, expecting a "While You Were Out" message to solve the puzzle. I wondered if, in fact, I would like what it contained.

But there was no message on my desk. Instead, there was a tall, blond, gorgeous werewolf in an Italian suit sitting in my chair. His back was to me, and he was on the telephone. His voice was clipped and authoritative as he said, "Yes, all right. And I expect it right away. I'll be at this extension for another ten minutes."

He hung up the phone and swung around in the chair to face me, scowling. I caught my breath.

It was Noel Duprey.

CHAPTER TWO

Noel

You wouldn't know me—not unless you are a king, minister or mogul in the world of human business and finance...or perhaps a fashion model or a rock singer or another member of the beautiful, fun-loving set with whom I used to roam. And even then you wouldn't really know me. You wouldn't know what I am.

My name is Noel Duprey. I like my music loud, my cars fast and my women leggy. I hate carrying a briefcase. Until six months ago, I was vice president in charge of research and development of Clare de Lune Perfumes, and I ran my division in accordance with my personality—brilliantly, creatively and with a great deal of laissez-faire.

It may surprise you to know I held a position of such responsibility, but I come from a family of high achievers. I was also, if I may say so, a very good chemist and an inspired researcher; no one gets to be a vice president in the St. Clare Corporation without demonstrating exceptional ability.

The fact that I could have achieved so much so young and still have time left over for the indulgent life-style I so enjoyed is not unusual among our kind. What we do, we do very well and with a definite flair.

I applied myself and I was pleased with what I had achieved. I had a secure future, high status and just enough responsibility to keep me from growing lazy. I even had hopes of one day becoming second-in-command to Michael St. Clare, who was heir to the entire St. Clare empire.

Instead, *I* am now heir to the empire, and I'm sometimes still not entirely sure how it happened.

Until six months ago, my life was perfect. I had a job I liked and excellent prospects for advancement. I had a fabulous town house in London and a black Ferrari. I worked maybe three days a week, and let me assure you, when I gave a party it wasn't the kind where anybody worried about which fork to use. I climbed the Matterhorn. I raced the Grand Prix. I spent weekends on the Riviera, where even now, in the midst of all this craziness, memories of a certain nude beach can put a smile on my face that no one else can understand.

I still have the town house, of course, though I never see it. The Ferrari is gathering dust in a garage somewhere, for now I'm chauffeured around in a Rolls with no less than two bodyguards everywhere I go. The Riviera is a thing of the past. The Grand Prix? Forget it. I'll be lucky if I get a chance to watch it on television. And now I carry a briefcase wherever I go.

I once had something of a reputation as a playboy—or playwolf, if you will—and why not? I'm only thirty-two years old, which is young among our kind. I had plenty of time to settle down. Or so I thought.

I never lacked for female companionship, and taking advantage of that fact was one of my primary leisure activities. To those unfamiliar with our nature, this may be shocking, but I assure you, in comparison to the way the human world conducts its courtship rituals ours are practically sedate.

We mate for life, and take the matter of finding a suitable companion very seriously. The physical consummation of the love of two werewolves for each other always takes place in wolf form, and results in a telepathic and empathic bond that only death can break. This does not mean, however, that a variety of sensual pleasures cannot be enjoyed in human form between consenting males and females in the meantime, and I have done my best to discover them all. After all, how is one to know when the right woman comes along if one isn't willing to look with an open mind?

But that was then. These days I am far too busy to have much energy left over for recreation of any kind. And besides, as I am constantly reminded by everyone around me, I have a certain image to uphold.

Sometimes I'm not at all sure I was cut out for this life.

For over four hundred years, the pack has been ruled by the St. Clares, and without great complaint. Sebastian St. Clare, our present venerable ruler, is well liked, as far as I can ascertain, and certainly well respected. His son Michael was scheduled to succeed him, and we as a people looked forward to another hundred years or so under peaceful St. Clare rule.

Then Michael St. Clare fell in love with a human woman, and everything changed.

Oh, yes. It's shameful but it's true. And I, in my efforts to bring Michael back to his senses—he is my cousin, after all, not to mention that I was under orders from no less than Sebastian St. Clare himself—only made matters worse.

A centuries-old rule of succession was invoked requiring the two of us to do battle for the throne—a battle to the death. Every werewolf in the empire was there at the amphitheater at Castle St. Clare to witness it, cheering us on, and what was I to do? I never wanted to fight Michael

St. Clare. Hell, he's twice the werewolf I'll ever be. I'm lucky he didn't kill me.

But…and this is where I still have difficulty believing it…not only did Michael not kill me, he forfeited the battle, and the throne, to me. Sometimes I wonder how history will remember that moment; already I see it being rewritten by those who, to honor me, I suppose, forget that it was Michael who first bared his throat to me. They remember only that I refused to kill him when it was my right, and even brought him under my protection when the keys to the kingdom, so to speak, were mine.

So that is how I came to this position of great importance. Accidentally, unwillingly, and, some say, unfairly. As for *what*, exactly, my new position is…well, that's still a matter of some debate, particularly in my own mind. Michael St. Clare, the natural heir, is alive and well and living as a human in Seattle. Sebastian St. Clare still rules us all firmly and fairly from Castle St. Clare Alaska. And I, the heir designé and newly named CEO of the St. Clare Corporation, spend a great deal of time flying from one city to the other, attending meetings, plowing through great tomes of corporate documents and scanning gigabytes of computer data…but doing, for the most part, nothing at all. I haven't been in a research lab in months. Some new man has taken over my office at R & D. The things I knew and enjoyed are all behind me. What lies before me is anyone's guess. Like the human Prince of Wales, I suppose, I am little more than a man in waiting.

As for what I was doing here, in the cramped little cubicle of the most junior account executive in our Montreal office…well, my head was still spinning. The phone call had come in the middle of the night less than forty-eight hours ago, putting me on the corporate jet for Alaska almost before my eyes were open.

My first clear memory of that flight was of Castle St. Clare, erupting in all its Gothic magnificence from a cloud of mist and ice fog like a well-planned miracle. I love that first view of it from the air, and whenever I think of home that's how I see it. Carved into the side of an ancient mountain in one of the most rugged, isolated parts of Alaska, the castle has been a fortress for and a monument to our kind from time immemorial. The sight of it never fails to take my breath away.

By that time, we had transferred to the helicopter, for Castle St. Clare is accessible only by air in winter. The whole way, we fought wind sheers and temperatures that were minus twenty in calm winds, and no one but a werewolf pilot could have made that landing safely.

Even under the uncertain circumstances, I was glad to be home. I had been born here, spent much of my childhood here, and even after my education at Oxford and the assumption of my position within the corporation, I never missed a clan gathering or a birth celebration or even a board meeting if it meant a chance to come home. My roots were here, and even covered in ice, battered by killing winds in twenty-below temperatures, it called to me. Always before, I had answered that call with a light heart.

But these days when I returned home, I did so as the heir designate to the entire St. Clare empire, the man who would one day assume the cloak of responsibility for the financial, personal and moral well-being for every werewolf, dam and wolfling in the clan. There were many who were uneasy with that concept. Sometimes I myself was among them.

The helicopter pitched and dropped several times on its way to the freshly cleared landing pad atop the tallest roof of the building. The blades whipped the surrounding snow into a blizzard-like frenzy that pelted the bubble of the helicopter and reduced visibility through the clear panels to zero. I knew we were on the ground when the floor stopped pitching and the sound of the blades was reduced to a mere ear-shattering whine. The pilot grinned over his shoulder and gave me the thumbs-up. I pulled on my coat.

Within seconds of stepping out into the icy air, I was surrounded by a phalanx of guards. Some of them veered off to retrieve my luggage. One of them took my briefcase and shouted, "Welcome home, sir," while the others formed a living circle around me, shielding me from the wind, escorting me toward the door a few dozen yards away. They walked quickly, heads down, mindless of the ice-slick stone beneath their feet. Surefootedness is another advantage werewolves have over humans.

The warmth of the building was a shocking, if welcome, contrast to the bitterness outside, as was the silence of the carpeted corridor after the roar of the wind and the screech of the chopper blades. Though I had only been exposed to the elements for a few moments, my skin was chapped and my coat was stiff with cold.

Had I been in wolf form, of course, I would not have suffered any of those discomforts. In our natural state, we are all perfectly adapted to this environment.

"Do I have time to freshen up?" I asked, pulling off my gloves.

"I'm afraid not," the young man who had taken my briefcase replied, "He's waiting. However," he added, as though hopeful of making up for bad news, "there's a bottle of very good Madeira waiting in your quarters, and we're having salmon cakes for tea."

"Well," I murmured, more to cheer my companion than myself, "that's something, I suppose."

The elevator was waiting. Three of the highest-ranking

bodyguards stepped in with me; the others took the service elevator with my luggage.

There was no reason to assume, of course, that any of this meant bad news. The abrupt summons, the short deadline, the air of urgency...Sebastian St. Clare was a man who was accustomed to having his orders obeyed and having them obeyed immediately.

In the past six months, I had received exactly this kind of summons no less than eight times, and each meeting, it seemed, had been more unpleasant than the last. I was beginning to suspect our esteemed leader was enjoying the power he held over me. One thing was certain: Sebastian St. Clare would never let me forget that I had come into my position by accident, not by right.

The elevator covered the twenty floors in as many seconds. I had reason to wish, as I almost always did these days, that the castle was not equipped with quite so much technical sophistication. It seemed to me that everything was moving too fast lately.

We stepped out into the corridor. Lushly carpeted in royal blue, paneled in gold-tipped mahogany, this part of the complex was, in fact, the heartbeat of the corporate headquarters. I was relieved. If the meeting was to take place in a business environment, at least it would be on a level I could understand.

I took off my coat and handed it to my escort as we started down the hall. The muted chirrup of telephones and the hum of office machinery from behind heavy paneled doors were the only sounds that accompanied our passage, though if I tried, I could hear the conversations that were taking place over those telephones—on both ends of the line. My hearing, even by werewolf standards, was superior.

I wasn't interested in eavesdropping, however, and I

was too anxious about this visit to play games. I said to my escort, "I don't suppose you have any idea—"

The young man shook his head. "I'm sorry, sir. I've only just been assigned to this level. I promise I'll be more prepared next time."

One corner of my mouth turned down dryly. I was quite certain that, by the next time I was called home, this co-operative young man would be reassigned. One of Sebastian's favorite tricks was to continually reassign my personal assistants, just to keep me on my toes…or off guard, as the case might be.

We reached the set of tall double doors at the end of the corridor. The inner sanctum. I took a breath, straightened my tie, and ran my fingers through my long blond hair, correcting what the wind had mussed. I held out my hand for my briefcase.

The young man handed it to me, then seemed to hesitate. I glanced at him.

"Sir," he said, looking tense and uncomfortable. "I just wanted you to know that…well, there are quite a few of us who think it's time for a change, and we're behind you. Sir."

Some of the tension went out of my shoulders, and I smiled. "Thanks," I said. "That's good to hear."

But there was no way to postpone it any longer. I straightened my shoulders, and opened the door.

The Keeper of the Gate—as I like to refer to her with a certain dry sarcasm, and then only in my secret thoughts—was built like a battleship in shades of iron gray, with a beak of a nose and jet-black eyes and an angular, jutting bosom that could intimidate the strongest man. Her official title was administrative assistant to Sebastian St. Clare, but I did not know a werewolf in the empire who would care to take her on in battle.

She did not like me. She had made that clear from the beginning.

However, protocol dictated that she get to her feet when I entered, and she did not defy it. "Sir," she said. Though the greeting might be interpreted as deferential, the tone never could. If anything, in fact, there was a glint of disdain in her coal black eyes. "Good afternoon. You are expected."

I refrained from replying that, since I had been awakened at 3:00 a.m. with a royal summons and had been traveling for almost ten hours, I certainly hoped so. Instead, I inclined my head and replied pleasantly, "Ms. Treshomme. You're looking lovely as always."

She did not bother to disguise a contemptuous sniff as she came around the desk and crossed to the inner door. She knocked once and opened it. "Monsieur Duprey," she announced, and stepped aside to let me enter.

I took another breath and straightened my cuffs, refusing to be rushed. I adjusted the weight of the briefcase in my hand, gave Ms. Treshomme my most charming smile and stepped inside.

No one from the human world had ever been here, of course. If they had been, they would have been astounded. Where once the castle had served as a fortress to defend its occupants from their enemies and shelter them from the elements, it was now a showcase for the enormous success we had achieved. On one wall was a simply framed postimpressionist canvas worth approximately five million dollars. On the other was an undiscovered Matisse whose value was incalculable. The carpet on which I trod was Persian and over nine hundred years old. The enormous glass pedestal desk in the center of the room was actually a sculpture by an artist who was at this moment exhibiting at the Metropolitan Museum of Art, New York.

Glass shelves, expertly lit, displayed artifacts and objets d'art whose age ranged from a few hundred to several thousand years old. Long ago, in times mostly forgotten, Castle St. Clare had been a sanctuary against outside persecution. Now it was an unabashed showcase of our triumph over the outside world.

The focal point of the office was a floor-to-ceiling window that looked out over a breathtaking vista of snow-shrouded mountains and windswept plains. Before that window with his back to me stood Sebastian St. Clare.

He was a big man, wide-shouldered and tall, with a magnificent mane of full white hair that fell below his shoulders. He was dressed in woollen pants and a fur vest with rawhide catches. As always, I felt overdressed and underprepared in his presence.

The elder werewolf certainly heard my entrance, but he chose not to acknowledge it for a full two minutes. I stood in the center of the room and waited.

When Sebastian St. Clare turned, there was no welcome in his face, or his voice. "You're late," he said flatly.

I replied pleasantly, "Good afternoon, Grand-père. You're looking well as always."

"Which must be a grave disappointment to you, my heir."

There was no acceptable reply for that.

Sebastian glared at me for a long moment beneath bushy, iron gray eyebrows, then gestured abruptly toward a wine-colored leather chair that was drawn up before the desk. "Sit down," he said. "We have some things to talk about."

Sebastian St. Clare was a legendary leader of strong and certain convictions. His shoes would be difficult to fill even without the twisted circumstances that had led to my succession. However, the task would have been a great deal easier had Sebastian made even the smallest effort to ease the transition for me, or at the very least, to make me feel welcome.

I glanced at the leather chair Sebastian had indicated, then deliberately chose the tapestry divan that formed part of an informal conversation group before a dancing, crackling fire. Keeping my expression determinedly pleasant, I placed my briefcase beside me and stretched my fingers toward the fire, warming them.

"To tell the truth," I said, "I was glad to get your call. London is deadly dull this time of year. The weather is frightful, the streets are someone's idea of a bad joke and I'm afraid the theater season is shaping up to be another disaster. It's good to get away."

Sebastian made no move to join me before the fire. He simply fixed me with that great, glowering gaze for several long moments. Meeting those powerful eyes without wavering for such a long time was a matter of physical effort for me, as it would have been for any other werewolf. Of course, no other werewolf would have dared try.

Sebastian said, "You are very clever, aren't you, Noel? I have relied upon your cleverness to deal with many a delicate problem over the years. Your solutions have always been—shall we say—inventive. One can't help recalling, for example, the solution you devised for bringing my son back to me when he was suffering from amnesia and lost in the world of humans."

My jaw knotted. This was the first time Sebastian had referred directly to the incident since it had happened. I could not help thinking that his doing so now represented some sort of test, but then, it seemed to me everything Sebastian did where I was concerned was a test.

I replied evenly, "It worked, didn't it?"

The faint softening of Sebastian's expression might

have been amusement, or simple surprise for my audacity. He said, still watching me, "So it did."

I went on, choosing my words carefully, "I think it's important to remember that Michael chose to leave his life here. If I hadn't brought him back the way I did, he never would have returned. If I hadn't challenged him, he would have abdicated."

Sebastian moved from the window to the fireplace with measured steps. He gave no reply. I hadn't expected one.

The older werewolf stood with his hands linked behind his back, gazing into the fire for a moment. Then, without turning to look at me, he said, "We live in troubled times. You'll have to learn to deal with those troubles if you expect to lead our people when I'm gone."

At last, I thought. *Something to do.*

Finally it sounded as though Sebastian was actually considering giving me some real authority, an assignment to carry out, a responsibility of my own. It didn't matter what it was, as long as it was something that would allow me to act as a second-in-command should, to prove my worth and my usefulness. I would do anything.

Or at least that was what I thought until Sebastian went on.

"You know, of course, about the trouble in New Orleans."

I nodded. Everyone knew about that. It was the most shameful thing that had happened to our kind in centuries. One of our own had gone renegade and had actually started killing humans, one a month for the past eight months, each killing coinciding with a full moon. Already, human reporters were calling him the "werewolf killer." What might happen if they knew how close to the truth they really were?

"He has to be stopped," Sebastian said matter-offactly, "and it's plain the human world will not be able to do so. Little surprise. They can't even control their own lawbreakers. No, this renegade is our responsibility. We will have to intervene to save both our worlds from further damage...and to preserve the peace we've kept with humans for all these thousands of years."

My throat went dry as I thought I understood what my assignment was to be. My tracking skills were only fair, but as Sebastian himself had pointed out, I was extremely clever. Could Sebastian mean to send me after this killer? I was not short on courage, but I had no desire to commit suicide. And if someone as unqualified as I should take on such a task, that was exactly what it would be.

On the other hand, if Sebastian wanted to get rid of me, there could hardly be an easier way.

And then Sebastian said, "However, that is not your concern, except to know that it's been dealt with...and not to complain," added Sebastian with a wryness so subtle that it was almost overlooked, "that the current administration is not keeping you abreast of the situation."

I was so surprised at my narrow escape—and so relieved—that it was a moment before I could focus on the next part of Sebastian's statement.

"What has not been nearly so well publicized among us," he went on, "and what you doubtless don't know, is that there is a far greater threat within our ranks than this renegade human-killer. One which strikes, you might say, a great deal closer to home."

He turned from the fire then, hands still clasped behind his back, and addressed me directly. "Over the past four months, Clare de Lune has lost the formulas to three of our newest products—MA471, SR389 and DL400. In addition, we've had to pull production on Tango and Cobalt because, quite simply, our competitors beat us to them."

I felt the color drain from my face. I was on my feet. "What? Why wasn't I informed?"

Sebastian made a small decisive movement with his wrist that gestured me back into my chair. I resumed my seat reluctantly, my hands tight on the arms of the chair.

Sebastian said, "The truth only came to light a few weeks ago. Since then, we've made a concerted effort to keep the knowledge of the fiasco as limited as possible. The more people who know about it, the wider the circle of suspects. However, the details have been uploaded under your access code now."

Because of the enhanced sense of hearing we all share, it is difficult to keep a secret in the werewolf community. Matters of security were therefore routinely handled through the written word, or these days, via computer. Not that security itself had ever been much of a concern among us, for pack loyalty is one of the few absolutes we hold sacred. We all work for the same company. We all share the same profits. Clare de Lune Cosmetics—and, by extension, the St. Clare Corporation—was not only our livelihood but our *life*. Why would anyone betray it? And more important, who?

As though reading my thoughts, Sebastian said, "We've been able to do some eliminating, and we think we have the source of the leak narrowed down to the Montreal office."

Some of the tension went out of my shoulders and I thought, *Of course*. The Montreal office housed the marketing and advertising division of Clare de Lune and it was staffed more heavily by humans than any other department. Although quite a few humans were employed in various capacities by the St. Clare Corporation, only in advertising were they actually able to rise to positions of authority—and confidence. And humans were infinitely corruptible, their loyalties easily purchased.

Of course, if a human employee had committed this perfidy, some werewolf was still accountable. That disturbed me deeply. How could anyone be so careless?

Sebastian watched the changing expressions on my face with detached interest, following the line of reasoning as it was reflected in my eyes. Then he said, "There's more."

He crossed to his desk and opened a drawer. He returned in a moment with a crumpled scrap of paper that looked as though it had been torn from a larger sheet. He handed it to me.

It was—or had once been—a sheet of office stationery. Most of it had been torn away, so that only scraps of words were visible in most places, and no identifying telephone numbers or names remained on the letterhead. Two consecutive sentences remained intact, however, and they were enough:

What I've given you so far is nothing, the real secret is how they do it. There are things about these people—if *people* is even the right word—that are difficult to believe, even for me.

I looked up slowly, frowning. "It sounds as though the writer is talking about..."

"Knowledge of our true nature," Sebastian supplied. "And he—or she—seems to indicate a willingness to share that knowledge."

"But that would be foolish. No human would believe what we are even if they were told. What point would there be in telling such a secret?"

Sebastian shrugged. "There are those who believe a

secret worth keeping is also worth telling—or selling, as
the case may be. At any rate, such a thing is simply unacceptable. Whether or not the truth would be believed is
immaterial. It will not be allowed to reach that point.''

I murmured, ''No, of course not.'' I was examining the
paper. ''How did this happen to be found? Why wasn't it
mailed?''

A spark of appreciation glinted briefly in Sebastian's
eyes, and I felt like a schoolboy passing approval on my
observational skills.

''It was in the trash bin of the fax room at the Montreal
office,'' Sebastian answered. ''Apparently, the sender attempted to destroy it after faxing the message, but wasn't
entirely successful. He should have used the shredder.''

''Doesn't the machine keep a log we could check?''

''Of course. But hundreds of faxes go out of that office
every day, many of them to competitors. Without knowing
exactly when this particular message was received, we
have no way of tracing it.''

''Which one of our competitors, I wonder, has been the
lucky recipient of our trade secrets?''

''An interesting question, actually. Two of our formulas
went to two different companies, one we haven't been
able to definitively trace yet, and the other two went to
Sanibel Cosmetics. That doesn't preclude one company's
buying all the formulas and selling off those it doesn't
want. Interestingly enough, Sanibel's corporate headquarters are in Montreal.''

I studied the half-torn paper again. It did not necessarily
mean what it implied. It didn't really even mean that the
author of this letter was the same person who had been
selling secrets to the outside. But it was certainly enough,
with all the other circumstantial evidence at hand, to narrow the search to the Montreal office.

It was then that I realized there was something I had overlooked. I looked up at Sebastian.

"If it's a human, if he's somehow managed to get his hands on these secrets, and if he's even by some incredible stretch of the imagination managed to piece together enough information to speculate on our true identity, how could he possibly have avoided detection? This human is surrounded by werewolves at least eight hours a day. Unless the Montreal office is completely staffed with incompetents, how has he avoided detection?"

Again, the faintest hint of approval in Sebastian's eyes, even less than a pat on the schoolboy's head.

He said, "Only a werewolf can hide from a werewolf—and then only with great difficulty. If these were the actions of an ordinary human, I should think someone would have heard or smelled or seen something long before now."

"So you're saying it is one of us, after all." My tone was flat, devoid of emotion. But what I felt was a slow cold rage, a roiling contempt, a furious sense of shame and betrayal that one of our own could stoop so low. The traitor had to be rooted out, destroyed like a blight on a shrub before it did any more damage. He deserved no mercy.

"It does seem logical. Did you have another thought?" Sebastian asked.

I hesitated, hoping that my next words wouldn't sound as badly motivated as they felt. I said, very carefully, "When did you last speak with Michael?"

The older man was a master at concealing his thoughts, and he betrayed neither surprise nor outrage. "Last week, I believe. He may no longer be my heir, but he is a dutiful son." The words *whose loyalty to the pack is unquestioned* remained unspoken.

But I pursued the issue, "He's doing well, then?"

"By some standards, I suppose. He's working with humans, building houses for them."

I managed a smile. "We'll be awarding him major industrial contracts before the year is out."

"Most likely," agreed Sebastian without a flicker of humor.

"And his wife…"

"The human," supplied Sebastian. Again, his distaste was carefully disguised.

"Yes. Agatha, isn't it?"

"They seem to be very happy."

"They probably have no secrets from each other."

"Probably not."

"You might want to check," I concluded with care and deliberation, "whether either of them has been to Montreal lately."

And Sebastian replied, with equal deliberation, "I think I'll let you do that."

I remained silent, not daring to speculate on what this might mean.

"There has never been a ruler who hasn't faced at least one crisis that threatened the very survival of his people. I needn't point out that this matter could do just that. I therefore suggest, for the sake of your regime and the future of all our kind, that you deal with this problem as quickly and efficiently as possible," Sebastian said.

I stood slowly. I couldn't entirely control the leap of excitement in my pulse and I was sure my elder heard it, but I didn't care. "Are you putting me in charge of the situation, then?"

"You will have complete responsibility. I expect to be kept apprised of your plans, however, and to be kept current on developments."

"Yes, of course." Already my mind was racing, devising schemes, formulating battle plans. "But I shall have complete freedom in dealing with the matter?"

Sebastian made a small dismissive gesture with his hand. "I have other concerns," he said gruffly. "I can't be everywhere at once."

And then I understood the full significance of what was happening. Sebastian, pressed by the troubles in New Orleans and having recently lost his right-hand man—Michael—had turned to *me* to handle this most delicate and dangerous problem within the company. That had to mean something, didn't it? This was not just a token assignment, or a test. This was the kind of responsibility that would only be given to someone Sebastian trusted, in whom he had confidence to solve the problem.

Sebastian was relying on me. Perhaps that meant that, after all this time, the older man was coming to accept me as his heir.

I inclined my head. "I shan't disappoint you, sir."

Sebastian scowled. "For your sake, I should certainly hope not."

I reached for my briefcase. "I'll leave for Montreal in the morning. Is there anything in particular I should familiarize myself with before I arrive?"

"It's all on your computer. If you have any questions, I'm sure Victoria will be able to answer them."

Already a dread I could not quite define was creeping to my stomach. "Victoria?"

"Victoria St. Clare. She's an account executive in the Montreal office. You'll be working with her. Didn't I mention it?"

St. Clare, I thought. *I should have known.*

I kept my face expressionless. "No, sir, you didn't. In exactly what capacity will we be working together?"

The slight arch of Sebastian's eyebrow was almost imperceptible. "In every capacity."

"I understood you to say I would be in charge of this operation."

"And so you will be. You should look upon Victoria as...a partner."

I translated, *Spy.*

"Surely you'll agree with the wisdom of having a confederate in the enemy camp."

I nodded stiffly. "Of course. I should have thought of it myself."

Sebastian almost smiled. "Yes. You should have. You'll report to her as soon as you arrive, then."

"Of course."

"Very good. That will be all for now. We expect you for supper. My wife sends her greetings."

I barely managed a polite reply and a gracious bow as I left the room.

I didn't know why I was surprised. I should have expected a trick like this from Sebastian. But if the older man expected me to be defeated or distracted by it, he was to be greatly disappointed.

I had a job to do, and I would get it done with or without Victoria St. Clare, perhaps even in spite of her. I would prove myself worthy of the command I was about to inherit, to Sebastian St. Clare and everyone else in the clan, if it was the last thing I did.

And that is how I, Noel Duprey, future leader of my people, ended up sitting behind the cramped metal desk of a junior executive in a corkboard-walled cubicle that wasn't even soundproof, gaping like a schoolboy at a woman in a white fur coat. I represent the strongest, the smartest, the bravest and the most noble of all our kind.

I am the standard against which all others are measured. Yet at that moment, as I turned to gaze at the female who had just entered, I was reduced to—forgive me—an almost human incoherence.

I was quite frankly astonished. I had just spent the entire flight from Alaska studying the personnel files of everyone in the Montreal office, most especially that of Victoria St. Clare. I thought I knew everything about her, but nothing had prepared me for this.

Victoria St. Clare—several dozen times removed from the direct line of descent, fortunately for everyone concerned—is what is known as an anthromorph. What that means, quite simply, is that through some genetic anomaly, she is condemned forever to retain her human form. She can never mate; she can never bear young; she can never know what it is to be one of us through the miracle of the Change. Of course one has to feel sorry for such a creature. I suppose it's only natural to regard those different from oneself with a certain wariness, but Victoria St. Clare's differences condemned her to a life of pity and scorn among her own people.

I had known that much about her as soon as I refreshed my memory on her name. There weren't more than a dozen or so anthromorphs among us, and I remembered her from childhood pack gatherings as the poor ugly duckling all the other children used to torment. According to her personnel records, fortune hadn't favored her much as the years progressed, either.

She was portrayed as a mediocre employee about whom the kindest evaluation report read, "Generally punctual." In a business where creativity, ambition and daring were prized, she displayed about as much imagination as a toad. In six years of employment, she had been passed over for promotion no less than two dozen times. Even humans held positions over her.

She was, nevertheless, the werewolf who had been assigned to work with me on the most delicate, volatile situation ever to arise within the St. Clare Corporation.

No werewolf would ever be fired from the St. Clare Corporation, of course, and no St. Clare would ever be demoted. But with this kind of record, what amazed me was that she had achieved the position of account executive in the first place. With the kind of record Victoria had, Sebastian St. Clare was either up to some devilishly clever trick by assigning me to work with her, or the man was utterly insane.

Because something else had also become apparent through Victoria's personnel file. She consistently rated low scores in job satisfaction tests. No one wanted to work with her. Other werewolves didn't trust her. She was well known for associating with humans—even business competitors.

It seemed evident to me that, if there was a traitor in our midst and if the source of the treachery was the Montreal office, Victoria St. Clare had to be a prime suspect.

With all of this in mind, I wasn't entirely sure what to expect when I met her. But it certainly wasn't this.

She was exceptionally, even strikingly, beautiful. She was tall with ivory skin and jet black satiny hair, which she wore pulled back from her face in a chignon at her neck, like a ballerina. She had the exquisite bone structure of a dancer, too: high cheekbones, delicate nose, aristocratic forehead. Her eyes were large and gray and deeply fringed with coal black lashes. Eyebrows arched gracefully over her brow ridges in a way that seemed designed to most easily express aloofness or disdain.

She was swathed from neck to ankle in a white fur coat,

and she wore it regally. Where the coat opened in the front, I could see black suede boots and a slim leggy figure hugged by a teal-colored jersey dress that left no secrets—flat firm abdomen, the delicate notch of hipbones, the dip of her waist, the rounded swell of her breasts.

I don't know. I suppose I expected her to be…unattractive.

Instinctively, I got to my feet, and at just that moment she recovered from her own shock and dropped her head, starting to bow. I suppose we both felt foolish.

She said, *"Pardonnez-moi, je ne sais—"*

And I said, *"Non, pas de—"*

We both broke off, and Victoria fell into a respectful silence, avoiding my eyes.

I released an impatient breath. There were certain things about my new status I would never get used to. Deference was one thing. Abject subservience was another.

"Are you Victoria St. Clare?" I asked.

She inclined her head. *"Oui, monsieur."*

I switched back to English, just as I had been doing since I'd gotten off the plane. Montreal was such an unpredictably bilingual city, even I was becoming confused. "I am Noel Duprey."

She shot me a surprised look. "I know, sir."

Of course she knew. Everyone knew who I was now, even if they hadn't before. Victoria St. Clare had rattled me more than I realized.

I pushed a hand through my hair and adopted a brisk air of authority. "All right, here are the rules. Speak English. I've lived in London for twelve years, and I think in English. And don't call me sir. I'm not the ruler yet. Call me Noel or Mr. Duprey. Now pack up your desk and be ready to get out of here in fifteen minutes."

She no longer appeared to be having any difficulty

maintaining eye contact. Her eyes flashed outrage, and I couldn't understand why, although if I had truly tried I probably could have put it together. I confess I was distracted, and by several things, the curve of her bosom being only one.

Her voice was cool and her manner remote as she said, *"Monsieur, comment*—I mean, sir, if I may ask why?"

I scowled fiercely at her. "I asked you not to call me that. As for why…" I gestured abruptly to my surroundings. "I should think that would be fairly obvious. Do you call this an office? There isn't even a door. You may be able to work like this, but I most certainly cannot. I'll be taking over the executive suite, and for as long as we'll be working together, you will have the office adjoining. Does that meet with your approval, Ms. St. Clare?"

Now her eyes widened with astonishment. Her eyes, I don't think I've mentioned, were one of her most captivating features.

She said, "I…excuse me, but I don't think I understand."

I had to admire her composure, which was a great deal more evident than my own at the moment. This was not the first time I had been thrown off guard by a beautiful woman, although it was, perhaps, the first time I had been so rattled by one so inaccessible, and I had handled the whole thing badly, blurting out details without giving any explanation. I was annoyed with myself, and with her. She, however, remained completely unruffled, regarding me with a cool and distant gaze that revealed nothing more than polite curiosity.

That only irritated me more. I was beginning to understand why her co-workers didn't like her. This was one woman who could intimidate the hell out of man or beast.

"You're not the only one," I said shortly. "All I know

is that the powers that be have decided you and I should work together on a special project. I assumed you would have been notified by now.''

''What project?''

My frown increased. ''They haven't told you anything? Well, no matter. It's best that I explain it myself, anyway, but not here. We need some privacy.''

Now it was her turn to frown. ''But who? Who assigned us to work together?''

I was surprised, though I couldn't say why. ''Sebastian St. Clare, of course.''

She murmured, ''Of course,'' but I could hear her heartbeat speed up. With shock, excitement, confusion? She controlled her body language well, and her emotions were difficult to read.

Victoria turned away casually to slip off her coat, and I thought it was in an effort to further hide her reaction from me.

I said sharply, ''Why are you hanging up your coat? I told you, you're moving. Call an office boy to help you with your things and meet me upstairs in fifteen minutes. Don't be late.''

''I'm never late,'' Victoria replied coolly.

I could barely prevent a rueful smile as I remembered the one flattering entry in her file. ''Yes,'' I murmured. ''I know.''

I picked up my briefcase and departed.

CHAPTER THREE

Victoria

When Noel was gone, I pressed my hands to my cheeks and desperately tried to control the quick, hot beating of my heart, knowing that he could hear it and hoping that he would attribute it to anxiety, uncertainty, guilt, anything except what it was.

Noel Duprey. Noel with golden blond hair, quick green eyes, sharp, patrician features, wicked grin and irresistible sex appeal. Noel Duprey, the standard against which all others were measured, the strongest, the quickest, the bravest, the smartest and the most noble of all our kind. Noel Duprey, the future leader of all our people. Noel Duprey, on whom I had had a crush since I was ten years old.

Even as a boy there had been something special about him. He'd excelled at sports and scholastic competitions, running second only to Michael St. Clare in every important test in his level. Even then he'd had hangers-on and admirers, and the young girls had been shameless about him. But despite his exalted status, he was never too busy to play with the younger members of the clan, and he was one of the few boys who had never teased or tormented me. In fact, on more than one occasion, he had actually been nice to me.

That kind of nobility of character, I supposed, was one of the reasons he would someday lead us all.

I had been there for the battle of succession. The event was so spectacular, so unprecedented, that the entire St. Clare Corporation had shut down its offices all over the world for the day—the stock market had plummeted—and even underlings like me had been given the opportunity to see history in the making.

Michael St. Clare, Sebastian St. Clare's son, had been a brilliant man with every indication that he would carry on the St. Clare tradition of inspired leadership—except for one thing. He did not want to be leader. He did not even, the rumormongers whispered, particularly like being a St. Clare. When he finally announced his intentions to turn his back on his legacy and, in fact, on his very nature, for the love of a human woman, many said it had been inevitable.

Of course someone had to challenge his right to succession, though how it came about that Noel was the one to do so I was not exactly sure. I only know that I watched the violent battle with my heart in my throat and when Noel, poised to strike the killing blow, had instead turned and helped his adversary to his feet, my eyes had flooded with tears of joy and breathless admiration. Four thousand years of civilization had triumphed over the nature of the beast and had taken the form of Noel Duprey. He was the man to take us into the twenty-first century, the embodiment of honor and reason, intelligence and fair play. May he live forever.

And now this magnificent creature, this most exalted one of all our kind, had come to me. And the truth was, he wasn't all that magnificent up close.

Physically, of course, he was as striking as ever. But he was just as autocratic, just as long-nosed and arrogant as any of the St. Clares had ever been, and I had somehow expected more of him. Why, I couldn't be sure, but I had.

This was hardly the first time I had been disappointed in anyone, however, and I did not spend a great deal of time fretting over it. The only thing I had to figure out now was *why* he had sought me out. Or perhaps more specifically, why Sebastian St. Clare himself had done so.

Unfortunately, I thought I already knew. A job offer from the Gauge Group and special attention from Castle St. Clare itself all in the same day? It could hardly be coincidence.

After all, even Cinderella only got one shot at the ball.

I had nothing from my desk to pack, and exactly fifteen minutes later I stepped out of the elevator that opened onto the executive suite. Immediately my ears picked up the gentle hiss of the white-noise machines, which were the only method of screening voices from the inner offices from sharp werewolf ears. I could not imagine what kind of business Noel Duprey could be conducting here that would require that kind of secrecy.

The woman at the receptionist's desk was human, and I knew her. I had that much in common with Michael St. Clare—I found it very easy to make friends with humans, even though members of my own kind considered me standoffish and strange.

"Hi, Sara," I said as I approached the desk. I lowered my voice a little, knowing that it wouldn't matter how loudly I spoke with the white-noise machines running. "Any idea what's going on?"

Sara shook her head, short brown curls bouncing, though her eyes were bright with excitement. "I think they swept the place for bugs, though." And she giggled at the face I made. "The electronic kind, not the crawly kind. And Mr. Stillman was highly upset to be put out of his office, which is now *your* office by the way. Are you being promoted?"

I was impressed…and a little intimidated. Greg Stillman was head of an entire department.

I said, "Um, I don't think so. More like temporarily reassigned."

She gave another bouncy nod of her head, as though that confirmed what she'd suspected. "Well, Mr. Gorgeous in there has got everybody jumping around like their tails are on fire and from what I can gather, he's not telling *anyone* what's going on. Even Georgette doesn't know."

Georgette was the private secretary to Paul Esteban, Sr., vice president in charge of the entire division.

"Who *is* he, anyway?" Sara wanted to know.

"Mr. Gorgeous?" I couldn't prevent a grin. I rather liked that nickname. "He's the new CEO."

"Of Clare de Lune?"

"Of the entire St. Clare Corporation."

"Whoa." Now Sara looked impressed. "I guess we'd better act sharp then."

"I guess."

"By the way, he wanted to—"

The door across the room swung open and Noel Duprey stood there, larger than life and twice as gorgeous, a ferocious frown on his face. "Ms. St. Clare," he said. He had a powerful voice; it practically rang across the room. "If you can spare a moment?"

"See you as soon as you arrived," Sara concluded quickly and, shrinking down a little in her chair, turned back to her computer screen.

Before the angry visage of the future leader of our people, I would have liked to shrink down, too. I was not human, though, and had no choice but to square my shoulders and precede Noel into his office.

His office was actually the executive conference room.

It smelled richly of Earl Grey tea, walnut oil furniture polish and Noel. A faint trace of human sweat lingered in the air from the movers who had been engaged in transforming the space from conference room to office, as well as the aroma of old ash from the fireplace, and copy paper, and the subtle machine scent of a small computer...and Noel. Snow melting on wool. Highly polished leather. Silk. The color of sunshine which was his hair. Power, authority, refinement, maleness. The essence of Noel. It permeated every surface, tantalized every sense. I thought irrelevantly that if we could bottle that scent, we would rule the planet.

Pale blue damask draperies were swept back from the floor-to-ceiling windows, flooding the room with brilliant, snow-reflected sunlight. In one corner of the enormous room stood two small damask-upholstered chairs, in the other, a mahogany and brass grandfather clock. In the center of the wall was a glass china cabinet displaying a collection of Spode ceramic ware; flanking it were two Rothko paintings. The room was elegant, airy and, at present, so empty it echoed.

The thick rose carpeting bore the indentation marks of an enormous table and twelve chairs, though how they had been dismantled and moved so quickly I couldn't begin to guess. Noel's briefcase was open on the floor in front of the two small chairs; a cup of tea and his laptop computer rested on the marble hearth of the fireplace, which was dark and cold-looking. Apparently he had been too busy sending the staff into a frenzy to think of ordering office furniture, or even of lighting a fire.

"I love what you've done with the place," I murmured, glancing around.

He ignored me, and walked across the room to the two chairs. "Come and sit down. I've called a meeting for two o'clock, and we have a lot to discuss before then. You might want to inform your human friends, by the way, that the white-noise screen only works one way. From inside this office I can hear everything that goes on outside."

I had noticed the absence of the white noise the minute I entered the office, of course, but I hadn't registered its significance until now. So, he had heard the comment about Mr. Gorgeous. I wondered whether he had been flattered or offended and decided, from the expression on his face, that it was the latter. I was disappointed. I had expected, for some reason, that my idol would have had more of a sense of humor.

I said, "You're spying on them? Why?"

"That's one of the things we have to discuss."

He picked up his laptop from the hearth and sat down with it in one of the chairs, tapping on the keyboard. I followed him slowly, listening to the sounds from outside the room that were no longer screened from my sensitive ears.

"It's not just humans," I observed, "but werewolves, too. Why would you want to spy on your own team? Unless you *enjoy* hearing Stillman whine about how badly he's being treated. It's not as though I asked for his office, you know, and I really don't need any more enemies here."

Noel looked up in surprise. "You can hear him?"

"Can't you?"

"But he's in the cafeteria. That's six floors away."

I thought it best not to respond to that. I had always known that my hearing was above average, even for a werewolf, but thought it best not to advertise the fact. There were some advantages to being consistently underestimated by one's co-workers—and enemies—and I had not yet decided which one Noel was.

He looked at me thoughtfully for a moment. Then he said abruptly, "There is a traitor in our midst. Over the past four months, the formulas for five new Clare de Lune products have ended up in the hands of the competition. We believe the leak is coming from this office."

My knees folded and I sank heavily to the chair, staring at him. "Tango and Cobalt," I said softly. "I wondered why they were pulled at the last minute."

Again he looked surprised, but his tone was brisk and matter-of-fact. "Just so. Sanibel beat us to the market by three weeks with both of them."

My eyes grew wider, betraying my own astonishment— and horror. Sanibel! Jason Robesieur handled the Sanibel account. Jason, with whom I regularly lunched; Jason, who less than an hour ago had offered me a job...

I was beginning to understand why I had been singled out for attention from Castle St. Clare. And it was worse than I had imagined.

I braced myself for the accusations, but Noel went on, "Obviously this situation has to be handled as quickly and as quietly as possible. Recent events..." And he hesitated only slightly there. "...have made the matter of morale a top priority."

I couldn't help wondering which "recent events" he might be referring to. The battle for succession, Michael's defection, the insanity in New Orleans? Perhaps all of them? One thing was certain, if it became common knowledge that the company was being threatened and that the threat came from inside our ranks...well, it was unthinkable. Chaos would erupt. Morale would grow too low to measure. It was bad enough that such a thing could have happened, but it must never, ever become public knowledge.

"It almost has to be a werewolf, doesn't it?" I said, thinking out loud. "The humans are watched closely, and one of us would have been sure to overhear something before now. And no one but a werewolf would have access to formulas—ad campaigns, maybe, facts and figures and lower-level material, but formulas..." And I gave a slow, disbelieving shake of my head. "It has to be one of us."

Noel looked both surprised and annoyed at my quick grasp of the situation. "That would seem to be the case, yes," he said. "Although it never pays to eliminate the obvious. I should point out, by the way, that in my experience it's not a good idea to associate too closely with one's inferiors."

At first I bristled, and then I understood. He had overheard my conversation with Sara, and he disapproved of our friendship.

"Then why are you associating with me?" I asked.

His expression, perfectly bland, showed not a hint of apology. "I thought I had made that clear."

"Because you were ordered to?"

"Yes."

My lips compressed tightly; I did not trust myself to speak. I barely trusted myself to think, but Noel must have read my thoughts anyway because he said, "I've studied your personnel file. I'm aware that you have had a singularly undistinguished career here at Clare de Lune, with no particular talent that qualifies you for this assignment. I'm also aware of your friendship with Jason Robesieur, and the fact that he is the account executive for Sanibel's new products division. It might interest you to know that

I'm aware he offered you a position with his company and yes, you are high on my list of suspects."

He held me with his gaze for a moment, allowing that to sink in. Then he went on, "I don't know why Sebastian appointed you to work with me, although I have my suspicions. Blood is thicker than water, after all, and I would be a fool to assume that, while I'm tracking down a spy, I'm not myself being spied upon. That, after all, is the essence of the espionage game."

He paused then, ran his long, slim fingers through the silky fall of his hair and added, "Having said all of that, I came prepared to work with you and work with you I shall...until you give me reason to change my attitude."

I could barely keep myself from gaping at him. I pressed the palms of my hands against my crossed knees and spoke very deliberately, "Let me make sure I understand. You don't like me. You don't trust me. You suspect me, at best, of being a St. Clare spy, at worst of being the very traitor I'm supposed to help you find. You don't think I'm qualified for the job. And yet you are prepared to take me into your confidence regarding the most sensitive matter that the company has faced in decades?"

He regarded me steadily. "I didn't say that. I said I would work with you."

I swallowed back a hot retort. "Do you mind if I ask exactly what you expect me to do?"

He returned with no hesitation whatsoever, "Whatever I tell you to."

My hands pressed down more tightly on my knees. "I see."

With only the slightest evidence of capitulation in his voice, he added, "I expect you might be useful as a liaison, of sorts, between myself and this office. You know the people and the routine. I'm sure you'll be able to serve some function as an adviser.''

He could hardly have chosen a less propitious person for *that* job, as he would know if he had taken the trouble to find out anything about me that was not listed in my personnel file. No one confided in me here—no one of any importance, anyway—and no one knew less, or cared less, about the people in this office than I did. However, I was not about to enlighten the great Noel Duprey, who knew so much and saw so much and who was obviously never wrong. Let him find out for himself.

He glanced at the gold watch on his wrist and said, "Now, if we could move on…?"

I leaned back in the chair. "By all means."

Noel tapped a few more keys on his computer. "We're in the first stages of developing a new fragrance. If all goes well, we expect to introduce it by Christmas. Here's the timetable.''

He turned the computer screen around and I leaned forward a little to read it. I was sure I must have only imagined that his eyes dropped to the swell of my breast as I did so.

I murmured, "Moonsong." I arched an eyebrow in surprise as I studied the timetable. "That's pretty ambitious.''

"More than you know." He swiveled the computer to face him again. "Moonsong is more than a perfume, it's a revolution in perfumery. What alpha-hydroxy did for face creams, Moonsong will do for the perfume industry.''

I sat back, my expression patient and interested. In fact, a graphic was already forming in my head: *Moonsong, A Revolution in Fragrance.* No. *Moonsong. A Revolution in Fantasy.* And in the background, a moon in a blue-black sky spins slowly through its cycles. *Not bad,* I thought.

Noel went on, "Moonsong contains a unique ingredient that's impossible to patent, which is why security on this project is so important...and why it will no doubt prove impossible for our traitor to resist."

"Ah," I said, understanding. "It's a trap."

Noel paused one revealing moment. "In all important respects," he answered, "Moonsong is exactly what it appears to be—the most important new product to be introduced to the perfume industry in the twentieth century. My job—our job," he corrected himself almost without hesitation, "is to track every phase of every step associated with its production for signs of an information leak. We begin with the meeting I've called—senior account execs and above only."

Which was another way of saying no humans. That was one way to narrow the field.

"How are you going to explain me?" I asked pragmatically.

He looked at me blankly.

I gestured. "The fancy office, the secret meetings, the special attention... People are going to talk."

He scowled, clearly irritated to have overlooked that detail. He turned to the computer and began tapping out numbers again. "Hell, I don't care. Tell them you're my consort."

My cheeks grew warm. To his credit, he realized his mistake immediately and looked up.

"I'm sorry," he said, though somewhat stiffly. I supposed he wasn't accustomed to apologizing for much. "That was tactless."

It had never occurred to me to wonder whether or not he knew of my status as an anthromorph; it was hardly a secret, and he had access to all of my records, medical and personal, for as far back as he wished to go. Besides,

I had been told, though whether it was true or not I couldn't say, that the scent of anthromorphs is different from that of regular werewolves. Still, knowing that he knew and *knowing* that I knew he knew were two entirely different matters, and I found it embarrassing to have the subject out in the open.

Apparently he did, too, because he said brusquely, "We'll tell them you're my personal secretary. Excuse me, administrative assistant."

My eyes widened. "But that's a demotion."

"Exactly." He gave a satisfied nod of his head. "No one will question that. After all, you're not exactly blazing a trail in your present position, are you?"

I inhaled slowly through flared nostrils, but released the breath silently. I supposed, given his opinion of me, I was lucky to have a job at all.

"That's all for now," he said. "Bring a pad and pencil to the meeting."

I rose. "I don't take shorthand," I told him coolly.

He looked surprised. "I didn't expect you would. We have voice recorders for that. However, you might as well look as though you have a function."

I decided then and there he was probably the most obnoxious man who had ever lived. I moved toward the door.

"By the way," he said without looking up, "I did order office furniture. It should be here within the hour."

I turned, a small supercilious smile on my lips. "Then where," I inquired politely, "will we have the meeting? This used to be our conference room, after all."

I stayed just long enough to see that he hadn't thought of that, and then left him to find a solution—alone.

CHAPTER FOUR

Victoria

"Well, the new office is great."

I stretched out on the sofa and swung my feet over the back, cradling the telephone receiver against my ear. My black Persian cat, Socrates, jumped onto my stomach, causing me to gasp for breath and push him away. He looked offended at my reaction and settled daintily on the sofa at my side, within easy stroking distance of my hand.

"Television, VCR, penthouse view, coffee bar, my *own* bathroom," I continued, running my fingers over the cat's silky dark fur apologetically. "And Stillman's got this CAD program on his computer that is absolutely out of this world."

Phillipe, my downstairs neighbor and closest friend, chuckled lazily. In the background I could hear the rattle of pots and pans as he prepared yet another one of his gourmet feasts.

"Precious, only you would turn a perfect opportunity for bricking the gold into a chance to get a little extra work done. What do you care what's on his computer? What is a cad, anyway? Sounds perfectly dreadful."

"I think the term is goldbricking," I replied. "And it's not 'a cad,' Phillipe. It's CAD, which stands for Computer Assisted Design. And I care because by tomorrow morning the lovely thing will be reclaimed by its owner and I'll be reduced to using pen and ink again. In the meanwhile, though, I used it to send our new boss a little present.''

"Now, there's my girl! Something dirty, I hope.''

I laughed. Phillipe was French Canadian and spoke English with phrases that he copied from American television and always made me giggle. I, of course, am flawlessly multilingual, as all werewolves are. A facility for language is just another one of those adaptive traits we've picked up over the centuries and have incorporated into our genetic code.

We were speaking English because Phillipe had just started a new job in a fur salon where a huge percentage of the clientele was American. And because, when rich Americans travel to Montreal to buy their furs in exclusive local salons, they expected the clerks to speak French, Phillipe was determined they should hear nothing but English pass his lips. Annoying rich Americans was one of Phillipe's greatest pleasures in life.

I said, "Actually, I sent him a graphic for a new campaign we're launching. It will, as they say in America, knock his socks off.''

"Lovely. You are hopeless. And I think you must be mistaken about what they say in America.''

"Socks, I swear it.''

He made a noncommittal, highly skeptical, perfectly French sound, and I could picture him mentally marking down the phrase for later use.

"So explain to me, if you kindly will, why is it you sent a new design for his campaign to your perfectly hideous boss? Ah, wait! It was a *dirty* design!''

"No. It was a fabulous design. And I did it because he *is* hideous.''

I had used Stillman's advanced computer design program to give substance to my idea for *Moonsong—A Rev-*

olution. Four-color display, 3-D effects, video-quality with an audio clip. I had logged it under my security code to be sent to Noel via the company network as soon as his own computer came on-line, which, as of five o'clock that afternoon, had not happened yet. His furniture had not been delivered, either, I had noticed a little smugly, when I left the office promptly at five.

"He thinks I'm useless," I explained to Phillipe's puzzled silence. "Also stupid. I wanted to let him know it doesn't pay to make snap judgments. Because it is a *fabulous* design, and as soon as he retrieves it, it's going to self-destruct. Let whoever he assigns to steal it waste their time reprogramming it."

He burst into loud delighted laughter. "You are a witch! Is it any wonder I treasure you? Now, I'm just putting the soufflé in the oven and opening a bottle of Beaujolais. Shall I pour you a glass or no?"

"No, you're having company and—"

He made a dismissive sound. "It's just Doug, and he adores you. Come down and eat with us, then be discreetly on your way."

"What kind of soufflé?" I inquired, tempted.

"Salmon, your favorite. And a lovely roulade for the main. Darling, you don't eat enough to keep alive a moose. I insist."

I giggled. "Mouse. Keep alive a mouse."

"That's what I said. I'm setting a place."

I was just about to accept, when I heard a distinctive footstep far below, caught a familiar scent. I swung my feet to the floor and sat up, dumping Socrates unceremoniously to the floor, my heartbeat speeding.

"Phillipe, I can't. There's someone at my door."

"I didn't hear the bell."

"He knocked."

"Don't you dare open without calling out for who it is."

"I know who it is. It's my boss."

"Monsieur Gorgeous?"

"Phillipe…" I looked anxiously toward the door, knowing that Noel, even in the lobby three floors below, could hear and hoping he wasn't listening.

"Ooh la-la. He got your message then. Oh, to be a flea on your wall. Call me."

"Tomorrow," I promised.

I hung up the phone and got quickly to my feet, checking my appearance in the mirror over the fireplace. I was wearing one of those thermal-knit unisuits that look like nothing more than a pair of long johns from the previous century and were all the rage in the trendy boutiques that winter. Mine happened to be gray with tiny pink flowers all over it, and it stretched nicely over my breasts and bottom. Not that it mattered; when I was at home I dressed for comfort, even if it was in men's underwear and big woolly socks. My hair was loosely braided over one shoulder and tied at the end with a pink bow, and my makeup had almost completely worn off. I had time to do no more than brush the cat hairs off my clothes and push back a few errant hairs of my own before I heard his long strides on the carpeted hall floor outside my door.

The doorbell rang in two sharp jabs. He sounded imperious, so I let it ring again.

I opened the door and he came in without waiting for an invitation. He not only sounded imperious, he looked it—and angry. Splotches of melted snow clung to his charcoal wool overcoat, which he removed with a swinging gesture reminiscent of a nobleman swirling off his cloak. He thrust the coat toward me with the kind of dismissive disregard that same nobleman might have used with a servant.

"Well, that explains one thing, anyway," he said.

I took the coat because if I hadn't, he doubtless would have dropped it on the floor. People like him were so accustomed to having someone around to attend to their every need, they didn't know how to manage when left on their own.

I said, my markedly polite tone in deliberate contrast to his, "What explains what, sir?"

He scowled. "I asked you not to call me that. And I was referring to your conversation with your friend on the telephone."

And that was enough. I had started across the room but now I turned angrily, clutching his coat in my hands. "Excuse me, *sir*." I practically spat out the words. "But I would very much appreciate it if you would kindly refrain from eavesdropping on my private conversations. I find it not only an invasion of privacy but a demonstration of exceptionally bad manners."

He looked surprised, if not exactly chastened. And while I held his gaze, my color high and my stance defiant, desperately trying to remember what I had said about him on the phone and wondering exactly how much of it he had heard, he was thoughtful for a moment or two.

Then he said, "You're quite right, of course. It is extremely bad-mannered of me—to tell you what I heard."

I didn't trust myself to respond to that. I whirled and proceeded to the closet, where I jerked out a hanger, draped his coat sloppily upon it and thrust it inside. "That," I said, with a broad gesture as I closed the closet door, "is where we keep our coats. I trust you'll remember that if you ever call here again. Otherwise, be good enough to bring your body servant.''

His eyes narrowed slightly. ''You have quite a wicked tongue on you, don't you?''

I was as shocked as he was at my impudence and couldn't imagine what had possessed me. I was quaking inside now, and did my best to keep him from noticing. I lifted my chin another fraction and replied, ''It comes from having nothing to lose. Sir.''

This time the emotion that narrowed his eyes was amusement. For the first time, he seemed almost, well, to say human would be an insult, but you know what I mean. He seemed almost like the person I had always imagined him to be.

He murmured, ''Yes, I can see that.''

Then the brief humor that had momentarily softened his demeanor was gone, and he said briskly, ''From this point on, Ms. St. Clare, please remember that you have a great deal to lose. We all do.

''I came here because of the graphic you sent me,'' he went on without pausing to give me a chance to respond. He plucked off his leather gloves and tossed them on the painted étagère by the door and strode into my living area without invitation. ''You could have saved me a trip through the snow if you had been at the office where you belonged instead of chatting on the phone with humans.''

I gaped at him. The man didn't seem to be able to open his mouth without infuriating me. ''I left at five o'clock!''

He glared back at me. ''When you work for me, you don't leave until the job is done.''

''I don't *have* a job. At least nothing that I could determine from that so-very-informative meeting this afternoon!''

I had him there. After seating eight high-powered ex-

ecutives in folding chairs and giving them portfolios on
Moonsong to balance on their knees, he'd spent forty-five
minutes briefing them on absolutely nothing. I've got to
admit, I've never witnessed such a remarkable facility for
making utter nonsense sound like the most important, interesting and vital message one has ever heard, and I admired him for it. It takes real talent to make certain people
leave a meeting more confused than when they entered,
and I could well imagine, even now, a bevy of werewolves tossing down Chivas at the local fern bar and trying to figure out what in the world the new boss had *said*
at that meeting this afternoon.

He had introduced me as his personal assistant, which
raised a few eyebrows, mostly because no one was quite
certain what that was. He'd then gone on to extol the
remarkable characteristics of Moonsong without ever
quite describing them, and explaining that he would be
personally overseeing the security on the project and that
everything concerning the campaign must first be cleared
through him, although he never quite got around to explaining what "everything" was. Oh, yes, those ferns at
the local bar would be rattling tonight.

He dismissed me to my luxurious new office—which
did have furniture, by the way—with absolutely no in-
structions whatsoever. So what am I, a mind reader? I
played with the computer, helped myself to tropical-
flavored mineral water and macadamia nuts from Stillman's private collection, and watched an American talk
show on television. At five o'clock, which coincidentally
was the time the talk show was over, I went home.

It's not my fault the man doesn't know how to handle
his employees.

His eyes narrowed again, briefly, and I could see him

trying to mentally rearrange his approach to dealing with me. I was glad to know I could keep him off-balance.

He said, quite calmly, "All right. Now I know why you destroyed the graphic. It was a clever joke. But not nearly as clever as the design itself. I hope you kept a copy, because I want you to present it to the account execs at the staff meeting tomorrow morning."

Fortunately, there was a chair at my back. I sank into it. My self-congratulation at keeping *him* off-balance disappeared in a puff of smoke. I couldn't even answer. I just stared at him like a tongue-tied child.

He glanced around the apartment curiously, and I could detect a faint aura of self-satisfaction in his stance now. "Is there anything to drink?" he inquired. "No, don't get up. I'm perfectly capable of serving myself."

I ignored the hint of sarcasm and got up, anyway. The activity helped to clear my head. "I, um, think I have some wine. And some cherry brandy someone gave me for Christmas."

He wrinkled his nose at that. "Wine."

He followed me into the kitchen. It was a big, old-fashioned room with a weathered brickwork island and copper pots hanging from a rack. There was a bay window filled with African violets and geraniums. I have good luck with flowers; I don't know why. While I rummaged around in a cabinet for the bottle of burgundy someone had brought to dinner once and never opened, Noel looked around appreciatively.

"This is a nice place," he said. "How did you find it?"

My apartment was actually one-third of a renovated warehouse—Phillipe had the second-floor space and the ground floor belonged to a female artist with two Dobermans. It wasn't just nice; it was spectacular. The walls were ancient brick, the arches that led from room to room were part of the original space; the floors were gleaming hardwood. Every room had a fireplace, although the one in the kitchen didn't work. The huge, arched windows in the living room looked out over the water, and I rarely bothered to draw the curtains. Perhaps its most enchanting feature, however, was the garden bathing room, featuring a cedar whirlpool, a separate sauna and a glass roof. One could sink into a haven of warm, frothing bubbles and count the stars at night.

The apartment was eclectically furnished with castoffs from the attics of aunts and cousins, siblings and grandparents. To my family, I have always been "poor Victoria" as in, "Darling, when the Limoges arrives, let's give the old china to poor Victoria," and "Poor Victoria, sleeping all alone on that cheap cot. She should have Grand-maman's bedroom suite." My relatives are well-to-do and have excellent taste, so "poor Victoria" was not a designation to which I objected in the least.

There was a beautifully carved antique armoire that hid a cheap department-store television set. A reproduction Duncan Phyfe table had been distressed and painted to look like a badly treated original. The sofa was big and old in a faded tapestry print with feather-stuffed cushions that practically embraced the body when one sank onto it, and there were two big, overstuffed chairs drawn up before the fireplace, one in plum-colored velvet and one in worn and often-brushed emerald green. Both the chairs and the sofa were liberally draped with colorful shawls, which disguised Socrates's persistent attempts to sharpen his claws on other people's belongings. There were Tiffany lamps, some real, some not, and Oriental carpets on the hardwood floors, all of them faded and none of them real. The walls were hung with my own artwork—pen-

and-ink sketches of human nudes, an oil seascape, a colorful abstract, an impressionistic landscape depicting the lake at the foot of Castle St. Clare—all representative of my various artistic "periods." There was one painting in the bedroom that I hoped Noel Duprey never saw. Or perhaps, like most of us, he wouldn't recognize himself on canvas.

I was glad to know Noel did not have a completely atrophied sense of the aesthetic, and I was glad he appreciated my taste. But I knew what he was really asking was not how I had found this apartment, but how I could afford it. I made a good salary, but waterfront property like this was not cheap.

I finally answered him. "It's a sublet. One of the owners is an actor, and he's touring with *Les Misérables*. An advantage of making friends with humans—they have all the good apartments." I found the wine and blew the dust off the label, holding it up to him. "Is this all right?"

He took the bottle from me as I got to my feet. "What happens when the tour is over?"

"Nothing, probably. The other owner is the architect who redesigned this building, and she has apartments all over North America." I rummaged in a drawer for a corkscrew. "They'll probably move into one of her other buildings."

He murmured, "You do know interesting people."

I found the corkscrew and was perfectly willing to open the bottle myself, but Noel took it from me. I went to the china cabinet for glasses, and after only a moment's hesitation decided on the real crystal my grandmother had given me for my twenty-first birthday. After all, if one doesn't break out the good stuff when the heir designé of the entire empire drops in, what is it for?

After a surreptitious check to make sure they were

clean, I returned to him with the glasses. He took them both in one hand and expertly poured a measure of wine into each. He handed me mine.

"Shall we drink to our new association?"

Finally I gathered my flyaway wits about me and said, "Wait a minute. Before we drink to anything, let me make sure I understand you. Did you mean it? You want me to present my design to the group tomorrow?"

He met my gaze levelly. "It depends. Do you have a copy?"

And then I understood. The son of a cur thought I had stolen the graphic—from Stillman, probably. Stillman, who had never had an original thought in his life. Who couldn't produce a graphic like that in three years, much less in three hours. Noel Duprey thought I had stolen it from Stillman's hard drive, passed it off under my signature and destroyed it so that its true origins couldn't be traced. I wanted to throw my glass of wine at him.

Fortunately, I have excellent control of my temper. In fact, the angrier I get, the colder and more polite I become. It has always been my method of dealing with strong emotion—to retreat rather than advance. You would have to have had my childhood to understand why.

So I very calmly set aside my wineglass, went over to the rolltop desk that sat against the brick wall beside the fireplace and opened it. The desk had belonged to my grandfather. I'm sure Noel was wondering how I could afford that, too.

I moved aside a recipe folder, a file box of unpaid bills and the accordion file where I keep my tax receipts, and pulled out a diskette holder. I'm no fool. I back up everything onto floppy.

I held up the diskette. "The original," I told him. I took out another diskette and another. "Also the original project folder on Ambition for Men, the logo for Celestial and the entire campaign plan for Forgotten—television and print ads, graphics, slogan and even the bottle design, for God's sake. I must say, they must have really liked that one. They didn't change a thing.''

Noel held my gaze. His face revealed absolutely nothing. Then he said evenly, ''I know.''

There was no chair behind me that time. Somehow I managed to stay on my feet.

He must have taken my dumbfounded silence for lack of comprehension, because he repeated, ''I knew no one in that office was capable of coming up with a design like that in such a short time. Hell, most of them are still trying to figure out what Moonsong is. So I did some checking. I'll say this for your colleagues, they aren't shy about admitting how easy you are to steal from. Most of them were only too anxious to brag about how they'd taken your ideas and 'improved' them.''

The flesh around the corners of his eyes tightened, and he took a sip of his wine. Actually, he tossed it back like hard liquor, without tasting it. I had the feeling this was not something a man of Noel's refinement did lightly. He was angry—not at me, but for me.

I didn't know what to think.

His expression was hard when he turned his gaze on me again. ''Why did you keep doing it?'' he demanded. ''Why did you let them steal your work like that, not once but over and over? Why didn't you report it?''

I was surprised at his naiveté. ''To whom? My superiors were the ones doing the stealing.'' Then I lifted one shoulder in an uncomfortable shrug. I was aware that, when I put my reasons into words, I sounded like a fool. ''Besides, they were good ideas. I wanted them to be used.''

He looked at me for such a long time that I wanted to squirm. He has a piercing gaze, have I mentioned that? It's the kind of gaze you can feel even when your back is turned, going through you like a knife. No one could meet it for long.

Then he said, "What else haven't you told me? Rest assured, I can find out your secrets, as I trust I've already proven twice this day. But I would rather not be bothered. I have enough on my mind, as it is."

Oh, yes, I had no doubt he could find out anything he wanted. He knew about Jason. He knew about my purloined campaigns. What else was there?

Still, I might have made up something, so intimidated was I by him, if it hadn't been for that last comment. I prickled. I didn't like to think of anything about me, particularly my "secrets," as being a bother.

So I said, very sweetly, "I believe everyone should have *some* surprises in life. So why don't I just let you find out for yourself?"

I returned the diskettes to their holder, closed the desk, then brushed past him to pick up my wineglass.

He followed me back into the living room. "I didn't come here to spar with you, Victoria," he said in that clipped, authoritarian tone that I had begun to notice became more pronounced when he was not quite as sure of his position as he would like to be.

"What *did* you come for?" I demanded.

I lived a quiet, predictable kind of life and I liked it that way. In one day I had had more excitement than I generally endured in a year and I simply wasn't ready for any more surprises. I needed a chance to absorb what I had already learned.

But Noel was no longer looking at me. He had brought himself up short and was staring with a look of repressed disgust and disbelief on his face, at something on the floor. "What is *that?*" he inquired.

Socrates drew himself up to his full cat height, arched his back and hissed. He could hardly be blamed. He had never smelled a male werewolf before.

I regarded Noel with sublime patience. "That," I informed him, "is a cat."

Noel looked from Socrates to me, making no attempt to disguise his opinion of either of us. "You let a *cat* live here?"

I replied. "No. He lets me live here."

"That," Noel informed me, "is disgusting."

Many werewolves don't like cats. I've never understood why.

I fixed a gaze on my faithful friend and said mildly, "Socrates, kill."

Socrates, who often exercises better judgment than I do, merely flipped his tail and walked away.

I shrugged and sat down on the sofa, tucking one leg beneath me. "You were saying?" I invited of Noel.

He glanced again at the retreating Socrates, stepped carefully around the spot where the cat had been, and came into the living room. He moves with the most exquisite grace. There is something sensual in watching him.

He took a seat in the plum-colored velvet chair opposite me. Its loose, plump cushions molded themselves around his long body, its rich antique color brought out the lights in his hair. I have the eye of an artist; I notice things like that.

I also have the instincts of a woman. And no female could fail to notice Noel Duprey, wherever he was, whatever he did.

He took a sip of his wine, and he said, "In answer to your question, I came because we have work to do."

I lifted an eyebrow. "It's eight o'clock at night. Did I ask if this job came with a raise?"

He regarded me steadily through those unrelenting green eyes. He said, "I have been traveling since seven o'clock this morning. Before that, I had approximately four hours' sleep and before *that*, I was awakened at three o'clock in the morning to fly to Alaska. So please don't push me, Ms. St. Clare. I'm having a very bad day that has already lasted thirty-six hours too long."

I felt appropriately chastised. I dropped my eyes to my glass, cleared my throat a little, then glanced back up at him. "What do you want me to do?" I asked.

"It occurred to me that I just told a half-dozen experts in the field that I would be in charge of the Moonsong campaign," he answered simply, "and I don't have the first idea how to begin. I was hoping you did."

The grin that tugged at my lips was mostly from relief. He might be the bravest and the smartest, an excellent R & D man, probably a pretty good CEO, but he couldn't be expected to know anything at all about advertising. This, then, would be my job. I had been afraid he was going to ask me to do something hard.

"Sure," I said, and reached for the sketch pad I kept on the lamp table beside the sofa. "The first thing you do is assemble your team." I always think better with a pencil in hand, and I began to put it all down for him on the sketch pad. "If I were you, I'd put Leo Fabres in charge. He's not very creative but he's awfully clever with details, and he knows when to leave good people alone. Then under him you'll have a team of artists and a couple of copywriters, and Serena Renard is an outstanding video person."

He came over to sit beside me on the sofa, to better see the organizational chart I was sketching out for him.

His scent was so intoxicating that for a moment I faltered. It spoke of power, strength, sexuality, and it soaked into my pores like sweet oil.

"Go ahead," he said, looking at the chart and not at me.

I quickly focused my attention again and for the next half hour I told him about the advertising business and the structure of our division. He listened attentively, and I felt very important. I also felt strange and quivery and at times hardly able to concentrate for the simple excitement of being near him.

It's a hormonal thing. You'd have to be one of us to understand…or perhaps not. Perhaps you'd just have to be a woman who's had a crush on a man she can never have for most of her life and who, when she finally gets close to him, doesn't know what to do…or even to feel.

I heard the door close downstairs and Noel noticed at the same time. "Something smells good," he said.

"Dinner must be ready." I had been so absorbed in the essence of Noel that I had hardly noticed the other wonderful fragrances that permeated the building.

He smiled. "Ah, yes. Phillipe, the cook."

Phillipe was coming up the stairs. I excused myself and went to the door.

I opened it just as he arrived and his face was wreathed with delight. "You do amaze me, precious! How is it you always know when I'm about to ring your bell?"

"I can hear you coming," I said.

He had a plate in his hand covered with a cloth napkin—the source of the delicious smells—and he was doing his best to peer over my shoulder into the interior of the room. Phillipe is not a tall man, and this was not easy.

He said, indicating the plate, "I know you said not to bother, but the roulade turned out so divinely I simply had to share, and I put a *petit*-smidge of soufflé on the platter, too…"

As he spoke, he elbowed his way through the door and toward the kitchen. Now he brought himself up short and affected surprise as he looked at Noel. "Oh, *mais pardonnez-moi!* I did not know you had company."

Noel got smoothly to his feet and nodded a bow. "Good evening."

I could have kicked Phillipe in the shins. Instead, I put on my best company manners and said, "Phillipe Renoir, Noel Duprey. Noel is my new boss," I added totally unnecessarily.

Phillipe thrust the plate at me and went forward with his hand extended, appraising Noel from top to toe. "With pleasure I make your acquaintance, *monsieur*. I've heard so much about you."

Noel shot me an amused glance, and I smiled weakly. If Phillipe had been close enough, I *would* have kicked him.

The two men shook hands. Phillipe looked Noel over once more, then turned to me, approval in his eyes. "Well, I must flee. I'm expecting a guest."

"Thank you," I said, "for dinner."

"There's enough for two," he told me with a wink. And as he passed close, he murmured, "Precious, he *is* gorgeous. If you don't snap him up, I will."

"Trust me," I returned dryly under my breath, "he's not your type."

I saw him to the door and locked it when he was gone. Then I turned, holding the plate awkwardly in my hands.

Noel said, "I shouldn't interrupt your dinner."

And I said at the same time, "Will you have some?"

I should explain that in our culture, food and the sharing of such has a special significance. Two or three generations ago, simple good manners would have required that I, the lowliest member of the pack, silently present Noel, the elite ruler of us all, with the entire platter and then leave the room while he consumed it. The presentation would of course have been even more acceptable had I killed the lamb myself.

I am for the most part a vegetarian—although Phillipe's concoctions have been known to tempt me from my diet now and again—so the tradition seems as silly to me as it probably does to you. But it has its foundation in common sense. In ancient times, when most of our culture originated, the alpha leader was responsible for defending, sheltering and providing for the entire pack. If he himself were not well fed, we all would die. It's really rather stirring, when you think of it like that.

So these little rituals developed around food and status, especially where members of the opposite sex are involved. At a formal dinner, the order in which everyone is served is far more important than what is served; wars have been started over a mistake. During courtship, the gift of food is tantamount to a proposal of marriage; what is offered and how it is accepted determines precisely what kind of sexual liberties can be taken.

As for the sharing of a meal between two members of the opposite sex of widely divergent status...well, nothing is as simple as it sounds. It depends, you see, on whether one is orthodox or reformed, culturally liberal or conservative. I myself am a well-educated girl from a good family and I knew perfectly well how to behave. My Aunt Lucille, the werewolf equivalent of Miss Manners, would have fainted dead away had she seen me so casually invite the heir designé to share a meal. But many of us of the younger generation, having dealt so much with humans in our everyday life, have come to adopt some of their ways.

Obviously I am one of them, and sharing food seemed to me a friendly, sensible gesture, one I made without thinking.

There was no way of knowing what Noel Duprey's opinion on such matters might be, however. I held my breath for a sign I had given offense.

He glanced at the plate in my hand. "It does smell delicious," he admitted. "And I don't think I had lunch."

I'm sure my shoulders sagged with relief. "Come then," I said. "Would you like to dine before the fire?"

CHAPTER FIVE

Noel

All right, I probably shouldn't have agreed to share a meal with Victoria. As I may have indicated, there are still some of the protocols and formalities about my new status that make me uncomfortable, and sometimes I forget. Besides, I was alone in a strange city, too tired to travel, and starving.

Which covers every reason except the real one—Victoria St. Clare. She was fascinating, captivating, dangerous. I didn't understand her, I couldn't ignore her and I dared not trust her. But I was not ready to leave her.

I drew up a small table before the fire and brought two chairs from the kitchen while she found plates and silverware. She made a salad and I poured more wine. I enjoy these quiet domestic evenings occasionally; I always have. When I thought of the alternative—the corporate condo with its chrome-and-black decor and its silent, shadowy servants efficiently programmed to anticipate my every need—the warmth of Victoria St. Clare's fire was even more welcome.

Of course I knew better than to let myself get too relaxed with her. She took far too many liberties, as it was. And it was becoming clearer by the moment that Victoria St. Clare was more of a force to be reckoned with than I had ever imagined.

It had seemed so simple at first. Victoria St. Clare: a

distinct annoyance, perhaps Sebastian St. Clare's stooge, possibly even a minor-league spy. But surely not powerful enough to do any real damage. Now...the more I learned of her, the more worried I became. The woman who had created that graphic was talented, focused and self-directed. The mind behind the other campaigns that I had eventually discovered to be hers was brilliant.

Knowing how she had been abused, ignored, passed over and stolen from during her tenure in the Montreal office, seeing what she was capable of accomplishing with almost no effort at all...well, frankly, the only thing that would have surprised me would have been if selling secrets was all she was capable of.

At that moment it was clear that this case would either be solved in record time, or I had just stumbled into more trouble than I knew. Which was another way of saying that I didn't know what to think. If Victoria could keep her genius secret from her own colleagues all these years, what other secrets might she be hiding? Just how much damage was she capable of doing?

On the other hand, there was no real evidence against Victoria at all, and a great deal of cause to reserve judgment. It was entirely possible that Sebastian St. Clare had set up a devilishly clever trap into which it would be far too easy to fall. So I was proceeding very carefully. Innocent until proven guilty, and so on.

There was, of course, always the possibility that Victoria was nothing more or less than exactly what she seemed to be: bright, capable, woefully underacknowledged and completely taken aback by all of this.

There was a part of me that really wanted to believe that, and for absolutely no other reason than the fact that I have a weakness for beautiful women, whoever they might be and wherever they might be found.

She didn't make a fuss about lighting candles or breaking out the linen tablecloth, as some females would have done. She simply set the big bowl of salad on the table, along with a basket of crusty bread and a bowl of butter, and divided the contents of the platter between our two plates, although I noticed she took slightly less than she gave me. She had excellent manners, which shouldn't have surprised me. She is a St. Clare, after all.

The cat sat on the hearth beside her chair, and Victoria fed it bits of salmon from her plate. I was appalled. But my manners are excellent, too, when I remember to use them, and I said nothing.

"Do you have a place to live?" she inquired, spooning a large amount of lettuce and carrots onto her plate.

When she offered to serve me the same, I held up a staying hand. I do eat vegetables, but not when there is meat on the table.

"I'll be staying at the condo," I told her, doing my part to keep up polite conversation.

"Oh, you have an apartment in the city?"

"No, the company does. It's for visiting dignitaries or members of the board, didn't you know that?"

"Why should I?"

She looked unconcerned as she fished out another piece of salmon from the soufflé on her plate and sneaked it to the cat. I averted my eyes.

"No reason you should, I suppose." And then I observed, "There are no werewolves in this building."

"Of course not. This neighborhood isn't at all trendy enough for them."

"It's nice," I said. "The privacy."

She looked at me thoughtfully as she skewered some salad onto her fork. "Yes. I suppose it is."

Having made short work of the soufflé, I dug into the

roulade. "This is very good. Your Phillipe is quite a cook, for a human."

She tore off a piece of bread and popped it into her mouth. She had pretty white teeth, small and sharp. "He finds you attractive," she said.

That amused me. "I'm sorry I can't return the compliment."

Her eyes twinkled. "I think I speak for our entire population when I say I'm very glad to hear it."

I laughed. It felt good to laugh. I couldn't remember the last time I'd done it.

I took up my wineglass and leaned back in my chair, smiling at her. "And what about you?" I inquired. "How do you find me?"

It was habit, nothing more. I appreciate females, I flirt with them, I enjoy them. Generally, they enjoy me, too. I may have mentioned I have something of a reputation in that area. I don't mean to imply that the only way I know how to relate to a woman is sexually, but...I'm not sure I know how *not* to, either.

I'm not really a jerk. I just act like one sometimes.

She regarded me through cool gray eyes, her face as smooth and white as a glacier, absolutely expressionless. She said, lifting her fork, "You seem to have all the appropriate parts."

"I didn't mean to offend you," I said uncomfortably. "Sometimes I speak without thinking, especially where a pretty woman is involved."

She said, touching her napkin to her lips, "You didn't offend me."

That was all the encouragement I needed. I said, "May I ask you something? You needn't answer if it's too personal."

She said nothing, which I took to mean consent. So I blundered on.

"Your condition... Have you been tested? What do the experts say? Is there nothing that can be done?"

Her eyes were big and guileless. It was as though no one had ever before broached the subject with her in such a forthright manner, which, I supposed, was entirely possible. After all, how many others could possibly boast such natural tactlessness as I had just displayed?

But she surprised me by answering with nearly equal candor, "They poked and prodded me until I stopped being pleasant about it, and discovered absolutely nothing, of course. They really don't know what causes these cases, you know, and there's nothing to be done about it."

I murmured, mostly to myself, "Yes, I know. And a pity."

She paused with her fork half lifted from her plate, an eyebrow faintly cocked. "Oh? Why is that?"

I hardly knew what to say, although the response was obvious. However, having nothing intelligent to say has never stopped me from speaking, so I answered, blustering a little, "Well, you come from good stock, that's evident. I would think you would have a great deal to add to the genetic pool."

Her lips twitched faintly with the corner of a smile. "Yes," she agreed mildly. "A pity."

By then I was in too deeply to back away without looking the complete fool, so I held her gaze and I said deliberately, "And of course you are, on the surface, a very appealing female. To waste that..."

Her eyebrow rose higher. "Ah, you noticed, did you?"

"What?"

"My appeal."

I scowled, searching for composure. "Of course I did.
That is to say, just because you can't...what I mean is,
just because I'm not..." I was flailing about hopelessly
and sinking fast. There was nothing to do but throw myself on her mercy. "Look," I said, "I haven't spent much
time around..." I trailed off.

Her gaze was unrelenting. She wasn't about to let me
off the hook. She said, "No, I don't suppose you have."

So I plunged on. "What I mean to say is, I've never
worked with an anthromorph before. I'm not even sure
that's an accepted term."

She lifted one shoulder. "There are crueler ones."

"Would you rather be called something else?"

She held me in that cool gray gaze again. "I'd rather
be called Victoria."

If there were a prize for giving the most offense while
trying the hardest to give none at all, I suppose I would
have won it then. I saw no hope for it, so I decided to
abandon the subject entirely, casting about in my mind
for something neutral to say. Victoria turned back to her
salad.

"I remember you when you were young," I said at last.
"At clan gatherings. You were one of the best fly-ball
players in your level."

She finished chewing, swallowed, picked up her wineglass and sipped. And then, for some reason, she seemed
to decide to forgive me. She said, "I've never worked
with an heir designé before, either. So we can both be a
little uncomfortable."

And she smiled. That smile could take away the breath
of any male living, werewolf or human. I don't think I've
ever realized before that moment how cruel an arbiter fate
can be. For all that loveliness to be wasted on one who
would never know the wonder of taking a mate, the magic

of the Change, the miracle of bearing young. It wasn't fair.

And perhaps the most unfair thing of all was how all of that loveliness—all of that useless, wasted exquisite loveliness—affected me.

She said, "Actually, you're the only person who's ever been interested enough to inquire about my feelings on the subject, so I may as well tell you, I don't mind talking about it. And to answer your original question…I think you're very sexy."

I was taken aback and it must have shown, because she arched an eyebrow.

"Just because I can't do anything about it doesn't mean I don't notice," she said.

"Oh." I didn't want to let her know how much the subject fascinated me, so I took a sip of my wine and replied lightly, "In that case, may I return the compliment?"

She smiled. "Thank you."

She thought I was just being nice. I wasn't.

She finished her salad and what remained of the salmon soufflé. She offered me her portion of roulade, and it would have been rude to refuse. I was glad I had stayed, and because of more than the roulade. She had given me a lot to think about.

Victoria went to the kitchen and brought out a plate of ginger crackers and cheese, which I like very much. We sat there at the table before the fire, sipping our wine and nibbling on the cheese. The firelight made colors in her hair. The warmth and the wine seeped into my muscles and the knots of tension started to dissolve.

"Will you tell me something?" I asked.

"If I can."

We both reached for the cracker plate at once; our fin-

gers brushed. She withdrew her hand first, casually but
without a cracker.

I asked, "What do the other werewolves say about
me?"

She looked surprised. "They don't share confidences
with me."

"But you hear them." I spread cheese on my cracker,
glancing at her casually. "I'd be willing to guess nothing
goes on in the marketing division that you don't hear."

Her lips tightened at one corner, though what that sig-
nified I couldn't tell. She was debating, that much I could
easily see, how much of the truth to tell me.

"A lot of them don't think it was right," she said at
last, "the way you took the legacy from the St. Clares.
They're waiting for you to do something, you know, to
prove you can handle the job. I mean, it's been six
months."

That was not what I wanted to hear, but I wasn't surprised.

She added, "But there are others, younger ones, mostly,
who think what you did was romantic and, well, splendid.
They think it's about time we had someone in power with
energy and vision."

"Yet they're waiting for me to do something, too." My
tone was dry, and the old frustration rose. I fought the
urge to defend myself to her—how could I prove myself
when I wasn't given a chance to? I hadn't wanted this job
in the first place, and how could I do anything when I had
no power...all the old arguments. I focused instead on the
one important thing I needed to know. "Victoria, look at
me, please."

She did. I made her hold my gaze.

"If there was anyone in the Montreal office who meant
me harm, would you tell me?"

She thought about that, but she didn't try to evade my eyes. "Do you mean physical harm?"

"I mean any kind of harm."

"If you were in danger, I would tell you. Just because my name is St. Clare doesn't mean I wouldn't like to see some changes made, too," she said with her big gray eyes firm and steady.

Once again, she'd caught me off guard. It had never, ever occurred to me that Victoria St. Clare might be among my supporters. At best, I had imagined her to be indifferent to political machinations. Not, of course, that I accepted her statement at face value, but it did give me something new to consider.

Then she said, "Now will *you* tell me something?"

I nodded cautiously. "If I can."

"Am I still your prime suspect?"

It would have been easy to lie. I'm very good at it. But that would have been such an unnecessary insult to a woman who had been so often insulted in her life that I simply couldn't bring myself to do it.

So I answered honestly. "Yes. You are."

She might have been enraged; she might have been hurt. But to show either emotion would have been undignified. So she looked at me thoughtfully, turning it over in her mind, following my logic. Then she said, "You have character, Noel Duprey. A lot of people would have been seduced by Phillipe's roulade."

That was, I think, the classiest thing I've ever heard anyone say. It almost persuaded me to change my opinion, but I found myself in the oddly perverse position of trying to live up to her opinion of me.

She got up and began to clear the table. I sipped my wine. "Will you answer me one more question?" I asked.

She gave me a look over her shoulder that suggested cautious acquiescence.

"Why," I asked, "are you wearing men's underwear?"

She laughed. It was a trilling, delicious sound that reverberated in the pit of my stomach with an almost sexual pleasure.

And she said, "You are not at all what I expected, Noel Duprey."

That made two of us.

I was growing entirely too comfortable sitting there before the fire, sipping wine, watching the alluring curves of Victoria's closely clad figure as she moved back and forth between kitchen and living room. Finally I finished my wine, refused another glass and got up to replace the furniture we had rearranged for our dinner.

When she came back from the kitchen, I said, shifting the tenor of our relationship back to the workplace as casually as I could, "You didn't ask what the unique properties of Moonsong are."

She sank onto the sofa with one leg folded beneath her, picking up the sketch pad again. Her braid fell forward and caressed one breast, her lashes formed crescent shadows on her cheekbones as she began to make notes on the paper.

"If you had wanted me to know, you would have told me," she answered.

"Everyone else asked," I said.

She shrugged. "That's what executives do. They think they'll be accused of not paying attention unless they ask questions. Of course," she added almost absently, "what they don't realize is that you'll give each of them a different answer, the better to trace down the source of the leak when it comes."

God, she was quick. It was a little scary.

"It's important that we run a serious campaign on this product. Anything less will sabotage our entire effort."

She nodded. "Of course. That's why I think you should put Donald Lassair on the team. He's one of the most original thinkers in the company and an absolute genius with computer design. I'd put him in charge of the creative team, as a matter of fact. For a product like this, the campaign should be absolutely leading edge, at least as revolutionary as the perfume itself. "Yes," she finished with a decisive nod. "Definitely Donald."

I frowned a little. "I don't know him."

She met my eyes with something of a challenge in her own. "He's human."

"I'm sure he's very fine, but not for this project." I reached across and took the sketch pad from her, making a few notes of my own.

She sat back, looking at me suspiciously. "I think," she said slowly, "that you are a racist."

"Racist is a human term."

"Xenophobe, then," she said, scowling. "Whatever the word, it's a very unbecoming characteristic, particularly for someone who is supposed to be responsible for the moral welfare of his entire people."

"I'm sure you're right. As for your Donald, no doubt he's very competent, but there's simply no room for him on this team." I made a final change to the organizational chart and turned the sketch pad around for her to see.

She took it from me slowly and studied it without a word for a time. Then she raised her eyes to me. Her face revealed no expression at all.

"You've put me in charge of the creative team."

"That's right."

"I thought I was going to be your secretary."

"Personal assistant. Until now your duties weren't defined. Now they are."

She held out the sketch pad to me and said flatly, "This is impossible."

"You're perfectly capable of doing the job. You said yourself we have to run an aggressive campaign, and you're the person best qualified to make sure it's done."

"That's absurd. I've never run a campaign before. I can't give orders to werewolves—"

"But your friend Donald could?"

The truth in her eyes was painful and infuriating: that even humans had more status in that office than she did.

"They'll never accept this."

"They'll accept it," I told her, "or they'll deal with me."

I got to my feet, walking toward the closet where she'd put my coat. I dreaded the drive across town to that black cold apartment, but if I stayed any longer, I was in very great danger of falling asleep before her fire. That would be undignified.

"I will be at the office at eight," I told her, shrugging into my coat. "I expect you to be, too. And it should go without saying that you will stay as long as necessary." I pulled on my gloves. "Is there anything you need to help you on your way?"

She was still sitting on the sofa where I'd left her, staring at the sketch pad in her hand in a rather dazed way. Now she got to her feet, her face clearing, and she said decisively, "Yes. Stillman's computer."

"It's yours."

You would think I had just made her a present of the Eiffel Tower. I couldn't help smiling.

"Good night, Victoria," I said. "You will have that

presentation ready for the nine o'clock meeting, won't you?"

"Yes. I—yes."

Her mask was back on, composed and dignified. But I could hear her heartbeat. It made me happy.

I was warmly tucked into the back seat of the limo when I heard her dialing the phone. Her voice was breathless and excited. "Phillipe, you won't believe it!"

I chuckled, listening. I was only sorry we were out of range before she stopped gushing about work and started gossiping about Mr. Gorgeous.

I'm only a werewolf, after all.

The presentation the next morning was flawless. Victoria was composed, prepared and looked good enough to eat in a cherry red sweater and long winter-white skirt that clung to her thighs and calves like a second skin. She wore a gold chain around her hips and another one around her neck, dangling between her breasts. I must have given those chains more attention than I probably should have because I found I missed a lot of the details of her presentation.

Not that it mattered. The presentation accomplished exactly what I wanted it to.

The senior executives listened indulgently, and when she sat down, someone said, carefully noncommittal, "Very nice. Who's idea was that?"

Victoria sat with her hands folded atop the table, her shoulders square, her head high. She replied, "Mine."

The look that went around the table was clear enough for even a human to read. They didn't want to offend me, who obviously didn't know better, but allowing Victoria to participate in any way at all in this campaign was utterly out of the question.

"Well," said Harrison, who had been in charge of every major perfume campaign to come the company's way in the past thirty years, "I'm sure we'll be able to do something with it. Now, I've been thinking about a team. With your permission, sir, I've drawn up a—"

"I've already assembled the team," I said. I opened a folder, took out a dozen photocopies and spun them down the table. "Sorrenson, budget. Cadet, print. Jacardi, audiovisual. St. Clare, design. As I told you yesterday, I will be personally supervising the campaign. Ms. St. Clare, as head of the design team, will be second-in-command. Any questions?"

Oh, their faces were brimming with them. But no one had the nerve to speak out loud.

I said, "Good. Let's get to work, then. Moonsong isn't the only thing we're trying to sell today."

I would have liked to have caught Victoria's eye, to tell her what a fine job she'd done, but I was too busy reading the body language of everyone who filed out the door. They were not, as they say in America, a bunch of happy campers. As a matter of fact, if we had been on-board ship and I were the captain, I would have slept with a pistol under my pillow that night.

It fell to Stillman to speak to me, as dictated by rank. We both acknowledged this in a congenial manner.

"I wonder if you could spare a minute," Stillman said, smiling.

I glanced at my watch, but my expression was pleasant. "Just. My office?"

My furniture had arrived sometime during the night, an eye-jarring collection of Louis Quatorze and Pennsylvania Dutch that smelled as though it had been sitting in a warehouse the better part of the century.

I led the way from the audiovisual room, where we had

held our meeting, into my office, acknowledging Stillman's reaction to the furnishings with a vague wave of
my hand. "I'm going to have it replaced," I said.

Stillman quickly turned his attention back to me, his
big smile in place. "My wife and I had hoped to have
you to dinner last night. We feel awful leaving you on
your own your first night."

"I managed to keep myself occupied," I assured him,
equally as pleasantly, and settled in behind my desk.

This was his signal to sit. "Well, we insist you join us
Friday night. A small dinner party, you know, just a few
people you should know in the city. And please, bring a
date."

"Thank you."

I glanced surreptitiously at my watch.

He took the hint. The time for small talk was over.
"Sir, your arrival yesterday was so unexpected, I'm afraid
none of us had an opportunity to express what we feel,
which is how pleased and proud we are to have you single
out our little operation here for attention. I personally
would like to assure you that if there's anything at all I
can do to assist in your understanding of our procedures
here, I stand ready."

I folded my hands across my chest in a polite listening
posture and thought, *Liar. You resent the hell out of my
being here, and you're scared to death I might find out
something. What, I wonder?*

Stillman went on, so smoothly I had to admire his gall,
if nothing else, "On that subject, sir, I'd like to speak a
moment if I may about the St. Clare female. I feel it's my
duty to spare you embarrassment, and I hope I haven't
delayed too long but—"

"Yes, I'm glad you brought up the subject." *You patronizing fool,* I thought, but kept my demeanor calm and

businesslike. "I spent some time last evening going over the records, and frankly I was shocked by the St. Clare situation."

He looked relieved, the foolish dog. "Well, sir, I know that we've allowed her far more latitude than is normal but she is, after all, a St. Clare. Not that that means anything at all now, *monsieur*. Of course not. And may I say that I for one am looking forward to the day when the name St. Clare does nothing to buy special favors."

If he had licked my face and puddled on the floor, he could hardly have been more obvious. I despised him.

I slid open the top drawer of my new desk and removed several file folders, which I slid across the shiny uncluttered surface of the desk to him. "Greg," I said congenially, "I wonder if you would be good enough to take a look at these."

He made a show of putting on his glasses and examining each folder. "Ah, yes," he said, "some of our most successful campaigns. There are two Clios here, and the television run for Ambition must have netted forty million in North America alone."

"I was particularly interested in the creators of each campaign," I said helpfully.

He flipped open a couple of the folders. "Well, they're all different, naturally. It only goes to show what an unsurpassed collection of creative talent we have here at Clare de Lune, which should of course come as no surprise to you, sir."

I wanted to punch him in the mouth.

Instead I said, "But the truth is that those campaigns *weren't* all created by different people, were they? In fact, they all—including the two Clios—originated with the same person, didn't they? Victoria St. Clare."

He looked as though he didn't quite follow my reasoning. "Well, yes, I suppose there may be some truth to that, but you have to understand, sir, there is a wide gap between *originating* an idea and developing it. I certainly hope, sir, that you don't take whatever complaints the St. Clare woman may have made too seriously."

I don't know if I've mentioned it, but I hate being called sir.

"What I take seriously, Greg, is your apparent disregard for the future of this company," I said, very politely.

His shock was absolute, but I was too enraged to appreciate it. I went on in a deliberately even tone, "You have here one of the most inventive, incisive, brilliant minds it has ever been my surprise and pleasure to come across. Talent like this could make us all very rich, Greg, it is the stuff upon which our preeminence in the world of business thrives. This is the kind of genius we encourage, Greg, we nurture it and exploit it to the benefit of us all."

He was losing color with every word I spoke and I could see his knuckles whiten on the folder he still held in his hands. I enjoyed his discomfort, reveled in it.

"But you," I said, leaning forward a little to add emphasis to my words, "you haven't nurtured this talent, you haven't used it the way it was meant to be used. You've stolen it, haven't you? And in doing that, you've stolen from us all."

Stillman's face was as white as marble now. I was surprised he had the wherewithal to speak, but he managed it. "Sir, I'm afraid you don't understand how our division operates—"

"I understand, all right." I cut him off. "I understand that it operates inefficiently and dishonestly. I understand that *you* don't understand exactly how serious is the crime you've committed against the welfare of this company."

His mouth tightened. He straightened his rounded little shoulders and he looked me in the eye. "Sir, I apologize. I didn't understand the, ah, nature of your interest in Ms. St. Clare. I had heard your appetites were well, eclectic, but I had no idea they might be quite so bizarre."

Six months ago I would have lunged across the desk and gone for his throat. I would have ripped out his kidneys and had them for breakfast. I would have...well, never mind what I would have done, and forget that remark about the kidneys. It's just a figure of speech.

The truth is, I am a civilized man and I knew exactly what I had to do. Get the son of a cur out of my sight, out of my office and out of the position to do any more damage.

I said in a tone that could have frozen steel, "Greg, old chap, it's been a pleasure chatting with you. But I'm afraid your usefulness—"

My telephone rang.

I couldn't believe the impudence of the interruption, and I stared at it until it rang again. I snatched it up. "I'm in conference," I snapped. "No calls."

Victoria's voice, smooth as silk, said, "A wise old human once said, 'Keep your friends close, and your enemies closer.' You asked me to tell you if you were in danger."

I looked at Greg. My hand tightened on the receiver. It tightened so much, in fact, that I was surprised the plastic didn't crack. I said, very slowly, "My office. Five minutes."

I hung up the phone.

CHAPTER SIX

Victoria

Noel could hardly have made me more of a target for the werewolves in the office had he tied a piece of liver around my neck. The presentation was possibly the most thoroughly humiliating, excruciating thing I've ever been through, but I could hardly fail to rise to the occasion, could I? He was testing me, obviously. I had no intention of failing. But that does not mean I was grateful for the experience.

Still, he was my boss and I owed him my allegiance. I expected, at the very least, *he* would be grateful for my warning. When I passed Greg Stillman in the hallway, he was looking smug and satisfied, so I assumed my intervention had accomplished what I'd intended—to keep Noel from deposing the most influential man in the Montreal office and making enemies of, not only Stillman, but a dozen or more subordinates.

I'd just done the man a favor he frankly did not deserve. I didn't expect him to send me jewelry—although flowers and candy would not have been refused—but neither did I expect the ice-cold fury in his eyes when he rose from his desk to greet me. In fact, one could say that was the last thing I expected.

"How the hell," he demanded in a low, terrifying voice, "did you hear what I was saying?"

At this juncture, I should point out that I did notice the

way his office was furnished, and it was hideous, like a bad accident in a gypsy caravan. It smelled like mildew and wood rot and I did not see how he could think it was acceptable.

But even as I was taking all this in with an automatic, background observation, my more immediate attention was focused on Noel, and his extraordinary reaction to me. I stared at him, dumbfounded, for a beat too long. He came around the desk and it was all I could do to hold my ground. He was magnificent in a rage. And deadly.

"How did you hear through the white-noise machines?" he repeated, raising his voice. "Answer me, and don't bother lying because I'll know it. Answer me, damn it!"

I couldn't have thought of a lie even if I'd wanted to. I replied, stammering a little and feeling stupid, "There—there's no screen on the telephone lines. I just picked up my extension and—heard you."

Now it was his turn to stare. "You what?"

My courage returned and I replied impatiently, "I assumed you didn't mask the line between your line and mine. I really don't understand—"

"You didn't dial an extension?" I had the satisfaction of seeing some of the color drain from his face. "You just picked up the telephone?"

Now that he put it that way, it did sound odd. I nodded. "Who debugged this office, anyway? Wouldn't you think they'd remember the phone lines?"

Noel didn't answer. He turned instead and turned on his stereo, then strode out of his office.

I watched him snatch up the telephone on Sara's desk and listen, scowling, while Sara watched him with polite puzzlement. "Could I help you make a call, sir?" she inquired.

Noel slammed down the phone without answering and crossed the reception room to my office. I leaned against the doorframe of his office with my arms folded, waiting, and when Sara cast me a questioning look, I simply rolled my eyes and shrugged. I knew perfectly well what Noel could hear from my office; I wasn't about to say anything out loud to her.

In a moment he returned from my office, his eyes dark with anger, and as he strode past me, he caught my arm and pulled me inside his office with him, slamming the door behind us. And that was enough. Certain indignities I am not required to suffer, even for the sake of protocol, and I jerked away irritably.

"Stop manhandling me! What's the matter with you, anyway? Do you think I came back here last night and rigged the phone system? Listen, I was just trying to do you a favor, warning you about—"

Swiftly, he was beside me, his hand tight on my mouth, his scent sharp and spicy, his muscles tight. I stared at him with eyes that were wide and outraged, but he did not remove his hand. He put his mouth close to my ear and he said, in a very low tone, "Not another word."

Personally I thought he was carrying this James Bond routine a little too far. After all, it wasn't as though I was about to give away the secret to Moonsong, or anything else, for that matter. It wasn't as though I was about to say anything of much importance at all.

He spoke again in that same low tone close to my ear, "Just tell me quietly. Is there anyone else in this building whose hearing is as sharp as yours?"

When he removed his hand, I just glared at him, trying to repair the edges of my smeared lipstick with my fingers. And I didn't bother to keep my voice low at all as I snapped back, "How should I know?"

He held me with those eyes, though, and in a moment I was forced to admit, however grudgingly, "I don't think so. Probably not."

The stern demand in his eyes turned to thoughtfulness as he continued to look at me. I was beginning to grow uncomfortable before he finally spoke. He said, "You are a puzzle, Victoria St. Clare."

He went over to the stereo and turned it up a notch or two. The *Brandenburg Concerto No. 2* sailed along in the background, but did not interfere with our conversation.

"I could barely hear the stereo over the telephone line," he said. "Your ears must be extraordinary if you could hear my conversation. Why do you suppose no one ever mentioned that to me before?"

I really didn't like the way he was looking at me. "Why, I really can't imagine. Perhaps for the same reason no one mentioned to you that I could occasionally, when left to my own devices, come up with an idea or two that wasn't entirely worthless?"

He looked at me so solemnly and for such a long time that I felt compelled to add—although, again, grudgingly—"I appreciate what you said before to Stillman. It was…" And I chose my word carefully because I didn't know exactly how I felt. No one had ever defended me before. "Unexpected."

His lips quirked, and he went to his desk. "I hope Stillman appreciates what you did for him. He was about to find himself transferred to a botanicals collection team. The jungles of East Africa, I thought, would suit him particularly well."

He sat down at a desk that looked as though it had served as teething fodder for several generations of pups and began working the keyboard of his computer, adding offhandedly, "The phones will have to be screened. It's nothing personal, but you might be wrong, you might not be the only one in this division whose exceptional hearing has gone undetected.''

I realized, of course, that the action was very much personal, but it was hard to resent that after he'd so nobly stood up for me with Stillman.

"So why did you do it?" I asked.

There was no need to explain what I meant; he knew. He finished typing his memo, put it on the network and answered with only a slight tinge of impatience, "Surely I'm not the only one who sees the stupidity of letting talent go to waste. It's a crime against the company, and the fool deserves worse than East Africa. We need every resource we have working at maximum creativity all the time. To allow anything less is the same as tossing shiploads of supplies overboard, or setting prototypes out to spoil in the sun. It's stupid.''

His outrage, though carefully controlled for my benefit, was genuine, and I understood then why he was our leader. He cared about us all, and with a larger vision than the rest of us ever troubled to encompass.

And then he swiveled his chair away from the keyboard and looked at me. "Why did you stop me?"

"Greg Stillman is stupid about a lot of things," I agreed, "but he can be helpful to you. And he commands a certain amount of loyalty in the division. Punishing him for something he can't help—his own inbred prejudices— would have made both of us a lot of enemies in this office. Maybe you can handle that, but it's something I don't need. I'll have quite enough of that to deal with after this morning's presentation.''

He looked genuinely surprised. "You did a fantastic job. That presentation would have impressed anyone. Why would you think anyone would object?"

I stared at him. Could he possibly be that far removed from the realities of office politics?

Though he had not invited me to do so, I sat down in the chair in front of his desk, folding my hands atop my crossed knees. I didn't miss the way his eyes traveled over the shape of my legs, briefly, and returned to my face.

I said, "Let me ask you something. Why do you think I've been passed over for promotion, had my ideas stolen or ignored and received poor evaluation reports for the past six years?"

He wasn't entirely naive. "I assume it's because of your status."

He was too polite to be more specific. The status of a nonbreeding female was the lowest in the pack; we both knew that.

"The only reason I got this job was because my grades at school—human schools—were too high to ignore. But in the werewolf world, I'm playing by entirely different rules. I may be talented, and I may be smart, but my status doesn't change when I go to work every morning."

"Your status has nothing to do with whether or not you can design an effective campaign," he replied sharply. But the truth was uneasy in his eyes. For all his progressive ideas, he couldn't change what should have been into what was, not now, and perhaps not ever.

I said, quite calmly, "I understand the way the company works, and I accept it. I'm satisfied with my job the way it is."

He looked me straight in the eye and said, "Liar."

"Maybe." I got to my feet. "But one thing is certain. I wouldn't want your job." I hesitated before turning toward the door. "What did you tell Stillman after I hung up, may I ask?"

"I told him that I admired the way the division was

being managed and would appreciate any help he could give me while I was here. Also that I would appreciate his discretion regarding the research I was conducting in which you were involved.''

I lifted an eyebrow. He was entirely too smooth a liar for my liking. "Research? What kind of research?"

He regarded me with a superior look. "I," he replied, "am not required to say."

I barely hid a smile. That, of course, accounted for Stillman's smug look when I'd seen him in the hallway, and I suppose it bought me some time, though to what purpose I couldn't say. "Do you still want me to pretend to work on the Moonsong campaign?"

What extraordinary eyes he had, as green as the sea on a sunny morning and, when he wanted them to be, just as unreadable. It was hard to gather one's wits when pinned by those eyes.

"What makes you think it was ever a pretend job?" he asked me levelly.

I frowned. "Isn't it obvious? Didn't you and I just have a conversation about what I am and am not allowed to do in this office? I agreed to the presentation but I told you last night, I don't have the experience or the power to be in charge of an entire campaign."

He looked at me steadily for a long time. I didn't know what I had said to arouse his suspicion—at least not lately—but I certainly had done something. I hovered there in the center of the room uncomfortably, wanting to leave but not daring to walk away, and then he said abruptly, "Would you like to have lunch with me?"

"No." Sheer surprise made the word abrupt. Then I felt my cheeks grow warm. "I mean—I can't. I have plans."

He tilted a graceful, light-colored eyebrow at me. "One of your human friends?"

He made it sound like an insult. Reactively, my chin went up a fraction, even though my cheeks grew hotter. "Those are the only friends I have," I replied.

With absolutely no change of tone or expression to indicate a switch of subject, he said, "Stay on the campaign. Block out a strategy and have it to me this afternoon."

I wondered if that was his subtle way of suggesting I work through lunch. If so, he had overlooked a few rather important details.

"In that case, I'll need a complete product description."

He just looked at me.

"A prototype," I suggested helpfully. "A chemist's report. A focus-group study, a test sample, a *photograph.* Or are we supposed to just guess what the damn stuff smells like and go from there?"

Still, his expression didn't change. Cool green eyes, aristocratic forehead, sharp nose. That mane of sun gold hair swept back from his shoulders, full lips that could so easily curve into a sneer or relax into devastating sensuality. God, he was beautiful.

He said, without a flicker of a smile, "Guess."

He turned back to his computer, and I was dismissed.

I turned for the door. But I couldn't resist having the last word. "Find the person who was in charge of debugging the office," I advised. "There's your spy."

With the greatest degree of self-restraint, I said nothing at all about his furniture.

If I must say so, I was quite proud of the way I'd handled myself. I mean, the arrogance of the man! First, he designates me his partner in his undercover case, then he informs me *I* am his prime suspect. Then he asks for my help in identifying his enemies, and when I try to prevent him from making a very powerful one, he all but accuses me of top-level, high-tech spying—on *him*. It's fortunate I am not a person of strong emotion. Outrage could have persuaded me to rash behavior as I left his office.

And what was that nonsense about having me continue to work on Moonsong? Only a fool would put an inexperienced junior account exec in charge of something that important. He must think I'm an idiot not to realize that. Assuming, of course, that I have a product to work with, which it was becoming apparent he had no intention of giving me.

Sara flagged me down as I sailed by her desk. It was hard to remember she was now my receptionist. She took one look at my face, which I do not like to think of as revealing, and inquired sympathetically, "Everything go okay in there?"

I tried to shrug away my pique. "He's no more irritating than any other boss I've ever had," I said. I thought about that for a second and corrected, "Yes, he is. Do you want to go to the Brasserie for lunch?"

A confession. I lied about having plans. But really, what was I supposed to do? Last night had been pleasant enough, despite a few awkward moments, but in the workplace? I hated being thrown off guard, and he was constantly doing that to me.

"I'd love to," she replied, "but you're otherwise engaged." She handed me a pink message slip. "Jason Robesieur asked to be penciled in, and I told him I'd try. You *are* traveling in fast company these days, aren't you?"

"Jason? We've been friends for ages."

I scanned the note absently, wondering if Jason was getting to be a little too pushy. True, he had told me he was going to be in town for several days, but didn't he know anyone else? Should I really let him think I was at his beck and call?

"Yes, but isn't he a senior partner in the Gauge Group?" Sara insisted, lowering her voice a little. "How did you get to be so popular all of a sudden?"

I was beginning to wonder that myself.

I glanced at Noel's office, then at the note in my hand. I made up my mind. "Call Mr. Robesieur back and—no, never mind, I'll call him myself." I started toward my office, then turned back. "Say, Sara, how would you like a promotion?"

Her eyes brightened. "You don't have to ask me twice."

I gave a decisive nod. "Then you're now my personal secretary. Move your things into Miss What's-her-name's office, and your first assignment is to find someone to replace yourself here."

Greg Stillman had, of course, taken his own secretary with him, leaving the tiny office next to mine empty. I had no need for a private secretary, and didn't have the faintest idea what to do with one, but I liked Sara and wanted to do something nice for her.

"Of course," I cautioned, "the job only lasts as long as I do…which may not be much beyond this afternoon."

She grinned. "I always did like playing house."

Smiling, I went to call Jason.

I asked him to meet me at the Lotus Room of the Waterfront Hotel. It was rather far for me to go on my lunch hour, but werewolves never went there, so unless I was being followed, there was very little chance I would run into anyone I knew. Besides, the Lotus Room served excellent Polynesian food, and with my new promotion I was entitled to a long lunch.

Jason arrived before I did and got a table; he was always thoughtful that way. He rose when he saw me coming and kissed my cheek. "You look stunning, as always."

Humans do have such delightful manners. But I had to remind him, only half teasing, "I can't have changed much since you saw me yesterday."

He didn't try to dissemble. "I don't mean to monopolize you," he replied as we sat down. "And I appreciate your giving me your time again today. As you might have guessed, there was something specific I wanted to talk to you about."

"Something related to business, I hope?"

He gave me an odd, almost cautious look. "Well, yes, as a matter of fact."

"Good, because this is now a business expense, and you're buying."

I picked up the menu, and he smiled.

I noticed he already had a scotch in front of him, and when the waitress returned, I ordered a Manhattan.

Jason looked surprised. "You never drink at lunch."

"Ah, but that was when I was a lowly junior exec with a cubicle and a secretary I shared with three other people. Penthouse executives, however, with private secretaries and VCRs, quite often have a drink or two with lunch."

"You got a promotion?"

I wasn't sure what it was I heard in his voice. Incredulity, disappointment, worry and all of it masked by a hastily composed expression of pleasure.

"Congratulations," he added quickly. "You deserve it."

I lifted my shoulders modestly. "Actually, it's more a temporary assignment than anything else. But I'm going to enjoy it while I can."

He looked strangely relieved. He sipped his drink. "Victoria," he said abruptly, "I have enough respect for you not to beat around the bush about this thing. Maybe I've made the wrong decision, but I thought it was best to come right out in the open and approach you directly."

The waitress brought my drink and I accepted it with a pleasant nod of thanks. Jason waited until the woman was gone before he spoke.

"There's a rumor going through the industry," he said, "that Clare de Lune is about to launch a new fragrance."

I stirred my drink, returning nothing more than a curious smile. But my heart was pounding. Any werewolf within half a block could have heard it. "We're always introducing new fragrances," I said noncommittally.

He sat hunched over his drink, and the way he looked up to meet and hold my eyes made me feel like an actor in a spy movie. He said, "This is more than a new fragrance. This is a revolutionary new product."

I deserved an Academy Award for the way in which I kept my composure. I removed the little plastic straw from my drink and calmly took a sip. I didn't even choke.

"Where did you hear this rumor?" I asked.

He shook his head. "It wouldn't be a good idea for me to tell you that...for your sake or mine. Anyway, it's all over the industry."

In a mere twenty-four hours. I was impressed.

"And you believe this rumor?"

He made a dismissive gesture with his wrist. "The new CEO flies in without warning to take over the marketing department, people are being reshuffled right and left, fired and—"

"No one's been fired," I objected.

"Promoted," he said, finishing meaningfully.

I took another sip of my drink, thinking rapidly. "Do you have any idea what this..." I chose my words carefully. "New product is?"

His quiet, steady expression indicated he was willing to play my game only so far. "I know," he replied, "that there are people out there who would give a great deal to know. And you and I both know that with a project like this, the marketing department is the last line of defense."

The waitress arrived. I cheerfully ordered a teriyaki chicken salad with extra sesame dressing and Jason said something about shrimp. My mind was reeling with a thousand different notions, all to be assimilated at once. Noel was right. There was a spy among us, a treacherous conniving crawling worm of a thief, and it was one of *us*, a werewolf. It had to be because only werewolves had been at the briefing yesterday, only werewolves—and high-level ones, at that—could possibly have had any access at all to the information about Moonsong, even by accident. But who? And how had it been accomplished so fast? And why was Jason coming to me? What was his role in this and what did he expect of me now? How was I supposed to react, what would Noel want me to say, what did *Jason* want me to say? How could this ever have happened, and how did I end up in the middle?

When the waitress was gone, Jason looked at me solemnly. I sipped my drink. And I knew no other course than straight ahead. One should never play one's weaknesses, and I'm simply no good at subterfuge.

"Why are you telling me all this, Jason?" I inquired.

It was a moment before he answered. I could smell his tension, hear the slow, calculating beat of his pulse and see the flickering shadows in his eyes as he chose his words.

"Preliminary reports indicate," he said, "that this is something big. Maybe the biggest thing to hit the perfume industry in two hundred years. Fortunes are at stake, futures on the line. Obviously there's some debate over whether St. Clare should be entitled to keep it all to itself."

I said pleasantly, "Since they're the ones who invented it and they're the ones who have the formula, I really don't see how anyone can stop them."

He had tried to appeal to my sense of fair play and failed. Now he tried a different tack. His voice hardened, just a fraction. Possibly the change in tone would not have been noticeable to anyone but me. "As I said, fortunes are at stake. Certain people are willing to pay a lot of money for the inside edge on this thing."

I lifted an eyebrow. "You wouldn't happen to be one of them, would you, Jason?" I asked softly.

To his credit, he didn't flinch. He said, "The offer I made you yesterday still stands. We wanted you then for your talent, and we still do. But for anyone who came aboard with information on this new product, there would of course be a substantial bonus, as well as an immediate position as senior account exec. If we happened to land the account on the new product from whoever might be developing it…"

Heavens, how slippery humans can sometimes be! And how easy it is to forget, when caught up in their charm.

"That person," he finished meaningfully, "would of course be assigned full charge of the campaign."

I sipped my drink complacently. "You're in advertising, Jason," I said. "Why in the world would you want to get involved in something like this?"

"Millions, darling," he replied simply. "Millions."

The waitress arrived with our food then, and there was nothing I could do but smile. "Well, it's all very interesting, but I really don't see what it has to do with me."

"Think about it," he advised. "Maybe something will come to you."

And think about it I did.

I am not a complete idiot. I knew exactly what kind of opportunity was before me, and I would have been a fool to reject it out of hand.

From the day of my birth, I had been mocked, tormented, scorned and ignored by members of my own kind. In the workplace, I had endured blatant discrimination and overt harassment. No matter how hard I worked, no matter how good I was at my job nor how much genius I displayed, I would never, ever rise above my present position with Clare de Lune; that was a simple fact of life.

I had at my fingertips the means to avenge myself on them all. Moreover, I could secure for myself a future, a position of importance and recognition, a chance to use my talent and do what I loved, and surely everyone deserved that. All I needed was the secret to Moonsong, and I was confident I could obtain it eventually, either through Noel or some other means. All I needed was Moonsong, and the willingness to betray my people and turn my back on the only life I had ever known. Then all I had ever wanted would be mine…in the human world.

It was like a bad fairy tale.

Shall I pretend I wasn't tempted? Shall I protest I didn't consider Jason's offer? The truth is, when I knocked on Noel Duprey's door at four that afternoon, I still wasn't sure what I was going to say. I would like to think that even if I had known the secret to Moonsong, I would have been just as undecided.

When he bade me enter, I closed the door behind me and leaned against it for a moment while he finished a telephone conversation. I needed the moment to compose myself, and it was not just because of the dilemma with which I wrestled. As always, seeing Noel caused in me an almost physical thrill.

He was lying on the sofa, his jacket and tie discarded and his vest undone, one leg swung over the back of the sofa—a hideous, humpbacked, curry-colored monstrosity—and the other stretched out long upon it. He frowned as he cradled the cordless phone to one ear and gestured me to come in with his opposite hand. He said into the phone, "I really don't see that any of that is my problem, do you? No, of course not. Indeed. And next time, I expect more positive results."

He punched a button on the phone and spoke tersely to his secretary, "Get me Sansonere in Paris. Don't buzz me. Keep him on hold till I pick up."

He disconnected with another punch of a button and swung his feet to the floor, simultaneously running his fingers through the gold cascade of his hair in a gesture that I found almost unbearably sensuous. He looked at me with eyes that were as green as a spring day, sharp and alert.

"Did you have the phones screened?" I asked, simply because I couldn't, at that moment, think of anything else to say. I could barely remember why I had come here.

He replied, "You tell me. Did I?"

I nodded and pushed away from the door. "As far as I can tell."

I could see the light on his desk phone blinking. Estelle, the human secretary who had been assigned to him, had reached Paris. It gave me an odd sense of power to know that I was keeping the president of the Paris office waiting, but also, if the truth be known, it also made me a little nervous.

There were two stiff-backed chairs drawn up before the sofa in an awkward imitation of a conversation group. I took one of them, and it was as uncomfortable as it looked. Something really had to be done about his furniture.

"Do we have a prototype for Moonsong?" I inquired.

Something flickered in his eyes, then grew still again, alert and watchful. "Why?"

"Because Jason Robesieur just offered to buy it from me."

He leaned back against the sofa, his expression thoughtful. I was not disturbed by his lack of reaction; he was far too well schooled to reveal emotions to a junior staff member. But I couldn't help wondering whether he was surprised, either by what I had told him, or the fact that I had told him anything at all.

"What else did he say?" Noel asked after a moment.

"Only that the news about Moonsong was all over the industry. He wouldn't tell me who told him, but I got the feeling it wouldn't help much to know. Jason is the kind of man who doesn't act on information unless he's confirmed it at several levels, so I believe he was telling the truth. Everyone knows."

Noel templed his fingers beneath his chin, gazing at me. I couldn't be sure whether he was really looking at me, or through me. "Rather haphazard of our traitor, wouldn't you say? Almost like something a human would do."

I was surprised. I had expected him to make more of the fact that it was Jason—*my* friend—who had been the first to approach us.

Or perhaps Jason wasn't the first. Perhaps I was just the only one who had reported the contact.

I said, "But it wasn't a human. Only werewolves were at that meeting."

And try as I might, I simply could not imagine any of them selling our secrets to humans.

Again, Noel nodded.

"So this confirms it." My voice was heavy, though I didn't mean it to be. "It is a werewolf, and he's in this office."

"And he wastes no time putting out the word that he has something to sell."

"But he doesn't," I protested. "None of us know anything about this so-called revolution, not even what is revolutionary about it."

There was no visible sign that he had made a decision, or, in fact, that he was about to say anything of moment at all. He replied, in the most casual tone, "You will. I want you to gather your team this afternoon for the first planning meeting. The product you are selling is more than a perfume. It may be, in fact, the first genuine aphrodisiac in the history of the world."

I stared at him, my disbelief evident.

He smiled. "I isolated the formula myself several years ago, but it's taken this long to distill it to a level fit for public distribution. Also, there have been problems with the FDA which makes it impossible to use any of our manufacturing plants in the United States."

"FDA?" I parroted, my eyes widening. "Food and *Drug* Administration? Since when do they have anything to say about the manufacture of perfume?"

He made a dismissive gesture with his wrist. "As I said, it's been a series of misunderstandings. At any rate, we will be using our facility in Paris, and we intend to start production this month…under the tightest possible security of course. The plant is being refitted now with special equipment to protect the laborers, but that shouldn't take more than another two weeks. We have got to be ready to go into production immediately, and that means we've got to catch this spy.''

I got to my feet, trying to control my agitation. ''Wait a minute.'' I paced a few steps away, pressing my fingers briefly to my temples as I tried to organize my thoughts. ''FDA, special equipment…'' I turned to him, almost afraid to ask the next question. ''Just exactly what do you mean by aphrodisiac?''

There seemed to be genuine amusement in his smile. ''Nothing irresponsible, I assure you. Although in its unrefined form, the prime ingredient is, in fact, capable of driving humans—and werewolves—into a sexual frenzy. Obviously this would hardly be suitable for a perfume, particularly as a commercial venture. No, what Moonsong does in its present state is stimulate the pleasure centers on an almost subliminal level. It makes people feel good when they smell it, or when they wear it. It makes people happy to be around it. And, of course, it makes people want to buy more of it.''

I blinked several times to clear my head. And, even though I should be ashamed of myself, the main thing I was trying to clear my head of were the dozens of delightful, innovative, *revolutionary* advertising concepts that were tumbling over themselves in their eagerness to be developed.

''Is it addictive?'' I asked.

Noel gave an impatient shake of his head. ''Of course not. And neither, as far as we can tell, does one develop a tolerance for it. Each time you smell it is just as delightful as the first. I hope you don't think I would ever involve this company in anything immoral.''

I didn't know what to answer except the truth. ''I don't know you,'' I said carefully. ''No one does, really. There are bound to be some rather demanding questions when the secret to Moonsong comes out.''

''Of course,'' Noel agreed mildly. ''But most of those questions will have answered themselves in the way Moonsong is received…as we watch the way people react to it.''

I swallowed hard. I had to ask. ''And the board approved this?''

He arched an eyebrow ever so slightly, at my impudence. ''Of course.''

I released a long, slightly unsteady breath. ''Well,'' I said at last. It was all I could manage. Who was I to question the board? Who was I to question Noel? But then, there were so many questions.

Fortunately, there were also one or two answers. I knew now why he had insisted upon putting me in charge of the creative team. A) He needed someone he could trust overseeing the most sensitive portion of the campaign, or B) He wanted to keep all of his suspects together. And the people working on this campaign comprised his shortlist of suspects. I understood that now. I also realized that he was carefully releasing information about Moonsong to us, one small bit at a time, so that he could more easily trace exactly when—and perhaps how—that information was leaving this office.

I said, ''I'll assign each member of my team a security code. They'll use it for everything—to log in and out on their computers, to access the fax machines, to request research and supplies. The telephone calls are already logged. If anything leaves this office regarding the campaign, we'll know it.''

I could tell he was impressed. His tone was brisk. "That's good. I won't be able to attend your meeting this afternoon, but I'll listen in. You understand that you're responsible for every member of your team?''

"I do.''

There was a lot more I wished I understood, but I wasn't ready to ask yet. I glanced at the light still blinking on his desk phone. "I'd best get to it then.''

He stood and started toward his desk. I turned toward the door. "There is one more thing,'' he said.

I looked back.

He picked up the receiver on his phone but didn't push the button. "Greg Stillman is throwing a party Friday night. I'd like you to come with me.''

Well, he couldn't have caught me more off guard if he had literally pulled the rug out from under my feet. I practically gaped at him. And before I could stop myself, I blurted out the stupidest thing.

"Why?''

Why? It was a reasonable question, wasn't it? He had asked me on a date, hadn't he? Why would he want to do such a thing? He knew about me, didn't he? A man in his position, a man with his reputation, to take me to a party—a party at Greg Stillman's house—the scandal it would cause, the outrage... How could I accept? What was he asking of me?

He glanced at me, his expression implacable, and he answered, "I have a feeling that party is going to be a loaded situation, and I can't be everywhere at once. I need you to be my ears.''

"Oh.'' I should have been flattered, I should have been

relieved. Certainly the last thing I should have felt was disappointment.

And to hide it, I answered, "I'll need a new dress. I don't suppose there's any overtime in this for me?"

His eyes glinted amusement as he replied, "You suppose correctly. Wear an old dress."

He punched the button on his phone and spoke to Paris. I left the office in a daze, with too much to think about and not enough time in which to do it.

CHAPTER SEVEN

Noel

I am a nice guy; ask anyone. I'm the first one to reach for the check. I always leave housekeeping a big tip, even if my party didn't destroy the room. I hold doors, I'm courteous to my elders and I've even been known—though not often, I admit—to smile at small children in crowded airport waiting rooms. I honestly didn't mean to hurt Victoria's feelings with my answer. *Why?* she'd asked. What was I supposed to say?

It did not occur to me that I might have put her in an awkward situation by asking her to accompany me to Stillman's party. Why should it? When I ask a woman out, she is generally delighted. I am an excellent date, if I do say so myself. The last thing I expected was that she would ask me *why*.

Why? Because I wanted to, of course. That, for the most part, is the reason that I do anything. Because she is lovely and funny and smart and because I frankly couldn't imagine going with anyone else... Which is odd, now that I think of it. There are dozens of gorgeous were-wolf females in the Montreal office alone, and, if it came to that, one phone call would put me in touch with any one of a directory full of other eminently eager female companions. But I asked Victoria because I wanted to.

Why should I have imagined she would be in the least bit uncomfortable by what was to me at best, a natural invitation, and at worst, a logical request? She was supposed to be my partner, after all. One could even say I was walking into a politically volatile situation with Stillman's party; naturally I would want an ally there. And hadn't she noticed that I hadn't been in town long enough to make any friends? What did she mean, *why?*

Because I wanted to, that was why. So why did I tell her that I wanted her to accompany me because I needed her ears? The crestfallen expression on her face before she disguised it with her usual cavalier humor pricked me like a knife point. I felt bad. But I think I didn't tell her the truth because I didn't really know what it was.

Why *did* I want her to come with me? I was still turning the question over in my mind, looking for a suitable answer, when I arrived at her house on Friday night. Need I point out that I was gentleman enough to call for her at her home, rather than leave from the office or ask her to meet me at the party? I even brought her roses—yellow, which, according to some long-forgotten human poet, mean friendship. I chose them because they are unique—particularly for Montreal in winter—much like Victoria herself.

She opened the door and the first thing I saw was the damn cat. It arched its back and hissed at me. I restrained myself from doing the same only because my eyes were fixed, at that moment, on Victoria's shapely ankles, and began to travel inexorably upward.

She was wearing a skimpy little white cocktail dress that would have sent any human male into a dead swoon. It had a flared skirt that fell to a point just above her knees and made her legs look a mile long, then proceeded to hug every curve and plane on her body all the way up to her barely covered bosom. A spray of rhinestones crossed diagonally from one shoulder to the opposite breast, accenting the sweet swell of her décolletage and leaving me dry-mouthed. Her hair...she had done something incredible to her hair. It cascaded in a riot of curls and waves from a glittering barrette at her crown to her shoulders and midway down her back. Her lipstick was cherry, her skin like porcelain. She smelled of silk and a vanilla-based fragrance called Enchantment (Clare de Lune, $142 per ounce without the employee discount, of course) that could have been made with her alone in mind. Try as I might, I could not see a panty line.

I thrust the flowers at her, wordlessly, and was gratified by the genuine delight that lit up her eyes. "Roses!" she exclaimed softly, and buried her face in the bouquet. "Oh, they're exquisite! No one has ever given me roses before."

How to describe the emotions I felt then? The surge of triumph for her pleasure, the outrage that no one had ever sent this magnificent creature roses before; the burgeoning admiration for her simple, piercing beauty; the stark confusion for the intensity of my own emotions.

"You look—stunning," I said huskily.

She lifted eyes to me that were pleased and anxious, though she made her voice flippant. "This old thing?" She pirouetted for me once, and the skirt flared to tease me with a glimpse of the comeliest thigh it has ever been my extreme pleasure to observe. "Just a little something I found in the back of my closet."

But when she finished her turn, her face was uncertain behind the bravado. "Is it all right, do you think? I could change."

"It's perfect," I assured her, and stepped inside, closing the door behind me. I hoped the cat might have taken the opportunity to escape, but no such luck; it followed me, glaring, as I crossed the room toward Victoria.

She pressed her face into the bouquet again, briefly, reveling in the scent of it, and said, "I'll just put these in water. Would you like a drink or anything?"

"No, I have the car downstairs." "The car" was the company limo, of course, a black Rolls with a bar more fully stocked than most commercial airlines and, unless my nose deceived me, a warming oven supplied with hot canapés as well as the usual caviar and goose pâté. "The driver tells me Stillman lives about half an hour outside the city, so we should probably leave."

She was smiling as she returned. "I doubt they'll start dinner without you."

"Probably not," I agreed. "But the sooner we get there, the sooner we can leave."

She took her white fur coat from the closet. "Is there anything in particular you'd like me to do tonight?"

Saints, she was taking this seriously. She really thought this was going to be a working evening. Well, in a way, I suppose it was; from now until we caught the spy, every moment would be a working moment.

I took the coat from her and held it while she slipped her slender bare arms into the satin-lined interior, experiencing a moment of pathos for this beautiful creature who, with no hope of ever having a coat of her own, had to wear manufactured goods to keep warm. I said, resting my hands for just a moment on her shoulders, "I want you to be lovely and charming and quick-tongued and bright. In other words, I want you to be yourself, and dazzle the hell out of everyone in that room."

She turned to me slowly, confusion and apprehension in her eyes. She was nervous, that much I could tell. But I was far too self-centered to understand the real reason why.

"You want me to be...distracting," she suggested, "while you make character assessments?"

Again, it was work for her. "I want," I told her, barely keeping the exasperation out of my voice, "you to have a good time. Enjoy your dinner. Chat with the ladies, show off for the men. Act like my date."

A faint line of puzzlement appeared between her eyebrows, but she nodded, pulling on a pair of white kid gloves. "I'll do my best."

She picked up her evening purse and called, "Good night, Socrates. Be a good kitty."

To my astonishment, the cat actually made some kind of vocalization in reply. It then leaped onto the sofa and began to groom itself, spreading black hairs all over the velvet upholstery.

The night was bitter cold but star-bright, and the warmth of the limo welcome. Victoria's eyes reflected awe as they quickly scanned the luxurious surroundings—the dove gray leather seats, the built-in computer terminal, fax and modem, the cellular phone and miniature television and VCR, the bar and walnut tray tables that also served as folding desks—but to me she looked perfectly natural in such an environment as she settled in across from me, a snow queen swathed in white fur.

"Champagne?" I offered. "Or something else?"

She hesitated, as though not quite certain whether she felt comfortable in this unfamiliar role, but then apparently decided to enjoy it. "Sherry," she said. "Champagne gives me a headache. And what is that marvelous smell?"

We nibbled on canapés from the warming oven and toast points with caviar, and she told me about Greg Stillman and his wife, Avril, both originally from Ottawa. "They have a wonderful house," she said. "Or so I've heard. One of those huge mansions way back in the woods with a gated entrance and hundreds of acres. I've always wanted to see it.''

As a matter of fact, the acreage was a minimum of five hundred, all fenced and heavily wooded to protect us from the curious. Werewolves do occasionally need room to run, and there were several such complexes in every major city in which we had offices. I explained this to Victoria, adding, ''The house is a company holding. Greg only keeps it in trust for as long as he holds his position here. And of course, the grounds are available only to higher-level executives.''

Her face, illuminated by the distant lights of other automobiles, looked thoughtful as she bit into a canapé. ''So,'' she said a moment later, ''executives like Stillman are highly motivated to maintain their positions within the company. If they don't, they lose everything.''

I did not entirely follow her logic. ''Well, no, not necessarily. I suppose it is conceivable that one might become attached to a particular house, but all the executive quarters are luxurious. A transfer to Europe, for example, might mean—''

But she interrupted me with a shake of her head. I could see the gleam of excitement in her eyes even from the depths of the seat opposite and it was captivating. ''No, I don't mean transfer or promotion. I mean failure, demotion, being passed over or even reprimanded, like you were about to do to Greg the other day. I suppose I always knew it, but I never really thought about it before. He would be humiliated, ruined, his status broken…but he would also lose everything he's accumulated. His house, his club memberships, his car—even his running space. Everything.''

I nodded slowly, still not completely understanding.

"Fortunately, that doesn't happen very often, particularly at this level."

"But don't you see?" She leaned forward a little, the excitement now penetrating her voice. "I could never understand why a werewolf would betray us before, particularly to humans. I mean, what would be the point? The company is our life, it gives us everything. To hurt it would be to hurt ourselves. But the company can also *take away* everything, especially on the highest executive level. And if it did, if an executive lost everything, where could he go except to humans? Where else could he ever expect to achieve the kind of success he once had known? Don't you see? That's the motive!"

I sat there in the silently gliding limo with a glass of champagne in my hand and the ghost lights of other cars flickering past, wrestling with the implications of her words and absorbed by the vision she made sitting across from me swathed in white fur and framed by that cascade of satiny black curls, when suddenly it struck me: I could trust this woman.

Yes, I know. The time for such an epiphany, if it were to come, should have logically occurred when Victoria had reported to me the offer made by Jason Robesieur. That proved her innocence, didn't it? If she had been our spy—and what a perfect setup, considering the Robesieur connection—how could she have resisted the temptation he offered her?

On the other hand, I had an empire to protect, a future held in trust. She would have expected me to know about her meeting with Jason—which I did, incidentally—and by dutifully and truthfully reporting to me, intended to throw me off her trail. Already I knew she was exceptionally clever; such cunning would not have been beyond her.

My eyes, my ears, my senses for all things devious told me the chances were better than eighty percent that Victoria was innocent. With all my heart, for whatever that's worth, I wanted to believe it. But so much was at stake; I refused to be led astray by a pair of gorgeous legs. So I withheld judgment, clinging to my skepticism with more determination than reason.

There was no more reason now to believe her than there had been earlier, but suddenly I did. Suddenly I saw in her eyes genuine concern, heard in her tone the conviction of the honest, smelled on her skin the sweet breath of utter innocence. This woman was on my side. She could help me. She was not the problem, but very possibly the solution.

Or perhaps that was, once again, simply what I wanted to believe.

I said, narrowing my eyes a fraction as I tried to sort out my thoughts, "Interesting. So you think Stillman could be the one we're looking for?"

She sat back, sipping sherry thoughtfully. Her coat was open, and I could not help noticing the glitter of rhinestones against creamy skin. I reminded myself my judgment might not be all it should be. It had not, in fact, been particularly accurate since I got here.

"I don't know," she admitted at last. "It seems a little too obvious, doesn't it? But I think he bears keeping an eye on."

"I agree."

She had given me a lot to think about, and a mile or two passed in silence as I sipped my champagne and gazed out the window, seeing, mostly, the reflection of Victoria, all elegance and beauty, superimposed upon the passing night.

At last I said, frowning a little, "I never really thought

about it before, but perhaps you're right. Our policy toward high-level executives does provide a motive for discontent, and a great deal more, I should think. St. Clare always provides an opportunity to make a living, and no one among us will ever starve...but shouldn't there be something beyond that? If a man works faithfully for twenty, thirty years, it doesn't seem fair that he should lose everything for one mistake, great or small. A man should be allowed to keep some of what he's accumulated, shouldn't he?''

I was thinking of Michael St. Clare, who once had been—on paper if not in fact—one of the wealthiest men in the world. He had been the second most powerful werewolf among us; a lift of his finger would have brought him anything he desired, accomplished anything he wished. Admittedly, his circumstance was not common and his transgression not small, but look at him now: working with his hands for humans, collecting their paltry wages, driving—I winced at the thought—a pickup truck. Of course, by all accounts he was happy, but he was a St. Clare, and it didn't seem fair.

I wasn't aware I had spoken that last out loud until Victoria responded, ''It's not fair, but that's the way it's always been. The welfare of the pack is the first priority.''

Imagine that. Victoria St. Clare being my conscience.

I said, ''That's right, and it should be. But maybe the principles that worked four hundred years ago aren't appropriate in the twenty-first century. Maybe we should look toward restructuring the justice system in this company.''

''Maybe you should.''

''Someone should appoint a task force.''

''Why don't you?''

I was taken aback. ''Me?''

Her eyebrows went up gently. "Who else?"

It struck me like that sometimes, unawares: *I* was in charge of the company. *I* could do it.

I lifted my champagne glass, a little overwhelmed by the concept, and murmured, "Indeed."

Stillman's estate was as Victoria had described it: a stately brick structure well removed from its neighbors, arranged in the middle of a parklike expanse of snow-covered lawn and fortified by intricately carved wrought-iron gates that slid open silently at our approach. The grounds were decorated with strategically placed garden lights that made the lawn look like a winter wonderland, and the house itself was ablaze with cheerful lamplight. I was amused by the way Victoria turned her gaze from one window to the other, trying to take in all the sights but determined not to reveal her eagerness.

"Would you like to live in a house like this?" I inquired.

"Good heavens, no," she replied flippantly. "I could never keep the floors scrubbed."

But then she glanced at me and admitted, with more longing in her tone than I suspect she wanted me to hear, "Who wouldn't?"

I wouldn't, for one. But then, I had a town house in London. And a villa in France and a chalet in Switzerland and a penthouse in New York. I had Castle St. Clare. The fact that I hadn't asked for any of them—except the town house—didn't make them any less mine. It was all still difficult to grasp sometimes.

The driver pulled the car in front of the freshly swept front steps and opened the door for me first, and then Victoria. Alternating blue and white spotlights illuminated the portico and the evergreen garden that surrounded it. I could hear a string quartet inside, ice cubes clinking in glasses, a myriad of separate conversations, none of them particularly interesting, caterers scurrying in the kitchen, the snap of matches as candles were lit, the ping of crystal brushing the rim of a bone china plate. Stillman had pulled out all the stops.

The steps were covered with a red runner to welcome important guests, and to absorb the melted snow from their expensive shoes. I offered my arm to Victoria and we ascended the stairs. I could feel her tension and see it in the stiffness of her smile, but I supposed—rather arrogantly—that she was intimidated by such an unaccustomed display of wealth. Had I forgotten that she was a St. Clare? For certain members of her family, a dinner like this would have been a casual evening at home. Besides, if I knew nothing else about Victoria, by now I should have at least realized she was not easily intimidated.

The door was opened by a butler—although I believe they prefer to be called housepersons or domestic supervisors or something of the kind. This one was polite and very well trained. He took our coats gracefully and advised us our hosts were awaiting our arrival in the grand parlor to the left.

Grand parlor. I was beginning to enjoy Stillman's pretension.

I placed my hand lightly on Victoria's back as we moved toward the crowd. The grand parlor was, actually, rather grand. It appeared to be two rooms, in fact, which opened into one another via a series of pocket doors. The ceilings were high and the decor muted in tones of mauve and federal blue. There were a great many plants and a few very fine paintings.

Intimate conversation groups were drawn up around spindly legged tables, but most people were standing, chatting in free-flowing groups from one to the other. You can always tell a gathering of werewolves from a human party; we are a gregarious, social people who never form those exclusionary little conversational knots that are so common in human gatherings.

The air was redolent of whiskey and white wine, chafing dishes and brie and an almost intoxicating mixture of St. Clare perfumes. There was laughter and the crackle of a fire dancing in the grate, the tinkle of dangling earrings and scraps of genial conversation. Then our host spotted us from across the room and everything changed.

To be fair, absolute silence did not fall. The quartet continued to play and the caterers continued to work in the kitchen. The fire continued to crackle and the ice cubes continued to clink in glasses held by unsteady hands. But one by one, word by word, conversations faltered and ceased as all eyes turned slowly toward us.

Since assuming my new office, I've grown accustomed to receiving a certain amount of notice when I enter a room. Sometimes, in fact, I feel like a headmaster on a playground, or a priest in a brothel, with the way I can subdue a crowd just by appearing. But I had never been the cause of this kind of reaction before. And, granted, Victoria was a beautiful woman, but not even that dress could account for the way people were staring. Besides, they couldn't be staring at her...but they were.

I'm not sure exactly when I realized that. Perhaps it was in the contempt that flickered across Greg Stillman's eyes when he looked at her, or the way his wife touched the pearls around her crepey neck as though afraid Victoria might steal them. Maybe it was the way the other werewolves glanced at me, then at Victoria, then at anyplace other than the two of us. But mostly I knew from the cool, curving smile that touched Victoria's lips, and the cold shield that rose over her eyes.

Greg Stillman came toward me, his hand extended, his expression welcoming and his voice a little too boisterous. His wife, following as though on a short leash, was a step behind, her own smile strained and her eyes disdainful.

"Well, Noel," said Stillman loudly, "so happy you could join us. Do you know my wife, Avril?"

I shook his hand and bowed over Avril's. "Thank you for inviting me," I said. You may recall, my manners are excellent. I turned to Victoria. "Do you know—"

Stillman interrupted me. "Did I mention Leonard White was flying in from New York? He's most anxious to meet you. You'll find him very useful when it comes to market research, the best in the business, they say."

I stared him down. I would like to say I shamed him into silence, but the man had no shame. It was fear pure and simple. I turned back to his wife. "*Madame,* as I was saying…?" I waited a polite beat. "Have you met Victoria St. Clare?"

The older woman avoided my eyes. She toyed with her pearls once more. She didn't look at Victoria, either, except for one or two curious, almost distasteful glances as she spoke. "Oh, yes, the little…" She cleared her throat. "From the office. Of course. Well, we weren't expecting—but I'm sure we can find a place…"

I said, "Excuse me, did I misunderstand? Didn't you ask me to bring a date?"

Stillman laughed loudly and gripped my arm in a far too familiar way. His wife tittered. Stillman said, "A date, yes! But you should have told me if you were that hard up, old man." He lowered his voice confidentially and started to lead me away. "I could have put you together with…"

Coldly, I pulled my arm from his grasp. The voices of other werewolves, murmuring in the background, now reached me in infuriating snatches. "I mean, really, the nerve of the little bitch. She thinks she can just push herself in anywhere…"

"How distressing! Poor Avril! Now the seating plan will simply be ruined."

"What can *he* be thinking, can you tell me that?"

"Perhaps he doesn't know."

"Well, if he can't tell the difference between a female and one like that, I think the pack may be in serious difficulty!"

"I've never seen one up close before. She looks rather normal, doesn't she?"

I looked at Victoria, stoic and calm, her face composed and her eyes devoid of emotion. I looked at my host and hostess. I looked at guests around the room, who avoided my eyes and sipped their drinks, suddenly finding other things of great interest to discuss. And all the while my fury grew.

I should explain that strong emotion, when we allow ourselves to experience it fully, is one of the things that triggers the Change in us from human to wolf. Anger is one of our most powerful emotions, so when we say, "I was angry enough to rip out his throat," it is not entirely a figure of speech. We do not, of course, generally act on our emotions; if we did, what kind of society would we have? We are trained from childhood to control our emotions and use them at our will; it's called civility.

I have never, however, been quite so close to involuntarily relinquishing control as I was at that moment. Only the steely press of Victoria's fingers on my forearm reminded me of my duty and my surroundings.

So, instead of launching myself at Greg Stillman and

his entire bigoted crew in a display of absolute idiocy, I said in a voice that could have cut diamonds, "Perhaps we had better leave."

I turned to Victoria, but there arose such a flutter of protest that I was forced to look back. Stillman looked utterly flabbergasted; his wife near tears. He said, "I'm sure I don't—" And she, "Oh, please, you mustn't!"

I realized they had no idea they had done anything wrong. In fact, no one in the room saw anything wrong with the way they had reacted to Victoria, not even Victoria herself. That in itself infuriated me, and I might have left, anyway, but for the steadying pressure of Victoria's fingers on my arm, the quiet strength that flowed from her. As far as she was concerned, she had come to do a job. So had I.

I made my muscles relax, I slowed the beat of my heart. I said in quiet, polite French, but distinctly enough for everyone to hear, "It is not my wish to make anyone uncomfortable. Please remember, however, that when you insult my guest, you insult me."

Stillman avoided my eyes, clearly confused. His wife tugged at her necklace in increasing distress. "Sir, I don't understand what you mean. Of course—"

And then, to my surprise as much as anyone's, Victoria spoke up. Her voice was cool and clear and held only the slightest tinge of impatience, nothing more. "What he means," she said, "is that he is the heir designé. If he brought a trained monkey to dinner with him, he would expect it to be seated at the table. Is that really such a difficult concept?"

"Oh." The faces around me cleared. "Oh, yes, of course." Avril Stillman bowed deeply, as did her husband. "Our pardon, sir. We intended no offense."

I turned again to Victoria, raising an inquisitive eyebrow as I offered her my arm.

She lifted a dismissive shoulder and murmured, "You just have to put it in terms they can understand."

There was a great deal more I would have liked to have said to her on the subject, but within moments we were separated by the demands of good party behavior. I didn't hover or force my presence on her; to have done so would have been to suggest Victoria St. Clare couldn't take care of herself—which, as I had just seen, was patently absurd. Besides, selfish as it was, I couldn't be everywhere at once, and I did need her ears.

I remember that the roast beef was excellent and abundant, so rare it could have walked away with a little encouragement and served with a flavorful Cabernet Sauvignon, of which I drank rather much, I'm afraid. There were many things of interest going on around me, I'm sure, but I paid them little attention. I was far too concerned with Victoria.

To their credit, once instructed in how to behave, the werewolves at the gathering conducted themselves suitably. They were careful not to snub or denigrate Victoria in any way, though neither did they go out of their way to make her welcome. Whether or not Victoria was hurt by this, I couldn't say. She sat beside me at dinner—at least Avril Stillman had gotten *that* much right—and responded politely when I addressed comments to her, but otherwise she was so unobtrusive as to almost blend into the woodwork. How this could be I couldn't imagine. Victoria St. Clare was the most beautiful woman present. How could anyone fail to notice that?

On the other hand, the ability to become invisible was a very useful characteristic for a spy. I supposed I should be grateful that, tonight, she was working for me.

The Silhouette Reader Service™ — Here's how it works:

Accepting your 2 free books and gift places you under no obligation to buy anything. You may keep the books and gift and return the shipping statement marked "cancel." If you do not cancel, about a month later we'll send you 6 additional novels and bill you just $3.99 each in the U.S., or $4.74 each in Canada, plus 25¢ shipping & handling per book and applicable taxes if any.* That's the complete price and — compared to cover prices of $4.75 each in the U.S. and $5.75 each in Canada — it's quite a bargain! You may cancel at any time, but if you choose to continue, every month we'll send you 6 more books, which you may either purchase at the discount price or return to us and cancel your subscription.

*Terms and prices subject to change without notice. Sales tax applicable in N.Y. Canadian residents will be charged applicable provincial taxes and GST.

If offer card is missing write to: Silhouette Reader Service, 3010 Walden Ave., P.O. Box 1867, Buffalo NY 14240-1867

NO POSTAGE
NECESSARY
IF MAILED
IN THE
UNITED STATES

BUSINESS REPLY MAIL
FIRST-CLASS MAIL   PERMIT NO. 717-003   BUFFALO, NY

POSTAGE WILL BE PAID BY ADDRESSEE

SILHOUETTE READER SERVICE
3010 WALDEN AVE
PO BOX 1867
BUFFALO NY 14240-9952

GET FREE BOOKS and a FREE GIFT
WHEN YOU PLAY THE...

Lucky 7

SLOT MACHINE GAME!

Just scratch off the silver box with a coin. Then check below to see the gifts you get!

YES! I have scratched off the silver box. Please send me the 2 free Silhouette Intimate Moments® books and gift for which I qualify. I understand I am under no obligation to purchase any books, as explained on the back of this card.

345 SDL DRM6

245 SDL DRNN
(S-IMB-10/02)

FIRST NAME	LAST NAME

ADDRESS

APT.#	CITY

STATE/PROV.	ZIP/POSTAL CODE

7 7 7	**Worth TWO FREE BOOKS plus a BONUS Mystery Gift!**
🍒 🍒 🍒	**Worth TWO FREE BOOKS!**
♣ ♣ ♣	**Worth ONE FREE BOOK!**
🔔 🔔 🍒	**TRY AGAIN!**

Visit us online at www.eHarlequin.com

DETACH AND MAIL CARD TODAY!

After dinner, we drank port and nibbled on Stilton cheese and sweet biscuits before the fire in the small parlor, which was one half of the grand parlor, with the pocket doors closed to create a more intimate atmosphere. I was just trying to decide how soon I could make my escape, when Stillman said boisterously, "What a fine moonless night! The snow is hard frozen in the woods, I checked it myself only this afternoon. Shall we run?"

The Run is a necessary ritual among werewolves, celebrating our uniqueness, our sense of play, our exuberance for life. The essence of it is exactly what it sounds like—except that it involves nudity, the transformation from human to wolf form and back again, and, more often than not, the expression of natural affection and high spirits which doubtless could not be understood by anyone outside our species.

The Run is a form of recreation, of exercise, of self-expression and stress reduction; it is also essential to our physical and mental health. To be perfectly honest, after an evening such as this, with the cold clear air beckoning and a black sky sparkling with stars close enough to catch in one hand, a run was exactly what I needed. And it seemed to me the height of bad taste for Stillman to suggest it in front of Victoria, who could not participate.

On the other hand, it would be wrong of me to deny the pleasure to the others, so I stood and said, "Thank you, I wish I could. But I have an extremely early conference call from Japan, and I'm afraid I must take my leave."

I turned to Avril. "*Madame,* the dinner was excellent. Thank you for your hospitality."

She colored prettily and offered me her hand. "You honor us, sir. You are, if I may say, more than I ever expected."

I wondered what she meant by that.

Stillman walked me to the door. I caught Victoria's eye across the room and beckoned to her.

"I've wanted to ask," Stillman said, "whether you're finding everything to your liking at the office. You want for nothing?"

"Everything's fine, yes." I wanted only to be away from there, and alone with Victoria.

"You know if you need anything at all, all you have to do is ask."

"I know."

"I was wondering…" Now he spoke a little more slowly, choosing his words with care. "Whether you have any notion yet as to how long you will be gracing us with your presence here in Montreal."

Ah, now I understood.

"Not yet," I said. We had reached the foyer, where the butler was waiting with my coat. Victoria was approaching from the right.

I held out my arms and the butler slipped the coat onto my shoulders. "However, I do appreciate your generosity in giving up your office. You're finding the new accommodations satisfactory, I hope?"

"Oh, eminently, eminently."

Everything about his body language declared him a liar. His smug smile grated on my nerves.

"I hope you're not finding your staff too much of a trial," he went on. "I'd be happy to advise you if you decide to make changes, or I would be happy to serve as your assistant myself. No job is a small job if it makes your job easier, sir."

The man had brass-plated gall, I'll say that for him. Victoria had arrived by then, and was slipping into her coat. I couldn't be away from there soon enough.

"Thank you for the dinner," I said again. "I appreciate your efforts."

And Victoria echoed sweetly, "Yes, it was delightful."

The look of contempt he cast her when he thought I didn't see made me want to backhand him across the room on my way out.

The night was cold and dark and as clear as crystal. I ached to run. Holding Victoria's arm lightly as we descended the stairs, I felt a brief and surprising prick of resentment, accompanied almost immediately by a surge of shame. I could run anytime I chose. She could never even know the desire.

We did not speak until we were in the back of the limo with the privacy screen up and the white noise on. Then she said breathily, "Well, what an evening!"

I wanted to apologize to her. I didn't know where to begin.

She went on with a kind of subdued eagerness, "First of all, you may have noticed, Greg Stillman is absolutely furious about losing his office...and humiliated over the fact that he lost it to *me*. What puzzles me is why he hasn't made a bigger fuss over getting his computer back. I know he has an identical unit now, but a computer is a personal item and it just seems to me like the kind of thing he'd take a stand on... Is that coffee I smell? Could we have some?"

I stared at her. "Victoria...did you have a good time tonight?"

She seemed surprised by the question. "Was I supposed to?"

I didn't know how to answer that so I concentrated on trying to figure out how to work the coffee dispenser, and on finding cups.

"Go on," I invited briskly.

She gave me an odd brief look, then resumed her report. "Well, that PR man from the U.S.—what was his name? Singleton? He doesn't like you in the least. He thinks you're far too liberal and potentially dangerous. The others were a bit kinder, though it was probably because they knew you were listening. On the whole, I have to say bringing me to the party did you more harm than good, though it did throw quite a few people off-balance."

I handed her a cup of coffee, black, and settled back into the shadows of the seat with my own cup, fascinated by her.

"No one, absolutely no one, talked about Moonsong, did you notice? That in itself seems odd to me. I mean, what else were they there for? However, I did learn several interesting things. Mikail Salinski went to school with Alvin Rolander, head of R & D at Pavlova Perfumes... and they ended up with one of our formulas, didn't they? Their wives keep in touch—the recipe for the crab dip came from Marissa Salinski who got it from Sandra Rolander only last week—so one can assume the husbands do, as well."

I was amazed. "And you think more than recipes could be changing hands?"

She shrugged. "Then there's Pierre Tuscan, who seems to be very afraid for his job for some reason. His wife told Leanna Devlin they canceled their ski trip to Europe this year because—and I quote—their financial future is so uncertain."

She sipped her coffee. "In fact, half the executives on the Moonsong team are more than a little uneasy about their futures, mostly just the natural nervousness that comes with a change of administration, I think. I mean, they've modeled themselves all these years to please Michael St. Clare and now everything they've done could end up being for nothing. Anyway, it occurred to me that the thefts seem to have begun right about the time your succession was announced, and I couldn't help wondering if there was a connection.''

''Well,'' I murmured. ''I'm impressed.''

She gave a small deprecating lift of her shoulders and sipped from her cup again. ''I didn't learn much, I'm afraid. Some possible motives, but no real suspects. And, oh, this was interesting… I almost forgot. Did you know Greg Stillman has a direct line to Castle St. Clare? I noticed it in his study.''

''You were in his study?''

I saw the flash of small white teeth as she grinned in the shadows. ''People are used to overlooking me. There aren't too many places I can't go. It was scrambled, too.''

''What?''

''The line. Is that routine for department heads?''

''Oh…yes, I suppose.'' I was still marveling over the fact that she had gained entry into Stillman's study—a werewolf's most private den—without notice. ''You are really quite remarkable. I'm beginning to suspect we're not paying you nearly enough.''

She chuckled throatily and crossed her legs. My eyes were riveted on the shapely knee as her coat fell open, the curve of thigh. ''That,'' she said invitingly, ''sounds like something we can discuss.''

I can't explain what happened next, not even, adequately, to myself. I put my coffee cup aside. I leaned forward until our knees touched. I framed Victoria's face with the thumb and forefinger of one hand and I kissed her, tenderly, on the mouth.

It was a gesture of affection, of friendship, of gratitude, even of apology. Or that's what I intended it to be. That's how it started out. That's what it *was* until I drew her fragrance into my nostrils, tasted the satin of her lips, felt her softness, heard the leap of her pulse and the catch in her breath. And then I started to melt into her. I could feel my very soul swirling round and round in the sensations that suffused me, caught in the essence of her, drowning in her. She was a drug, swift and potent and thoroughly unexpected, soaring through my bloodstream. She was a fever, slow and long. She was overwhelming, consuming, absorbing. She was everything I had expected and nothing I was prepared for.

My mouth opened on hers, helplessly, and her lips parted to my insistence. I pressed the flat of my tongue against hers, tasting her with all my senses. My skin ached to open itself and draw her in. Pleasure? Ah, it was so much more than that. It was a universe of sensation and discovery, an entirely new dimension of wonder; a moment in time that spanned all time, as though nothing had existed before us and nothing would exist after, only this kiss, only this marvel.

When at last we parted, we both were dazed, I think. At least I like to think she was as bedazzled as I. I could hear her heartbeat, rushing and loud, but only a little more so than my own. I could feel her heat, enveloping me like a shawl, even as I sat back against my own seat, and see the light caught in her eyes. And she murmured, ''I hope that's not in lieu of a raise.''

I adored her at that moment. I truly did.

I realized then that the car had come to a stop in front of her building. ''I'll walk you up,'' I said.

She lifted a hand to stay me. I noticed a slight unsteadiness, which gratified me. My own hand had been none too steady as I reached for the door. ''Please don't,'' she said. ''Phillipe will want to gossip, and it will be much easier if I know you're not listening.''

I smiled in the darkness. "Then I promise not to linger."

I pressed a button on the console and heard the driver get out to open her door. She turned to leave.

"Victoria."

She looked back, all swathed in white and glitter, looking like a Russian princess about to embark upon some mythical, magical journey. My heart caught.

There were things I should have told her. Things that, to be fair she deserved to hear. In my own defense I can say only that I *wanted* to tell her. But the future of our race was in my hands, and the responsibility weighed heavily on me. Too heavily.

So I merely smiled and said, "When you speak of me to Phillipe, and you will…be kind."

The smile she returned lit up her eyes and completely captured what was left of my heart. Donning her role like an elegant cloak, she kissed her fingers and waved them at me as she got out of the car.

I instructed my driver to see her safely inside, and then, true to my word, did not linger. As soon as we were under way, I put on the white noise again and made a long-overdue phone call.

Robesieur answered on the second ring.

"Jason," I greeted him. "Noel Duprey here. I hope I'm not calling too late. I wanted to thank you for planting that story with Victoria. I know you were reluctant at first but she behaved just as you predicted, and it was important that I know who I could trust."

I wanted to tell her, honestly I did. But I couldn't.

Hell, I guess I'm really not such a nice guy, after all.

CHAPTER EIGHT

Victoria

Of course I figured out that entire lunch with Jason was a setup. How? Elementary. First of all, it was entirely too convenient, don't you think? Noel holds a top-secret meeting to announce a revolutionary new product and the very next day *my* friend and competitor, about whom Noel had known in advance, offers to buy it from me? Furthermore, it didn't really seem like something Jason would do. There was something about the entire thing that just didn't ring true; perhaps it was in Jason's body language.

But most telling of all was the way Noel reacted—or didn't react. I had just given him the perfect lead to crack the case, as they say on American TV, and he'd ignored it. He'd barely even acknowledged it. How do I know? I called Jason and asked him. Jason, bless his heart, broke down and told me the truth.

This was of course several days after I had, like a good little werewolf, reported everything to Noel.

"Well, I think he's a beast, tricking you like that and then having the liver to put the heavy hands on you." This was from Phillipe, after I had finished unburdening myself to him.

"Gall," I corrected him absently. "He had the gall to put heavy moves on me, not hands."

"As I said."

It was Sunday afternoon after the party. Phillipe and I were finishing a bottle of wine while I did my nails and he braided my hair. Snow pelted lightly against the windowpane; Socrates snored before the fire. It was a perfect lazy Sunday.

"I don't understand why you tolerate his attentions after that," Phillipe went on, tugging at my hair with the comb. "I would be showing him the back side of the door if I were you. He's not *that* good-looking."

Here is where the differences between humans and ourselves are most pronounced. Noel had behaved in a devious, underhand, two-faced way; he had lied to me in deed and fact, attempted to entrap me and used my own friend as the bait, and he did it all without once blinking or displaying even a shred of remorse, completely discounting my feelings while he served the best interests of the pack. How could I help but admire that?

Phillipe expected me to be angry and insulted; I was impressed. In fact, when Jason finally confessed the scheme to me, I was delighted. It was a relief to know it was cunning, not stupidity or lack of ambition, that had caused Noel to ignore my information about Jason's offer.

But how could I explain this to Phillipe? I chose instead to address the last part of his statement. On the subject of the battle of the sexes we all speak a common language.

So I gave a little shrug and said, "I don't take his attentions, as you call them, seriously. He's not interested in me…as anything other than a possible spy, that is."

But oh, how his kiss had thrilled me. Was it possible for me to feel passion? I had never been sure until Noel had touched me, until the heat from his body had flowed through my veins and the pulse of his heart had taken control of mine. Passion, adoration, surprise, wonder, the dizzying heights and depths of unexplored sensuality all

in the space of mere seconds, all from the press of mouths
and the mating of tongues. This is what he had shown me
and, in the showing, had changed my world.

So you can perhaps imagine how difficult it was for me
to adopt so casual a tone when referring to that event, to
dismiss its significance so easily. I appreciated Phillipe's
outrage on my behalf.

"And why, may I ask, not?" demanded Phillipe with
such indignation that I had to smile.

"Well for one thing," I replied, examining my nails
from the distance of an arm's length, "he has a reputation
for being free with his favors, if you know what I mean."

True enough. I had spent the weekend reminding myself of all the known details of Noel's reputation with the
opposite sex. Again, this is a matter for admiration among
our kind, not condemnation. There is a reason, you know,
that a certain kind of human male is referred to as a
"wolf."

A male is expected to be experienced in the sensual
arts before he chooses a mate. It is not enough, after all,
to merely captivate a female, one must also hold her for
the family unit—and therefore, our species—to continue.

Phillipe sniffed expressively. "You missed a spot, dear,
there on the thumb."

"And for another..." I carefully touched up the spot
he had indicated with passion pink. "He's an important
man. He has no reason to be interested in me."

How to explain to Phillipe the issue of status, much
less the inviolate imperative that Noel beget an heir? His
would be a royal match, and as such, monitored by the
entire werewolf community. There was simply no possibility of a serious courtship between us. Even pleasure
games between us would be frowned upon if anyone
should ever find out.

Yet he had kissed me. *Me.* Noel Duprey had pressed his lips to mine and set my head to spinning and could I possibly pretend that anything would ever be the same after that?

"My dear, this is Montreal, gateway to the world!" Phillipe exclaimed. "This city is practically rolling with important men! Why, off the top of my fingers, I could put you together with—"

The ring of the telephone interrupted him. I looked at my wet nails and Phillipe considerately lifted the receiver for me and held it to my ear.

I answered in French.

"Are you alone?" demanded Noel's voice.

My heart speeded immediately and involuntarily. To hide it—for who knew what *he* could hear over a telephone—I responded flippantly, "Why, no, Phillipe is here. Would you like to speak to him?"

Obligingly playing my game, Phillipe started to transfer the receiver to his ear, but Noel's growl—it simply could not be called anything else—stopped us both. "Don't toy with me, Victoria, I'm in no mood. Tell your friend to leave. I'm in the car. I'll be there in five minutes."

Before I could respond, he had disconnected. I looked at Phillipe with wide eyes. He shrugged, replaced the receiver and returned with a hand mirror, which he held before me so that I could examine my newly braided hair.

"I don't know, *chérie,* too much froufrou?"

I examined the style, which was accented with many small wispy curls around my face and forehead. It was much softer than I usually liked, but today for some reason it appealed to me.

"I like it," I told him. "Is there any more wine?"

Noel arrived as we were debating whether or not to make popcorn. He scowled when he saw Phillipe, who obligingly offered him a glass of wine. Noel looked point-edly at me.

"I'd like to speak with you in private," he said, his tone as frosty as the day beyond my window.

But beneath his wintry demeanor his blood beat hotly; I could feel it. I could hear the firm heaviness of his pulse, like a hammer striking an anvil with determined impas-sioned strokes; I could see the tension in the subtle length-ening of his muscles; I could almost smell the adrenaline on his skin. I was curious. But I was also just as deter-mined in my own way to make my point.

"I wish you'd done that on the telephone," I told him pleasantly. "Phillipe and I were about to make popcorn. Of course, you're welcome to join us."

Phillipe protested politely, "Perhaps another time, pre-cious. *L'amour, toujours...*"

Noel shrugged out of his snow-splotched overcoat, still scowling fiercely. "This," he told me brusquely, "is busi-ness." He tossed his coat on a nearby chair and thrust an impatient hand through his damp hair, tossing it back from his face.

"Well, in that case," I said, staring meaningfully at his coat, "I'll be in my office at nine tomorrow. Or maybe ten. I'm having my hair done." After all, it was a nasty trick he had played on me with Jason. He deserved some punishment.

Phillipe exclaimed in mock dismay, "And after all my efforts. I am squelched!"

"Crushed," I corrected. "And I love your efforts, truly. But Raoul will be devastated if I disappoint him tomor-row. I've never broken an appointment in all these years."

Noel said in a low tone, "Victoria..."

Phillipe grinned and turned his cheek to me, apparently tired of our game. "Give me a kiss, *chérie*, I'm off. Tickets for the symphony, you know, and I don't have the first thought on what to wear.''

I kissed his cheek lightly. "Have fun. Thanks for doing my hair.''

When he was gone, I twirled once for Noel, still teasing him. "Do you like it?"

His scowl was gone, but the intensity of his look all but burned my skin. "You amuse yourself in very strange ways,'' he said.

I met his eyes and no one could have been more surprised than I at the reply I made. "So do you."

He did not pretend to mistake my meaning. The muscles of his jaw knotted and the very faintest flush of an almost human embarrassment warmed his skin. He did not, of course, drop his gaze.

He said simply, "If you find my behavior toward you objectionable in any way, you should tell me.''

Now *I* was embarrassed, and not just faintly. What could I say? "I will,'' I answered, and shifted my gaze from his.

A heartbeat or two passed before he said, resuming his brisk tone, "A problem has developed, rather serious, I'm afraid, that you should know about immediately.''

I took my cue and tried to put on my Monday-morning face for him. "What is it?"

He took a folded paper from his pocket and came toward me. "I took this off the on-line clipping service this morning. It's destined for the business news tomorrow.''

I took the printout from him and scanned it.

Perfume Wars: A Revolution was the headline. The article dealt in a general fashion with competition in the perfume industry, then focused on Clare de Lune's recent losses to rival perfumeries. Though industrial espionage was never precisely suggested, anyone with an imagina-

tion could have read between the lines. But most dam-
aging of all was the last paragraph, which spoke of Clare
de Lune's "valiant attempt to rally with a top-secret project billed as 'a revolution in the perfume industry.' The
new product, which has already met resistance from the
United States FDA and forced its manufacture abroad, is
scheduled for a Christmas release with the aid of a mul-
timillion-dollar worldwide advertising campaign."

I could feel the warmth drain out of my fingers as I
read, and my throat grew tight. I looked up at Noel. "You
were able to stop this from going to print, weren't you?"

He gave an impatient nod of his head. "Of course. But
that's mere damage control. Enough people saw it on-line
to start any number of rumors, some of them with genuine
potential for disaster. What I want to know is how such
a thing could have happened."

He paced angrily to the window and stood there for a
moment, silhouetted by the sun.

Did I mention how gorgeous he looked today? If not,
it was not because I hadn't noticed. He wore a tweed
sweater and silky wool slacks that draped over his thighs
and buttocks like a woman's caress. When he thrust his
hands into his pockets, as he did now, the material was
drawn tight across the most attractive portions of his anat-
omy, drawing my gaze, as well. It was perhaps inappro-
priate of me to be making these observations at such a
time of crisis, but I confess doing so nonetheless.

He turned abruptly, forcing me to just as quickly pretend my attention had been, all along, on the wrinkled
paper in my hand. "Damn it, *who?*" he demanded, scowling fiercely. "Who is doing this?"

I raised my eyes to him. Something was running
through my head about faint hearts never winning fair
maids, a human axiom, I think. I hoped it applied to fair

gentlemen, too, because I could hardly remain silent with an opening like that.

"I don't suppose," I offered consideringly, "it could be the same person who told Jason Robesieur about Moonsong, could it?"

He read the truth in my eyes, acknowledged it, and not a flicker of expression crossed his face. He said, "You know better than that."

I thought I did.

Then he added, "I had to do it, you know. I had to be sure."

Though there still was no regret in his tone, the words themselves surprised me. It sounded very close to an apology, and none was needed.

I said, with perfect honesty, "I would have done the same."

The glint of approval in his eyes was as warm as an embrace, and even more so because it was unexpected. He said with a nod, "Just so." He went to stand before the fire, stretching out his hands behind him toward the flames while he watched me turn my attention to the press release once again.

"It *could* have been someone from the creative team," I admitted doubtfully, "but unless one of them is not at all what he appears to be, none of them knew anything about the other things—the formulas we lost to the competition before Moonsong, and the problems with the FDA."

He nodded. "Precisely. So that brings it back to the highest executive level."

I asked curiously, "Who *did* know about the other thefts?"

A grimness came over his face that caused a chill to go through me. "Outside of Castle St. Clare," he said, "and you and me...I don't know. But you can be sure I intend to find out."

In other words, there were still no solid suspects...aside from me and, I suppose, him. I was beginning to understand his frustration.

"You've talked to the reporter who put together the story?"

"Some silly human," he replied dismissively, "who said he interviewed a public-relations rep from the New York office. Of course, the name he was given was phony, the telephone number has been disconnected and never belonged to anyone associated with St. Clare." He was thoughtful for a moment. "A blessing, I suppose. If I hadn't threatened him with a lawsuit over his nonexistent source, he might not have been so quick to pull the article."

He brought his hand to the back of his neck in a brief massaging motion, looking suddenly weary and defeated. The movement was revealing, and it touched my heart. "Ah, well," he said, sighing, "*C'est la guerre, eh?* Or perhaps there is some equally trite expression I could better employ for the moment but now I can't think of it."

He looked with undisguised longing at the glass of wine I had placed, barely sipped, on the mantel. "Is there any more?"

I got up swiftly and went to the kitchen, returning in a moment with a glass of Montrachet from a vintage Phillipe had recommended. Since I had discovered he liked it, I had started buying wine with a discriminating eye; foolish, perhaps, but I was glad I had.

He accepted the glass with a murmured thanks and I picked up my own. I wished I could offer more than wine; consolation, perhaps, or, even better, a solution to the dilemma that faced us both. But I didn't know what to say.

I took my wine to the chair where I'd been sitting, and sank onto it with my feet curled beneath me.

He stood with one elbow resting on the mantel, looking out the window, in profile to me. He sipped the wine, closing his eyes as he tasted it, but I could not tell whether the gesture was from appreciation or fatigue. I only knew I had never seen such bleakness on his face before, and I never wanted to again. I deeply regretted the flippancy with which I had treated him earlier, with which I had, as a matter of fact, regarded this entire project from the beginning.

He said quietly, almost to himself, "Sometimes I almost envy Michael."

I said nothing, but he glanced at me as though I had—or perhaps it was surprise at the fact that he had spoken out loud that compelled him to explain, "I know it sounds strange. Michael, the deranged one, living in disgrace with a human... Michael, the reason we're all in this bloody mess in the first place." Again he sipped his wine. "But sometimes I think he's the sanest of us all. He just threw up his hands and walked away."

It alarmed me to hear him say that. I had been an admirer of Michael St. Clare—he was the Golden Boy, the Coming Prince. Who among us had not pledged him our admiration and support? But there was no honor in what he had done. He had turned his back on the pack, betrayed us all. Whether he chose to live among humans or in a cave was not the point; the fact was he had rejected his heritage and abandoned his responsibility and we were only lucky Noel had been there to fill the gap. To hear Noel speak now as though Michael's behavior had been enviable was deeply disturbing.

I said sharply, "That's utter nonsense. You defeated

Michael in just battle for the sake of us all. You have nothing for which to envy him, nothing at all!''

He turned eyes on me that were astonished and amused. ''Just battle? Is that what you call it? I was a fool to challenge him and a damn lucky one to escape with my life—for which I have nothing but Michael's grace to thank.''

That made me angry. My hand tightened on the glass. ''Why do you say such things? I was there! I saw—''

''Then you must have had a very poor seat,'' he interrupted shortly, ''if you didn't notice that it was Michael who, for reasons of his own, allowed me to live.''

I was momentarily at a loss. In fact, I hadn't been able to see very well; I had heard many versions of the actual battle, but the outcome—the moment when Noel, clothed in the royal raiment placed upon his shoulders by Sebastian St. Clare himself, had raised a wounded and bleeding Michael St. Clare to his feet and covered him with his own cloak—*that* I had seen. It had been the single most powerful, most reverent and sanctified moment of my life. Even now, thinking about it brought a shiver of thrill to my skin.

Noel sat down on the hearth, sipping his wine. Socrates opened one sleepy eye toward him, yawned and curled into a tighter sleeping ball. Noel reached out a hand absently and, to my utter astonishment, began to stroke the cat. I doubt he was even aware of what he was doing, and I certainly didn't remind him.

He spoke in a contemplative tone, as though merely voicing his thoughts out loud. ''No one believes it, but there is a certain affection between Michael and me, always has been. I know we've been set against each other from youth as competitors for every important honor, but that was just sportsmanship. Damn it, he was my cousin and my friend. He was in trouble and I wanted to help. What I did was ill-considered and rash, but I thought it was the best for him…who could have guessed it would turn out to be the worst possible thing for us all?''

''What are you saying?'' I asked, astonished. ''What in the world can you mean? Of course it turned out exactly as it was supposed to! The better man won, just as ancient tradition dictates, and triumphed to lead us all!''

His smile was vague and mirthless, his eyes bleak. ''Did he?'' He drank from the glass. ''Did the best man win?''

''Of course he did!'' I was growing annoyed now. Pack loyalty, among other things—in fact, the *least* among other things—demanded that I defend my leader from insult by anyone, even if the insult came from himself. ''You're talking nonsense and I really wish you'd just stop it.''

He looked genuinely surprised at my adamancy, then seemed to dismiss it as female foolishness as he lifted his glass again. ''A great many people don't seem to think so.''

''Who?'' I demanded impatiently. ''Who dares to say such a thing?''

He gazed at me with a kind of grayness overlaying his cool green eyes. ''Sebastian St. Clare, for one.''

Well, there was a dilemma. To champion the future ruler against the current one would have been a display of bad manners at best, disloyalty at worst. And the truth was I resented being put in that position. I couldn't imagine Sebastian St. Clare seriously questioning Noel's competence; to do so would be to go against every tradition we hold sacred. Noel was his heir. To diminish Noel would be to diminish himself and, therefore, us all.

''Noel, are you sure you didn't misunderstand? What could he possibly have done to make you think that?''

There was noticeable tension in Noel's shoulders as he left the soothing touch of Socrates's fur and got to his feet. "Nothing," he said. He drank from the glass. "And everything. Of course he had a right to resent me, I understand that. I overthrew his flesh-and-blood son. But I would have abdicated for Michael's sake and *he* should understand that. It's Michael he should blame, not me. But from the beginning, he's done nothing to help ease the transition or make me feel welcome, not that he's required to, of course. He's given me no responsibility. I have a title but no function. I have a schedule it would take ten werewolves to meet but no concept of its purpose. When I'm not being ignored by Castle St. Clare, I'm being harangued or inconvenienced or ordered about like a puppy, and until this assignment, I didn't even have a job. Now I'm beginning to think…"

But he broke off, finishing the wine in his glass.

This was, needless to say, deeply disturbing to me to hear. Not only because it was unfair and unchivalrous, but because it suggested an uncertain future for the power structure of Castle St. Clare.

I got to my feet and went into the kitchen for the bottle of Montrachet. I returned and refilled his glass silently. "What?" I inquired gently. "What are you thinking?"

He looked into the glass of clear liquid. "That the first time I am given any real responsibility, I prove him right," he answered without expression. "Or perhaps you're right." He glanced at me, and sipped his wine. "Perhaps Sebastian never expected me to fail at all. Perhaps I'm just blaming him for what I know inside to be true."

I could feel the frown of confusion gather between my eyebrows. I put the wine bottle on the hearth and touched his shoulder lightly. "Noel…"

But he cut me off with a shake of his bright golden head and a squaring of his shoulders. "No, please. I'm tired of all this maudlin reflection. Too much self-examination always gives me a headache. Let's talk about something else."

I admit, I was relieved. I felt him relax as much as sheer willpower could enforce, and I turned to pick up my wine. "All right," I agreed. "What shall we talk about?"

He was thoughtful for a moment, gazing out at the snowy afternoon. "The swim-through bar," he replied after a moment, slowly, "at the Halekalani Hotel."

I gave a startled laugh. "I'm afraid that would be a short conversation. I don't have the first idea what you're talking about."

He turned to me, smiling. "Hawaii. You've never been?"

I shook my head. "I went to New York once. But that's it."

I watched amusement replace the strain that had haunted his eyes since he'd entered my apartment and was gratified to have some small responsibility for it. "Are you serious? You've never been to the tropics?"

I shook my head, stretching out a hand to stroke the sleeping Socrates. "Should I have been?"

A secretive, delighted smile curved his lips, replete with pleasant memories. "Oh, yes," he insisted. "You definitely should have." But the sparkle in his eyes denied the soberness of his tone. He sipped his wine and added, "We could be there in twelve hours."

I gave a surprised laugh, only half suspecting he was serious. "I suppose we could."

He turned to me and, in a single swift and graceful movement, set his glass on the mantel and bent to catch my arms, lifting me to my feet. "Let's do it," he insisted urgently, his eyes shining. "The jet is standing by—that's one of the advantages of being the future leader of our people, did you know that? Pilots on salary, runways cleared, jet fueled for anywhere in the world twenty-four hours a day. So let's make them earn their pay. Hell, as long as we're going as far as Hawaii, why not Tahiti? Or Fiji? It doesn't even matter. This time tomorrow we could be walking on beaches as white as sugar, trade winds on our faces, the sun baking our skin, the surf making that oh-so-delightful sound in our ears. Drinking those awful rum and sugar drinks, dining on seafood that was swimming in the ocean an hour before. Victoria..." His hands tightened on my arms. "Let's do it."

I said breathlessly, "I think you mean it!"

The blaze of his emerald eyes was my answer, the heat of his fingers on my skin. And for a moment—just a moment, mind you—I was swept away by the possibilities, the fantasies he could make come true because, to him, they weren't fantasies at all. Sunshine on exotic shores, expensive meals, luxurious accommodations, swimming pools with bars—he did say *bars*, didn't he—in them. And me, with him. *He* had asked *me*. Not some nubile young thing of his own status and background, not some sleek and gorgeous female who might one day become the chatelaine of Castle St. Clare, but *me*. He might already be regretting the impulsiveness of the invitation but he couldn't deny making it and how could I refuse?

I couldn't believe the words that came out of my mouth, tempered as they were with a light laugh. "I don't think so, Noel. But thank you, anyway, for asking me."

He insisted, undeterred, "Whyever not?"

Oh, he was not making this easy. I turned away, reclaiming my glass of wine. "Well, for one thing, what would people say?"

He started to make some brusque, impatient noises of dismissal but I caught his eye deliberately. "For another," I said gently, "we have responsibilities."

I felt like the evil auntie in the movies who tells the child there is no Santa Claus. Although I should not in any way wish to compare Noel to a child, it was painful to watch the enthusiasm go out of his eyes, and in another blink, the sardonic smile return.

He said, "I think, Victoria St. Clare, that you could use a few lessons in giving in to the impulse of the moment."

I knew he was right about that.

"I also think that I could probably use some instruction in the art of responsibility," he added with a lightness that was forced, underscored by an edge of weariness that broke my heart to hear. "Which I believe brings us back to the conversation we just left, and that must be my cue to depart."

He went to the chair on which he had left his coat, while I desperately tried to think of some way to entice him to stay...or to at least bring back the twinkle in his eyes. He picked up his coat and glanced out the snowy window with something like a grimace. While we had talked, the gray afternoon had faded into night, and it looked colder and emptier than before. I was glad to be inside.

He looked around my apartment, a brief sweep of his eyes that seemed to take in more than simply what he saw. "You have a pleasant life here, Victoria," he said, "with your funny human friend and your lazy Sunday afternoons." The note of wistfulness in his voice surprised me.

"It's not Fiji," I said, trying for a smile.

"True. But it looks pretty good to me right now." He started to pull on his coat.

"Noel." I took a step toward him, just a little hesitant. "I can't offer you a swim-through bar...but I do have a bathtub that's big enough for two."

Perhaps this shocks you. A human probably would not invite her boss to share a bath upon the occasion of his second, perfectly informal visit to her apartment. This is simply another cultural difference.

Our attitude toward nudity is, of necessity, far more casual than yours, and the sharing of a bath is something two werewolves might do with as little thought as two humans sharing a swimming pool or a hot tub. Certainly there was nothing sexual in my invitation, nor anything implicit in his acceptance—or rejection—of it.

Still, I didn't want him to think I was imposing upon our familiarity or forcing my company upon him. So I held my breath for a second or two while he appeared to think it over.

"Bubble bath?" he inquired quite seriously.

I nodded.

"And is there any more of that very excellent Montrachet?"

I relaxed. "Another whole bottle. And Godiva chocolates in the fridge."

He let his coat drop. "My dear," he said, "I am yours."

CHAPTER NINE

Noel

To say I was surprised by Victoria's invitation would not have done my emotions justice. Surprised, delighted, eager…surprised. And to think, only moments earlier I had accused her of a lack of spontaneity. If there was one thing for which Victoria St. Clare had demonstrated an amazing aptitude it was keeping me off-balance.

That's not an altogether undesirable trait in a female.

There are some among us who have an aversion to water; it renders our tracking senses useless and distorts our sense of hearing and can be, when cold and salty or falling from the sky, aesthetically disagreeable. However, exquisite sensualists that we are, few of us can resist the allure of a warm bath or a steaming hot tub or a well-heated pool…especially when shared with a friend.

She ran the bath while I found the wine and the chocolates. Following the sound of running water, I carried our refreshments through the darkened bedroom and into the bathroom. There I stopped, letting my eyes feast upon the sight, and I can't say whether I was more taken by the visual enchantment of the steamy, candlelit room, or by the sight of Victoria's naked form, bending from the waist as she sprinkled bath salts over the frothing jets of water that filled the wide, sunken cedar tub.

She was more beautiful unclothed than I had imagined her to be. Her skin was porcelain smooth, her muscles sleek and firm. The delicate knobs and ridges of her spine beckoned to be caressed, her slim waist and the bold flare of her hips were fashioned by an artist's hands. Her breasts were full and perfectly round, the nipples pink and rose-rimmed. They drew my gaze in tenderness and admiration as she half turned to me, giving me a smile over her shoulder.

"It's marvelous, isn't it?" she said, indicating the room.

I brought the wine and the confections to the ledge of the tub and gave my attention for a moment—the briefest of moments, I assure you—to my surroundings.

There were several fat, variously colored candles stacked at one edge of the rim of the tub, their fragrances mingling vanilla, raspberry and citrus with the herbal scent of the bubbling bath salts. In addition, there were two tall, painted iron sconces situated in opposite corners of the room, each holding six more wide, low-burning candles. The effect was ethereal and delicately romantic, a flickering glow of misty yellow light that seemed to become one with the steam from the water and the scents that mingled in the room.

After a moment, I realized that the ceiling above us was glass, and, using my night vision, I could see beyond the reflection of candle flames to the spatter of snow, some flakes clinging and others melting to form a lacework of light and dark over our heads. There was an enclosed shower and spa in the corners of the room, and I could smell the earth and greenery of tropical plants. But for the most part my attention was captured by the play of shadow and light on the walls and the ceiling and the curves of Victoria's body.

"It is impressive," I agreed, sliding off my shoes and stripping my sweater over my head. "Do you know, Vic-

-toria, you aren't a fraction as wealthy as I am, but there are certain elements of luxury to your life-style that, frankly, I've never even thought of, much less enjoyed.''

She chuckled throatily. ''They say you don't need money if you have enough imagination.''

I stepped out of my trousers and underwear. ''Who says that?''

She smiled and extended her hand to me. ''Some silly human.''

I took her hand, descending into the steamy bubbling water first, then helping her in. We steadied ourselves against each other on the slippery surface, thighs and abdomens brushing, then sank into the water, carefully arranging our limbs so as not to interfere with the other's space.

Ah, to describe the experience. Winter outside, dropping its musical little snowflakes against the glass over our heads. Steam and floating candlelight inside, liquid heat surrounding and enfolding us, seeping into every raw and aching muscle in my body. I sank back, closed my eyes and surrendered myself to the sensation completely.

''Better,'' I murmured. ''Better than Fiji.''

''Well, closer, anyway.''

She leaned forward and filled our glasses with wine, momentarily parting the froth of bubbles that covered her breasts and giving me an all-too-brief glimpse of their loveliness again.

The tub was large and easily accommodated two people who were as tall as we. I stretched out my legs on either side of hers, she nestled her feet against my thighs. We lifted our glasses to each other. I was more content at that moment, more relaxed and free of care than I had been at any time since Sebastian St. Clare had first sent me on the fool's errand to find his missing heir.

I smiled at her for no reason at all except that she had given me this peaceful moment, and the wine, and the shape of her breasts outlined by bubbles. "So this is how you entertain yourself."

She laughed and reached for a piece of chocolate. "Hardly. My human friends wouldn't understand."

Her gaze fell momentarily on the gold medallion I wore around my neck. It was etched with a shadowed moon, the emblem of the St. Clare Corporation, and all the senior werewolves wore them. She, of course, did not, which was only another subtle reminder of the difference in our status. I wished I had taken mine off, but there was nothing to be done about it now.

"One of the disadvantages of human friends," I observed.

She lifted one smooth, glistening shoulder in a philosophical shrug, but it struck me, for the first time, perhaps, how lonely she must be. A bath was one thing, a simple pleasure shared between werewolves, but how many other things, simple and complex, was she unable to share with anyone? The peculiarly sharp and clear view of the world that only werewolves can know. The camaraderie of being with others of one's own kind. The quick wit, the cultural heritage, the private jokes. The truth about her nature.

"How odd...and wrong, I think, that a person should be judged by her ability to reproduce. You are so very much more than that."

"How good of you to notice," she returned, teasing me.

I leaned back in the water, resting my elbows on either side of the tub, and smiled as I sipped my wine. "I try to be observant."

Her small white teeth bit into the chocolate, then she flicked a sliver off her lower lip with her tongue. It was a gesture I found fascinating, even—oddly enough—erotic. She noticed me watching her and hesitated. "Will you have some?"

I slipped my hands beneath the water and encircled her ankle, lifting her foot up out of the water to rest on my chest. I heard her sweet catch of breath, the quick light pattering of her pulse, and it thrilled me. Bubbles dripped from her leg and foot like meringue.

She watched me, curious and alert, as she popped the remaining morsel of chocolate into her mouth. I tugged gently on her foot, lifting it higher, and she let herself slide deeper into the water. I leaned forward and licked the last few bubbles off her toes, spoiling the taste of my wine, then drew my tongue along her instep. She giggled and curled her toes, pulling away a little. I took her heel in my mouth, encircling it with my tongue. Her giggles turned into a murmur of pleasure.

Smiling, I dragged the arch of her foot along my jaw, tickling her with the light stubble of my beard. I slid my hand over her leg, cupping ankle, calf, the slender, perfectly formed knee, as far as my arm would reach, and the tactile sensation was exquisite: satin and pearls, heat and suppleness. She closed her eyes with a sigh of pleasure and sipped from her wineglass. Her toes curved and caressed my face. I smiled.

This was not sex play, though it might seem so to a human. Still, to go further would have presumed an intimacy which I was not quite sure we possessed, even though I would have very much liked to. So it was only polite to inquire, as I lowered her foot back into the water and rested my hand alongside her calf, "Do you mind?"

She leaned forward to reach for another chocolate, the sparkle in her eyes playful and seductive. "Do you?"

I put down my wine on the ledge and in a swift move-

ment calculated to disarm, I grasped her thighs beneath
the water and pulled her toward me. She gave the expected startled laugh and squeal of protest and I felt eigh-
teen years old again; I laughed, too, as she settled her legs
around my waist and her arms around my neck. Her eyes
were like diamonds, her skin like velvet. She had pinned
her braid around her head in a deceptively innocent cor-
onet, but humidity had curled a multitude of damp, es-
caping tendrils to frame her face. Her lips were parted
with laughter and her breath was sweet with chocolate and
wine. I loved having her near me.

"My wine," she protested, and gestured toward the
glass she had left on the opposite ledge. "And you've got
bubbles on my chocolate."

She lifted the morsel to show me and I said, "Chocolate
isn't good for you, anyway." I wiped off the bubbles that
clung to the surface of the bonbon with a soapy fingertip.

"Isn't it?"

I lifted my wineglass to her lips. "So I'm told."

She sipped from my glass, pressing the confection
against my lips. I opened my mouth and took the chocolate inside…and her fingers, licking them, smearing
them with chocolate. When the outer layer of the rich dark
chocolate was softened with the heat of my mouth, I took
it out with my fingers and dipped it in the wine. I offered
it to Victoria, and she licked off the wine with a sweeping
circular motion of her tongue, bright eyes captivating me.
I took the morsel from her lips, and drew it across her
clavicle, down the fragile indentation of her sternum, and
across the swell of her left breast. I drew the slick chocolate trail in a spiral around the aureole and the nipple,
which became engorged with my touch. Then, flattening
my hand to melt the chocolate, I elongated the trail across

her chest and to the other breast, decorating it in chocolate.

"You," she murmured, her voice thick with delight, "are quite insane."

"Inventive," I corrected, and fastened my mouth to the quick hot pulse of the artery in her neck, drawing a moan of contentment from her.

I traced the path of chocolate on her skin, licking and sucking, teasing sometimes with quick flicking motions of my tongue or long slow circular ones. Salt and perfume and chocolate tantalized my taste buds, and underscoring all, the musky, evocative singular taste of Victoria. I could have inhaled it, drowned in it, lived on it and never hungered for more.

I could hear the flow of her blood through her veins, the pumping of her heart, powerful and sure, its rhythm guiding my own. Her breath, whispering through her lungs, sometimes quick and shallow, sometimes long and deep. The pop of tiny bubbles all around us, the music of the snow tinkling on the glass ceiling above, a symphony on a stereo far away, the rush of traffic, a foghorn, wind across the river, the hiss of flame meeting candle wax, the beat of Victoria's heart, faster now, her moan of pleasure as I licked the spiral of chocolate from her breast, teasing the nipple, suckling there.

Her hands threaded through my hair and tightened on my scalp, indicating her pleasure. Fingertips moved down the column of my neck and spine, a sweet caress that brought a tingling to my skin and a slow, melting heat to my muscles. Ah, her touch. Her intoxicating touch.

With our mouths and our fingertips we caressed each other, turning each other in the water, the sounds we made sometimes smothered laughter, sometimes groans of unabashed sensual pleasure. The candles guttered with the water we splashed, the sound of our intermingled breaths merging with the sound of falling snow and the murmur of the water jets, the hiss of melting wax, a sensory symphony, a feast for the ears.

With my fingers I explored the secret crevices of her femininity and felt her shudders of delight, her sighs of contentment. It broke my heart to think no one had ever done this for her before. And when she turned to me, stroking the sensitive area between my thighs, taking my nipples between her teeth...ah, she was so sweet, so guileless. Ecstasy swelled within me.

There is no secret to it, this playful dance of pleasure which we performed so effortlessly, so gracefully. The nipping, the stroking, the teasing, the caressing. Such an easy thing, a kind of innocent eroticism, if you will, that was nothing more than an expression of the natural affection for one another which is endemic to our species. I had enjoyed such play dozens of times, hundreds. Sometimes matters take their course and arousal leads to transformation which, for an unmated werewolf, is the pinnacle of a shared sensual experience. Most of the time, pleasure is simply that—delightful and entertaining, leaving both participants relaxed and renewed. It need be nothing more. With Victoria, I had certainly intended nothing more.

But I hadn't counted on the effect Victoria would have on me, on my mind, my body. I should emphasize that I am generally the epitome of discipline and self-control; for a male of my status it would be unacceptable to be otherwise. But the touch of her fingers, the caress of her lips, the steamy herb and floral scent of her that seemed to seep into my skin and ignite a fever in my blood...I didn't expect it.

Before I knew what was upon me, I clasped my hands around her arms, hard, pressing her into me. Wet naked flesh against hot flesh, softness yielding against hardness; my mouth covering hers and her tongue, boldly mating with mine, tasting her, drinking of her, drawing her inside and melting into her. My skin was tingling, stretching, my muscles hardening. Strength flowed into me, expanded inside me, power penetrated every fiber and cell.

I stood in the tub, bringing her with me, water cascading from our entwined bodies in a single gossamer sheet. Her arms and legs were tight around me, our mouths locked together, our hearts but a single, rolling thunderbeat. Effortlessly I lifted her out of the tub, and the fire in my blood was so hot the water dried on my skin, dried her skin. I kissed her, I drank of her, I inhaled her. And she responded; I know she did. Her muscles, longer. Her breasts, harder. Her temperature rising, her breath an ocean in my ears, her scent sharpening, her nails digging into my back, piercing the skin.

I tore my mouth from hers, pressed it against her ear. I drew the lobe into my mouth and she shuddered. My fingers tightened on her buttocks, I whispered into her ear, urgently, hotly, "How does this make you feel, Victoria? Tell me."

She twisted against me, arching into the caress of my mouth, moaning, pressing her abdomen into mine, winding her legs around mine. Dizziness soared, the room swirled. I teetered on the brink of control and for a moment, for one wild, impossible, utterly sublime moment, I imagined that she did, too, that it was possible for us to know more, to be more, to go further than either of us had ever imagined.

But then it was as though a switch had been thrown inside her. The tension seeped out of her body, the thunder of her heartbeat slowed; I could hear her, almost by force of will, regulating her breathing. Her hands, which had

been tangled in my hair with wild abandon, now loosened
and she nestled her face in my shoulder, sweetly. She
murmured, "Good. You make me feel...good."

Oh, how simple it would have been if I were a human.
To sweep that sweet pliant bundle of womanhood into my
arms and tumble her onto the bed. To inflame her with
my kisses, to arouse her fever and with a few swift, urgent
thrusts, to ease the fire that threatened to consume my
soul. It would be over in moments, and by morning I
would barely remember her name. If I were human.

But for me it was not so easy. I looked at her with eyes
that were already losing their focus; I held her with hands
that soon would grow too strong to trust with fragile flesh.
I whispered hoarsely, "Victoria...I must leave."

She dropped her eyes, bowed her head. She said softly,
"I understand."

But she didn't. How could she?

I made myself release her. I looked around distractedly
and found a large gray towel hanging from a seashell-
shaped hook. I draped it around her shoulders, pulling the
two corners tight near her throat. And then I couldn't stop
myself. I caught her face between my hands and I kissed
her hard on the mouth. It was almost my undoing.

I looked at her, trying to focus. The room was dissolv-
ing into candlelight and swirling heat, Victoria's face,
Victoria's eyes. I said, "I wish..." But my voice was
going. I couldn't finish.

She gripped my arm. Such pain in her eyes. It tore at
me, wrenched my heart. "I know," she said. And then,
"Go. Now."

I'm ashamed to say I don't remember leaving her. I
dressed, but just barely, and only for the sake of any humans I might meet in the hall. I gave my driver instruc-

tions and before the city was behind us, my clothes were off again.

There are places we know, in every city we go to, everyplace we visit. This is the first thing we learn, these places. The car stopped in such a place and I tumbled out, the crust of icy snow cutting my bare feet, the arctic air flowing over my skin. I spread my arms, I threw back my head, I breathed it in. The city lights were far away, the sky was black and swirling with snow. The field was wide and empty. I began to run.

How to describe the Change, this wonder, this magic, this miracle that comes over us and is ours alone? And do I want to describe it, or if I did, could any human understand? There are no words, not really. It is a becoming, a stretching and a reaching, an explosion of light and energy; it is, for most of us, a simple relinquishing of the discipline that keeps us in our human form and a return to that which is more natural, more beautiful, more right.

Few humans have ever seen this transformation. Living today, I know of only one: Michael's wife. She tells us that, to a human, the mere witnessing of the Change can be an almost spiritual experience, mesmerizingly beautiful, paralytic in its intensity. For me, it is a building of fever, a focusing of desire, a hunger that goes straight through the soul. That night, the desire had a purpose, the hunger had a name: *Victoria.*

A leap, a cry, a shudder of physical thrill that started in the core of me and exploded outward into the night. Starlight, snowflakes, wind and ice. *Victoria.* She was the fire that fueled my soul; she was the scent that clung to my skin; she was the hunger that ached in my belly. Cold wind rushed through my fur, snow flew beneath my paws, snow-laden boughs slapped my body as I ran, seeking and celebrating, experiencing the magic of my nature and

wanting more...wanting more. Because in my mind, another form ran beside me as the night streamed away, hers
was the heartbeat that pulsed with mine, hers the breath
that frosted on the cold air. Victoria. *Victoria.*

Before that night, I had never known desire. After it, I
would never be the same.

I was later than I liked arriving at the office the next
morning. The run had exhausted but not relieved me, and
all I could think about was seeing Victoria. What I was
going to say to her I had no idea.

When I reached the executive suites, I inquired of the
human secretary whose name I could never remember, "Is
Ms. St. Clare in her office?" I paused to scoop up some
message slips and pretended to be interested in them; the
only thing I was really interested in was the woman's
reply.

"**As** a matter of fact, there's a Madame St. Clare in
your office. She insisted upon being allowed to wait there.
I hope I did the right thing."

I frowned and went to my office, so distracted that I
honestly did not know who the child was talking about
until I opened the door of my office, and caught the scent
of home.

"Grand-mère!" I exclaimed in genuine delight, and
closed the door behind me.

Clarice St. Clare turned from the window, smiling, and
opened her arms to welcome me. She was wearing a designer suit and a wide-brimmed, fur-lined hat, kidskin
gloves and a single strand of pearls. Her thick silver hair
was beautifully coiffed in an elegant lover's knot, her
makeup lightly and flawlessly applied. She was close to
eighty years old and to me, as to most others of our kind,

she would always be the most beautiful woman in the world.

We embraced, and I let myself sink into the scents of childhood: warm fur and sunshine, baking bread and steamed milk, evergreen, wood smoke, eiderdown, wildflowers, a combination of all this and more that was the unique essence of her perfume. I kissed the corner of her mouth. She stepped back and patted my cheek, beaming at me.

She was not, strictly speaking, my grandmother, any more than her husband, Sebastian St. Clare, was technically my grandfather. But they were. in the grand sense, parents to the entire pack, and were thus addressed, informally and affectionately, as *grand-mère* and *grand-père*. To me, of course, because of our familial relationship, they were more.

In our culture, it is not uncommon for community, or pack, ties to be closer than those of the immediate family, particularly since we are often sent off to school or for other training at an early age. I adore my mother, who is a brilliant scientist presently stationed in Hong Kong, and have enormous respect for my father, who has achieved quite some renown in the world financial market. But we rarely see one another except for family or pack holidays, and in times of pain or crisis it is not to either one of them I turn, but to this woman. It seemed only natural, then, that she should be here now, when I needed her most.

Perhaps too natural.

I took her hands in mine, remembering to smile even though she would smell my uneasiness. "To what do I owe this most delightful surprise?"

She laughed lightly, reading through me just as I knew she would. "Darling, you are transparent, but at least your manners are as fine as ever. As a matter of fact, I was on my way back from the spring fashion shows in Paris, and you were on my mind. I hope it's not too inconvenient?''

I gestured her toward the small sofa by the fire, relaxing a little. I *was* glad to see her. ''Only if you can't stay. Then I shall be devastated.''

Tea was ready in the silver service, as it always was when I arrived, and the fire, aided by gas logs, burned merrily on the grate. She took off her gloves and I poured. When we were comfortably seated with our cups in hand, I inquired with as much sangfroid as possible, ''And how is Grand-père?''

She smiled and patted my knee reassuringly. ''Relax, *mon cher,* he didn't send me to spy on you. I should be very surprised if he even knows I'm here.''

I dropped my eyes in apology, though in fact I *was* relieved. I was sending him dutiful daily reports and I had enough on my mind without worrying about having him peering over my shoulder. I sipped my tea. ''So tell me about the fashion shows. Are hemlines up or down? Did you buy tons of lovely frocks?''

Her eyes danced with reproval and indulgence. ''Very well, you naughty boy, I'll come to the point. I didn't fly several thousand miles out of my way to talk bustiers and kick pleats with you.''

I murmured, ''I'm sorry to hear it.'' But I was not so sure how anxious I was to know the real reason she was here. It would have been pleasant to spend a morning immersed in nothing of more consequence than the world of fashion.

She sipped her tea. ''In fact, *chéri,* what I have to discuss with you is something of a personal nature. I had rather hoped you might bring it up before now, but then it occurred to me, with all that has happened so quickly in your life, you simply might not have had a chance to give the matter thought. So I hope you don't mind if I've taken the liberty."

I uncovered the plate of sweet breads on the tea tray and offered her one. She shook her head and I took one for myself. "I don't understand. I'm sure there are hundreds of things I haven't had a chance to give thought to yet. I hope this one isn't very important."

She smiled at me. "Only the most important thing you'll ever do in your life." She laid a hand gently on my arm. "Noel, darling, you can't delay any longer. It's time you took a mate."

The honey-flavored roll tasted gummy in my mouth. I stared at her a fraction of a moment longer than was strictly polite, I was that taken aback. Was it coincidence that the matter of my marital status should become so important to her just when my own emotions were in such turmoil, or had someone decided I was lavishing a bit too much attention on Victoria St. Clare? And did it matter? Whatever had brought her here, she was right. It was time we discussed this.

I swallowed the remnants of the sweet roll and sipped again from my cup. "I wasn't aware there was any hurry."

"But of course there is, love," she replied with another maternal pat of my knee. "You're at your reproductive peak. The pack is waiting for you to produce an heir. Until you do, or at least until you are well mated and ready to start your family, you will never be taken seriously. You will never be allowed to assume full command."

Of course. It was perfectly sensible. In all our civilized history, no unmated werewolf—male or female—had sat on the throne. It simply wasn't done. As for why, well, *I* wouldn't trust a ruler who couldn't attract a mate. Would you?

I had simply never thought of it in terms of myself before. Or if I had, it was far down on my list of priorities.

"Unless you have someone already in mind…" She hesitated inquiringly, but I said nothing. She went on, "I've been looking over some available candidates, all from the best families, of course. I thought the best way to do this might be to have a weekend at the castle, next month, perhaps, and invite them all."

Isn't there a human fairy tale about a prince and a ball and hundreds of young ladies coming from all over the kingdom to win his favor? I wonder if that poor fool could have possibly felt as awkward as I did at the prospect.

I said, disbelieving, "Do you mean…to audition?"

She laughed. "Not exactly. I'm sure you know most of them already. Stephanie Lafevre, Yvette Dansonier, Patrice St. Clare and her third cousin Delancy, both lovely girls…"

The list went on, and I had to get up, pacing a few steps away, as the names started to blur together in my head. Yes, I knew them, many of them intimately. None of them had made me feel even remotely the way Victoria had last night.

"How do I choose?" I asked.

I realized I had interrupted her, but was suddenly too disturbed to think of apologizing. I turned to her urgently. "How can I know which one to pick for my mate above all the others? How will I know which one is right?"

She smiled. "Well, the most reliable way is to listen to one's heart, I suppose."

"What if my heart says the wrong thing? What if I make a mistake?"

She must have seen something in my eyes before I

could hide it because there was a flicker of concern in hers, and she looked at me more closely. I made certain my face was unreadable.

She said carefully, "I wouldn't worry about making a mistake if I were you, Noel. As long as you choose a girl of good character and fine family…"

Who is capable of giving you an heir. The words hung unspoken.

"What if I don't love her?"

She smiled confidently. "You will love her, when you are mated."

"What if I don't?" I insisted, feeling a little desperate now. "What if I mate with the wrong woman and she's inside my head forever and I don't want her there? What if I *don't love her?*"

She set aside her cup and came to me, slipping her arm through mine, her face filled with tenderness and compassion. "Darling Noel, it doesn't happen that way. You won't choose foolishly or impulsively. You'll know when it's right. You'll choose some bright young lady…"

But not as bright as Victoria, I thought.

"Who makes you laugh…"

But who couldn't have Victoria's quirky sense of humor.

"And makes you ache when you think of her…"

Just like I do now.

"And you would give up the world for her."

I thought helplessly, *Yes.*

"You will love her because you can't help loving her, because you can't imagine a time when she wasn't a part of you, because, my dear, dear boy, once you are mated you will never be alone again in thought or deed, ever. This is your destiny and it's a beautiful thing."

Yes. My destiny. Because Michael had turned his back

on his destiny, I could not. I had what was his whether I wanted it or not, whether I chose it or not…and could I really say I would have had it otherwise?

I murmured, mostly to myself, "To never be alone again…how lovely that sounds. For I think I have been more alone these past six months than I ever have in my life."

Until Victoria, that is.

She squeezed my arm, pressing her face to my shoulder in a swift, firm gesture of affection. "My darling," she said. "You are loved. I know it's difficult now, and no doubt your life seems very confusing, but never doubt our care for you."

I wanted to believe her.

I gave her arm a single affectionate caress and returned to the fire, picking up my teacup. "I've been thinking of going to visit Michael." I hadn't, really, but suddenly it didn't seem like such a bad idea. Michael, who was to blame for all this. Michael, who had given up so much and caused so much pain for the love of a woman. Michael, who, with his human wife, surely knew deprivations of the flesh I could not begin to fathom. It began to seem, in fact, like a very good idea. Michael.

Her smile was, as far as I could tell, without artifice. "I am fond of his wife."

"But she's not," I said carefully, "what you would have chosen for your son."

"No," she agreed. Her eyes held mine steadily. "But then, it was not my choice to make, was it?"

She walked back to the sofa, where she had left her gloves. She began to pull them on, giving attention to the fit of each finger, and she said, "It's not a good idea to dwell on the past, Noel, for any of us. And the only way to prevent that is to move forward. Having said that…"

She stretched out her hand to check the fit of the glove, then looked at me. "I think we can all agree that Michael's *affaire du coeur,* however fortunate the consequences may have been for him, was a misalliance with disastrous potential, and the pack can't afford another such indulgence. Can we?"

I felt the muscles tighten at the back of my neck. But I held her gaze. "No," I agreed.

There was compassion in her smile, regret and genuine tenderness. She was my spiritual adviser, moral guide, mate to our ruler, symbolic mother to our entire race…but she was also, at that moment, my *grand-mère.* She came to me, and kissed my cheek. "It is not so difficult, *petit-cher,* you'll see. Just be careful not to mistake infatuation for adoration."

I was certain then. She knew about Victoria.

And I knew she was right.

She said, "Thank you for the tea, my dear."

I made some protesting noises about her leaving.

"But I must. You have a job to do and I have a husband at home…and several dozen boxes from designer houses arriving even as we speak!"

She turned at the door, her expression confident and relaxed. "So, shall we arrange our little weekend for next month then? Around the fifteenth?"

"That's less than three weeks away."

Again, her expression was sympathetic, but her tone was determined. "There's really no point in delaying, is there?"

And because I had no choice, I agreed, "No, there's not. The fifteenth is fine."

When she was gone, I went back to the sofa and sat down, and spent a long time staring into the fire. I felt very old.

CHAPTER TEN

Victoria

There is no such thing as prostitution among our kind; there are no sex crimes of any kind, as a matter of fact. The concept of one sex using another for anything other than mutual delight is one we find difficult to understand. I read a great many novels written by humans, however, and I know that the average woman, having been made love to and then deserted in the way Noel left me, would have felt very badly used indeed.

I, however, felt honored. I felt touched by a miracle, dazed with discovery, ecstatic and in awe...and more desperately unhappy than I had ever been in my life.

I have learned to be content with my lot in life; what would be the point of doing otherwise? But it's easy to be content when you don't know any better. It's easy not to want what you never knew existed before. But Noel had shown me possibilities. I hated him for that. And adored him.

You no doubt think I'm referring to the physical pleasures. Certainly that was a part of it. The sensations he allowed me to experience were wondrous, magnificent, utterly indescribable to one who has never known them...which, until Noel, I never had. He was as skilled as I had heard him to be, as he by rights *should* be, and I was delighted to have discovered for myself how he had earned his reputation. But werewolves do not become attached to each other over such things. To do so would be akin to falling in love with your tennis partner because of his excellent serve.

Did I say falling in love? Well, I didn't mean it. I'm sure I didn't.

What I meant to say was that the physical aspect was only the smallest percentage of our relationship; so small, in fact, that I'm sure to him it was inconsequential, and yet I could not even fulfill that.

He had shown to me the possibilities of a world I had never been sure really existed. He had reminded me of my nature and how wondrous a thing it was, he had allowed me, through his simple generosity, to share myself with another of my own kind. For one such as I, who spends her life constantly balancing between the society of humans and werewolves, a part of both but belonging to neither, this was a rare and inexpressibly beautiful thing. He made me feel alive and glad to be alive. He made me feel a part of something larger than myself. He made me feel special. He made me feel, whether he'd intended it or not, loved. And in return for all that, I had given him absolutely nothing.

This made me feel unhappy and confused, filled with yearning one moment and despair the next. And even though I would not have changed the night we had shared for all the world, I almost thought I would have been better off never having known it, never having learned to want things I could never, ever, possibly have.

I kept my hairdressing appointment, partly because Raoul really *was* temperamental about people who stood him up and partly because I didn't know what to say to Noel, how to behave around him or what to expect. I alternately wanted to postpone the encounter as long as possible and hurry to meet him, unable to bear another moment outside his presence. He made me happy, he made me sad. He made me nervous, he made me giddy, anxious and excited, pleased and frustrated; he fulfilled all my fantasies and he left me filled with longing. I couldn't bear to be near him nor could I stay away. Oh, this was a miserable feeling. And I wasn't even in love with him.

I was quite sure of that.

I could sense the undercurrent of excitement when I entered the Clare de Lune building and caught murmurs of conversation that led me to understand someone from Castle St. Clare was on the premises. It wasn't until I got off the elevator, however, that I caught her scent and I knew it immediately. Madame St. Clare.

I stepped back and held the elevator door for her, lowering my eyes in respect. Even if I had not recognized her by scent—a virtual impossibility—her appearance would have been enough to intimidate. She was tall, elegant and dressed to the nines. She carried herself with a queenly demeanor that seemed effortless, and she never failed to inspire awe in even the grandest of us.

She was flanked by four bodyguards, two of whom entered the elevator before her, giving me long hard looks, and two of whom remained behind her. One of the bodyguards pushed the Door Open button on the elevator and I quickly stepped out.

As I moved past her, Clarice St. Clare murmured, "Enchantment." It was my perfume. "Lovely on you, my dear."

A thrill went through me, and I bowed my head in acknowledgment and modesty. Clarice St. Clare had noticed *me*. The maternal symbol of all our people, the woman every little girl dreams of growing up to be, had said *my* perfume was lovely.

But as she moved toward the elevator, she suddenly looked back at me sharply. My heart started to pound.

She said, "You're..."

"Victoria St. Clare," I supplied quickly.

Her eyes narrowed fractionally, and I don't mind saying, I was terrified. Then she murmured, without ever taking her eyes off me, "Yes, of course."

She held me in that silent, assessing gaze for perhaps five more excruciating seconds, and without another word she and her bodyguards got on the elevator. I dared not raise my eyes, but I could feel her gaze on me even as the doors closed.

It probably all seems very meaningless and insignificant, but her behavior upset me...enough to make me recall that I had been singled out by a member of the ruling family once before, when Sebastian St. Clare had assigned me to work with Noel. And then I remembered what Noel had said yesterday about Sebastian St. Clare's setting him up for failure, and then *I* started to wonder, treacherous as it seems, just how deeply the powers that be at Castle St. Clare resented the outcome of the battle for succession. I hated myself for it, but I couldn't help wondering what had brought Madame St. Clare to Montreal.

Doubtless it all seems very silly and farfetched, but the truth is that without that chance encounter I never would have begun to form my theory about the identity of our spy.

My heart had yet to regain its normal rhythm when I reached my office. Sara was waiting for me eagerly. "Who was *that?*" she wanted to know. "She's had this place in a buzz ever since she got here. Wasn't her suit fabulous? And that hat! Your hair looks great, by the way."

I touched my coiffure absently. "Thanks. He put in red highlights, but I don't know. Too brassy?"

"No, I can hardly tell, really. Just in the light. It's gorgeous. Now, who was that woman? Do you know her?"

I explained briefly who Madame St. Clare was and added, "I suppose she was here to see Monsieur Duprey."

Sara nodded. "She was in there about half an hour, I suppose. He left a message for you to see him as soon as you came in." She dug around on her desk and produced the message slip.

My heart leaped and speeded again as I took the slip of paper from her. I was torn between wanting to go to him as fast as my feet would carry me, and wanting to postpone the meeting until I composed myself or at least decided how I was supposed to behave. Would anything have changed between us? Would he regard me differently today? Was he sorry he had shared intimacy with me, disappointed in the way the evening had turned out, regretting having confided in me at all?

But no, I decided briskly. I was being foolish. Today was different from no other day, business as usual, and that, undoubtedly, was precisely what Noel wanted to see me about—business. Either that, or he wanted to scold me for being late. Resolutely, I turned toward his office, but something caught my ear.

Anyone with my sense of hearing learns to screen out background noise; otherwise, I would surely go mad. A hundred thousand clatters, clinks and conversations cross my ears every day; only rarely does one catch my attention enough to make me listen.

The voice I heard was Madame St. Clare's, six floors below me. But it was what she said that made me listen.

"Greg," she said warmly. It was unlikely that any but the most talented of werewolves on the floor she was on could have overheard her. "I'm so glad I got a chance to see you. I wanted to convey to you personally how grateful we are for your help…"

Something—the high-pitched whine of a fax or an incoming computer call—interfered with my hearing, obscuring the rest of her sentence. The next voice I heard was Greg Stillman's.

"…nothing I wouldn't do to—"

The phone on Sara's desk rang piercingly, and I flinched and swore silently.

"My loyalty has always been to the St. Clares," Stillman finished.

"And don't think it won't be rewarded," Clarice assured him.

That was all I heard.

I turned slowly back to Sara, Noel's message slip still in my hand. She covered the mouthpiece of the telephone and looked at me inquiringly.

"Will you do me a favor?" I said. "Stall him for a few hours. There's this project I was supposed to have ready for him and it's not quite done."

She nodded sympathetically. "Sure thing. Anything I can do to help?"

I smiled at her gratefully. How could Noel *not* like humans? "I'll let you know," I told her, and hurried to my office.

It took me less than two hours to discover what I wanted and then I wasn't at all sure it was what I wanted at all. Even though my pulse was racing with excitement, I didn't trust my own judgment. I needed to talk to Noel. It was only the first step, of course, and it might mean nothing at all, but perhaps this could in some small way begin to repay him for all he had done for me. And make up for the other things I could never give him.

I was a little breathless as I stopped by his secretary' desk. "Is he in?"

She didn't glance up from the document she was tran scribing, nor did her fingers slow in their keystrokes. "H has a lunch appointment in twenty minutes."

I went past her quickly and, after a brief knock, opene Noel's door.

The room smelled of Earl Grey and hickory wood computer printouts and Clarice St. Clare. Noel stood in spill of sunlight before the window, wearing a charcoa and heather tweed jacket and black silk turtleneck, th molten flow of his hair glittering in the light, his hea bent over the sheaf of papers in his hand. He seemed t be absorbed in what he was studying, so I did not inter rupt, but took a moment to draw a calming breath an enjoy the view.

But the view took my breath away. Would I ever reacl a point where just looking at him did *not* make my hear race and my palms sweaty? And the scent of him, washin over me in waves so intensely pleasurable that I wante to open my mouth and taste it…spice and hardwood, ci rus and evergreen, sunshine on wool and beneath it al so subtle as to be detectable only by another werewol the feral, musky scent of power and virility. And beyon that, even more subtle, snow and wind, herbal bath sal and yes, my own scent, faintly intermingled with his…th memory of our time together clinging to his skin as it n doubt clung to mine.

And even as the pleasure of the memory began to war my cheeks, something else occurred to me, and I kne why Clarice St. Clare had stopped, and looked at me s oddly. She had smelled him on me.

What that might mean for either of us I couldn't begi to imagine.

Noel said, without turning, "Who was that human king who had such an excess of wives that he killed a few?"

The question caught me off guard—small wonder—and it was a moment before I could orient myself. "Do you mean King Henry VIII of England?"

"Yes, I think so." Still he didn't turn, but gazed out the window into the snow-covered city with absent absorption.

"I can't think how you graduated from Oxford without knowing that," I observed, but in fact I knew perfectly well. Our short-term recall is excellent, but our long-term memory can be highly selective. Noel had no use for extraneous information about human kings, so he promptly forgot what he did not need.

I was deeply curious to know what had triggered his sudden interest in such arcane subjects, so much so that I almost forgot—momentarily, of course—the urgency of the reason for my visit.

He said, still oddly reflective, "And before him no human king had ever married one woman while loving another?"

I was fascinated. "Well, no. Human males have always used females in the most promiscuous fashion, you know that. But I think the significance of this incident with Henry had something to do with religious law. He had to marry and produce an heir, but the Church would not allow him to divorce when the wife who was selected for him turned out to be unsatisfactory. The poor fellow really was in a bind."

"Still, it seems as though murder was a rather drastic solution."

I shrugged. "Humans are often given to grand drama."

"Which we, naturally, are not." Even in profile, I could see the sardonic curve of his lips.

"Not in recent history, anyway," I admitted. "Certainly we don't go around murdering our mates because we find them inconvenient."

"No, of course not." Was that bitterness I heard in his tone? "We are far too civilized for that."

"Or practical," I suggested.

"And do you think it was practical of Henry to spend his life wedded to a woman he didn't love simply for the sake of an heir?"

"I think he may have loved some of them."

He turned, frowning. "Who?"

"His wives. I think I read somewhere he was in love with Anne Boleyn."

"Who in the world is that?"

"One of the wives of Henry VIII," I replied on the edge of exasperation. "Isn't that who we're talking about?"

He gave an impatient shake of his head. "Human history is an absurd and bloody maze of treachery and deceit. I don't think there's anything at all to be learned from it."

And I replied, now desperately confused, "I don't believe I said there was."

He looked at me sharply. "What have you done to your hair?"

Self-consciously my hand went to my hair. "Nothing much. I went to the salon this morning."

He scowled. "The color's different. I don't like it."

I lifted an eyebrow, wisely biting back any one of a number of acerbic replies that were on the tip of my tongue. Fortunately, Raoul had assured me that the high lights would wash out with a couple of shampoos.

I linked my hands before me and said formally, "I had a message you wanted to see me."

"That was two hours ago."

"Well, I had that appointment—"

He stopped me with a cutting look. "I heard you come in, Victoria. Why were you avoiding me?"

I swallowed hard. Dared I think that the inquiry had some personal origin, that he *cared* whether I avoided him or not? That he had wanted to see me because...because he wanted to see me, and for no other reason?

And the answer was, I told myself firmly, no. No, I dared not think any of that.

Still, there was an uncomfortable pressure deep in my abdomen that felt like longing, a dryness in my throat, a quickening of my breath. I knew he could hear my heartbeat speed, and the flare of acknowledgment within his eyes only made it beat faster.

I took a deep breath and plunged in. "Did you also hear Madame St. Clare's conversation with Greg Stillman?" I demanded.

Those eyes, which had been so intent upon mine, like probes of hot green ice boring into my soul, now moved reluctantly away, reflecting surprise and annoyance. "What?" he replied. "What are you talking about?"

I breathed a little easier, although anyone, observing the two of us, would have been hard put to know why. Noel was clearly at the edge of his patience with me, and I was so tense—afraid I might be wrong and even more afraid I might *not* be—that I was sure he could smell it. Still, I managed to explain in a more or less reasonable manner, "As she was leaving, Madame St. Clare paused to thank Greg Stillman for all his help, and to assure him he would be rewarded for it. He in turn assured her that his loyalties had always been to the St. Clares."

His frown darkened, but I could see uneasiness there.

"It means nothing. His loyalties are properly placed. The St. Clares are our rulers."

"Yes, I know," I admitted. "What I heard could have had a dozen interpretations. But I was wondering, do you know of any project on which he might have been giving Castle St. Clare particular help?"

The line between his eyes deepened, and his lips tightened. "No."

"Or why he should have sent twenty-one e-mail messages to Castle St. Clare in the past two weeks under his personal code—sixteen of which were tagged Moonsong?"

He had half turned from me in silent preoccupation, now he swung back, his eyes flashing incredulity. I pulled the printout of the network log out of my pocket and handed it to him. He scanned it fiercely, the fine lines around the corners of his eyes growing more pronounced as he did so. His hand tightened on the paper, crumpling it a little as he looked up at me. "What did the messages say?" he demanded.

I shook my head. "I don't know how to access them," I admitted. "I only knew how to call up the log because my friend Sara—I mean, my secretary—had to do it one time to prove her then boss was handling something properly."

Noel paced a few steps across the room, his eyes returning to the paper. "Stillman's head of the division," he said. "Of course he'd be in touch with Castle St. Clare. He probably sends twenty-one messages a *day* to headquarters."

"Not under his personal code," I told him. "All routine e-mail is automatically send under the department code, unless someone deliberately changes it."

And when he tossed me another sharp questioning look,

I explained, "I asked Sara. And why all the messages about Moonsong?"

He looked back at the paper. His voice grew more thoughtful. "Not so unusual. Moonsong is the most important project we have going now. If he's in communication with headquarters about it, he might simply be doing his job."

"But you didn't authorize him to do that."

"No."

"In fact, you specifically ordered secrecy."

He looked at me. "Yes."

"Noel, you don't think—"

He interrupted me, and he was right to do so. Neither one of us had any business thinking, much less speaking out loud, what I was about to say.

"It would be interesting to know what was in those messages," he said, and held out the paper to me. "And also whether any similar correspondence existed regarding the other lost formulas."

I had no idea whether it would be possible to find out any of that. But I nodded as I accepted the paper, and knew I would move heaven and earth to get the answers for him.

He had moved close to me, and he seemed to tower over me, the mixture of body heat and intoxicating scent that was the essence of his presence enfolding me. I said, a little nervously, "I won't take up any more of your time. Your secretary said you had a lunch appointment."

And he said abruptly, "Why do you let humans play with your hair?"

I laughed, startled. "Who should I let play with it?"

Have I explained about our hair? It never needs cutting or setting. It grows to a length that is predetermined by a chromosome or two and stays that way for the rest of our lives. Should it be cut, it will grow back in a matter of hours. Curled and sprayed it will hold its shape, but permanents are useless. Most of us have hair that reaches our collarbones at least, but there is no truth to the myth about the link between a male's virility and the length of his hair. Michael St. Clare, for example, had hair almost to his waist, but look what happened to him.

Noel, on the other hand, and his magnificent mane...

"You enjoy it," he accused.

Again I gave a little laugh, confused. "What?"

"Letting humans groom you, and put their hands on you. Why?"

That was difficult to explain, particularly when he made it sound so shameful. Particularly when he was standing so close, muddling my thoughts. I looked at him. I had to tilt my head back to do so.

"Well," I said, answering the question for myself as much as for him, "I do enjoy it. It's nice to be petted and fussed over and caressed. It makes me feel...special."

And he said softly, "Didn't I do that last night?"

His eyes were like jewels in the sun, their color pure and hot. He was so close that every pore on his face was clear to me, every glistening strand of hair. I could taste his breath, the sound of his blood rushed in my ears. His heat made my skin prickle.

He reached up and plucked out one of the pins that held my hair, releasing a heavy lock onto my shoulder, then another. I could hardly breathe. I didn't breathe. And he didn't blink, he didn't flicker a muscle or move an inch until all the pins were loose and then, with a single long and hungry inhalation, he gathered my hair in his hands and buried his face in it.

I sank into him. The room swirled around me, I went deaf with the roar of heartbeats and mingled breaths, my skin flamed and I was helpless, helpless with the power of his touch.

I linked my arms around his neck because without his support I would have surely fallen, simply melted to the floor in a single flood of sensation too intense to endure. His hair was spun silk between my fingers. His scent flooded my cells. I parted my lips to drag in breath and tasted the roughness of his face, the contrasting texture of his neck, the salt on his skin.

He whispered my name and it sounded like music. He tugged at the buttons of my blouse, exposing the deep cut of my lace-trimmed bra. He cupped his hands beneath my breasts, pressing and lifting, and then dropped his face to the cushion that was formed there, kissing the sensitive flesh, inhaling deeply, adoring me.

Adoring me. That's what it felt like, this caress, this discovery, this unexpected and inexplicable gift of sensual exploration—adoration. For certainly that was what he evoked in me, and I responded greedily, thoughtlessly, helpless and hungry.

He wrapped me in his arms, his face against my neck and his hands caressing the curve of my bottom, molding our bodies together at every point of contact. He pushed one leg between mine and I twined my leg around his, feeling muscle and sinew beneath the silky flannel of his expensively cut trousers, the shape of calf and ankle and strong lean flank that I knew so well. We embraced like this, breathing together, drawing in the essence of each other through this contact, the scent and the heat and the strength of each other. I wanted to be naked against him, and him against me. I wanted to be wrapped in him, absorbed in him, conquered by him, and I was like a child, wanting more but not knowing what, exactly, it was that

I wanted. The intensity of the need frightened me, or perhaps it was the not knowing.

I'm not sure what would have happened then if his phone had not begun to ring. I'm really not.

For the longest time, he didn't move or seem to hear the telephone at all. And I didn't want him to. I tried to block out the sound with my will, with the sound of my breathing, with his heartbeat. But I was being foolish.

I whispered, "Noel…"

And he murmured, "I know…"

His hands, tangled in my hair, tightened on the back of my neck once, then slowly loosened. He moved away from me, and to the desk.

In the absence of him I was cold. I buttoned my blouse with clumsy, uncertain fingers, and tucked it into my skirt more securely. Then I began to try to twist my hair back into some semblance of order with the pins that I could gather from the carpet. Who was I trying to fool? The werewolves wouldn't even have to look at me to know what had just transpired behind the closed doors of the heir designé's office, and the human females would be smothering their smiles after one glance. And did I care? Would I have traded one moment in his arms for the secrecy of a monastery? I think you know the answer to that.

He spoke briefly and tersely into the phone but I didn't hear what was said. By the time he turned, I had almost finished rearranging my hair, but the heat of pleasure still scorched my cheeks and I had no way to repair my makeup. That was the least of my concerns.

I smiled at him briefly and uncertainly and turned toward the door. "You have a lunch appointment," I reminded him.

There was a tightness to his expression that had not

been there before, a gravity to the set of his mouth and an odd look in his eyes—somber and bleak, yet angry. I hesitated because I thought perhaps the phone call had contained bad news.

But what he said was, "You didn't ask me why Madame St. Clare was here."

I was surprised. "I—I assumed she came to see you. You are her heir, after all."

"Yes." His tone was clipped. He stood very erect behind the desk, and he looked me straight in the eye. "She came to tell me it was time her heir chose a mate. She has even chosen the date—the fifteenth of next month."

I felt as though I had been punched in the stomach. I couldn't speak. I could only stare at him.

"It's going to be quite an event," he went on, and a streak of cruelty crept into his expression that I never would have imagined from him. "All the available females from the best families will be there, a positive orgy of possibilities, if you'll pardon the double entendre, and I'll have an entire weekend in which to choose. It will no doubt be the social event of the decade."

Finally, I found my voice. It was hoarse and dry. "No doubt."

And then, though it took more courage than I had ever known I possessed, I met his eyes and I found a smile. I said, "I don't see any reason we shouldn't have your business here wrapped up long before then. In fact, the timing is perfect. We can celebrate the successful launch of Moonsong and the mating of the heir at the same time— it will do wonders for pack morale. Madame St. Clare's reputation for brilliance is well deserved. Congratulations. I'm sure you will be mated beautifully."

And with a final injection of sincerity into my smile, I turned and left the office, my heart breaking.

* * *

The ringing of the doorbell awoke me at midnight. When I am depressed I sleep very deeply, so I can't say how long the bell had been ringing. When I heard the voice, spoken softly from the other side of the door, say imperiously, "Victoria, it's Noel. Open the door, please," I was out of bed and on my feet in a single movement, pushing my arms into a heavy terry-cloth robe and my feet into fuzzy slippers as I stumbled toward the door.

"What's wrong?" I gasped as I pulled open the door.

He came inside, pulling off his gloves and looking surprised to note my state of dishabille, the darkened room. "Were you asleep? Is it late?"

I gaped at him, the adrenaline shock slowly receding from my body and leaving me shaky and irritable. "It's midnight! Of course I was asleep."

He shrugged out of his coat and dropped it into its usual spot on the chair by the door. "Well, I'm sorry to wake you, then."

I pushed back my tangled hair and tied the sash of my robe. "Has something happened? Why are you here?"

"No, nothing's happened. Well, perhaps something." But as he spoke, his eyes were going over me from tousled head to fake-fur-clad toe, and it was clear, even with my night vision, that he was not impressed with what he saw. "What *are* you wearing?" he asked.

I rubbed one ankle against the other, self-conscious in my flannel nightie and heavy robe. But I retorted defiantly, "A nightgown, perhaps you've heard of it? It's perfectly acceptable sleepwear in all fashion circles."

"Human fashion circles, maybe. You actually sleep in it?"

I crossed my arms in an unconscious defensive gesture. "I get cold."

"That's because you sleep alone," he observed.

"And you don't?"

"Occasionally," he admitted. "But I've never resorted to a getup as ridiculous as that to keep warm."

That almost made me smile. Damn him for doing that.

I tightened the sash of my robe. "What do you want?" I demanded ungraciously.

He hesitated. I was still a little groggy with sleep, or I might have noticed there was more to his demeanor than was obvious on first glance. But I had suffered through a great deal in the past twenty-four hours; I should be forgiven if I was less than sensitive to the nuances of his mood.

He said, "I came to tell you that I won't be in the office tomorrow. I have an early flight to Seattle, and I don't know how long I'll be gone."

Even at that hour I made the connection. "You're going to see Michael?"

What else, after all, was there in Seattle of any significance?

"Yes."

He seemed uncomfortable for some reason, and it took me another moment to understand why.

"Noel, you surely don't think that Michael... I mean, granted, we don't know much about his wife, but I can't think that she—or he—would ever be involved in this!"

"Probably not." He didn't quite meet my eyes. "But I can't say I've done a thorough job until I've talked to him."

"Well." I shivered a little, even in my robe. "I don't envy you that task."

He looked at me oddly for a moment. It was late. I was confused.

Then he said, "I also wanted to apologize to you."

"For what?"

His eyes narrowed. I felt the tightening of his muscles, and detected a slight change in the sound of the blood that rushed through his vessels, indicative of a rise in blood pressure due, perhaps, to anger. I couldn't think why he should be angry with me. But his next words, though spoken calmly, confirmed that he was, in fact, angry.

"Damn it, Victoria," he said, "don't you care about anything?"

I simply stared at him.

He took a step toward me. His hands were clenched at his sides and it took me a moment to realize it wasn't me he was angry at, but himself.

"I used you," he insisted tightly. "Last night—I deliberately tried to arouse you knowing it could lead to nothing, knowing we could never... And then again, this afternoon, when I knew I was to be mated to another in a matter of weeks! Don't you care? Doesn't that make you furious?"

I bowed my head. "I didn't think of it as being used," I said in a small voice. "I thought of it as...pleasure."

He grabbed my chin between his thumb and forefinger and jerked it up, forcing me to look at him. His eyes were blazing with a low dark fire I couldn't understand. "There can be no pleasure between you and me, don't you understand that? There can only be me, taking my pleasure from you and knowing that I can never keep any of the promises those pleasures make! Damn it, why don't you hate me? Are you so accustomed to being badly used, you take it as your due? Or don't you care what I think of you?"

I jerked my chin away, my heart pounding with hurt and alarm. "Why are you doing this? What do you want from me?"

He grabbed my arms and bent his head to me, the fire in his eyes low and intense. I could almost feel its heat. "Last night," he demanded, "when I left you, didn't you wonder why? Didn't you care?"

"I—I knew why," I mumbled, embarrassed. "I knew—"

"No, you didn't!" His hands tightened on my arms, hurting. He was incredibly strong. I thought sometimes he forgot that. "You didn't know that it was because of you—*you* aroused me to the point of Change. That's not pleasure, that's passion! You did that to me, don't you care?"

I was stunned. I didn't know how to feel, much less what to say. What was he saying? What was he implying? And how could any of it be true?

I pulled away, turning from him, but he caught my forearm and held it firmly. I refused to look at him, but he would not let me escape his words.

"I sent for your records, Victoria," he said. "All of them. I spent the afternoon studying them and you know what I found? There's nothing wrong with you, Victoria! Nothing! Our medics find no physical reason for you to be any different from the rest of us!"

I snapped my head around to face him, my throat growing tight, my heart pounding. "Why did you do that?" I cried hoarsely. "How dare you! What gives you the right to pry into my private affairs, my medical history. How dare you!"

He released my arm abruptly, and with such force that I staggered back a step. "This gives me the right!"

He tore out of his jacket and tossed it aside, then stripped off his sweater. My stunned, disbelieving eyes had a moment's glimpse of his magnificent chest before he turned, catching his hair aside with one hand and showing me his back. A series of parallel red lines marred the perfection of his skin across each shoulder blade.

"These are claw marks, Victoria!" he cried. "You started to change last night, you did! And then you stopped it! Why?"

I was gasping, my breath coming in great horrified gulps as I stared at him, incredulous, confused, terrified. "No," I whispered. And then I cried out loud, "No, I didn't, I can't!"

I turned from him then and ran. But there was no place to go, really, and he caught up with me in the bedroom. He caught my arms and I struggled against him, crying desperately, "Why are you saying this? Why are you doing this to me? You know it's not possible, you know what I am! Why are you tormenting me?"

"Because I want you to care, damn you!" His voice was hoarse and the emotion emblazoned upon his face was raw, powerful, terrifying. "I want you to let go of that composure you manage so well and just *feel* for once, just want as much as I want and hurt as much as I hurt and *care,* for God's sake, just care about what we've lost!"

His words were like knife wounds to my spirit. Bleeding and aching, I pulled away from him, turning so that he had to follow, to look where I was looking. And I said brokenly, "I care."

I directed his attention to the portrait over the bed, the one I had never imagined he would see. Noel, as a magnificent silver blond wolf, superimposed upon Noel in sleek, naked human form. Each incarnation was equally as powerful, equally as beautiful. I had painted it in colors of fire and ice, magic and mystery, because that was what he was to me. I had never wanted him to see it, not because I was ashamed of my work, but because this was my most guarded secret. He could not look at that painting without knowing that I had loved him forever.

I thought he would be embarrassed, that he would withdraw from me in silence and leave. Instead, he turned to me, slowly, and drew me into his arms.

I lost my heart to him then. I truly did.

He cradled me against his chest, his one hand spread over my skull, fingers threaded through my hair. He rocked me gently back and forth, soothing me. And he murmured into my hair, with all the pain and helplessness of any lost lover who has ever lived, "I don't know what to do, Victoria. I just don't know."

I wanted to cry, but I didn't know how, any more than I knew how to experience the Change. So I just clung to him, loving him, surrendering all I was to him and knowing it would never be enough.

Then he stepped away, and pushed back my hair from my face. He looked deep into my eyes, telegraphing what he was about to do. My heartbeat grew heavy with anticipation as he dropped his hands, untying my sash, pushing the robe off my shoulders. He said softly, "Take off your clothes, Victoria. Let me lie with you tonight. I promise I won't hurt you, or take you anyplace you don't want to go. Just let me sleep with you, and keep you warm."

I watched as he unfastened his trousers, and stepped out of them. He was beautiful in his nakedness, the slim waist, flat abdomen, the thatch of light hair that cupped his sex, strong muscled thighs and golden-furred legs. I wanted to touch him all over. I wanted to claim him as my own. I wanted to be everything he needed me to be...everything I could never be.

I unbuttoned the small pearl buttons at my throat and pulled the nightgown over my head. My skin prickled with the temperature of the room and immediately he drew me against him, warming me. Oh, it was so wonderful, his heat penetrating me, enfolding me. His body molding itself to mine, blending with mine. His hands, stroking my back, caressing my hair. His breath, whispering in my ear. His musky scent enveloping me. The beat of his heart reaching out to mine and capturing it. Oh, how I wanted this. How I wanted it to last forever.

I whispered, "What does it feel like—the Change?"

His muscles tightened, his heartbeat speeded. He slipped his hand between our bodies and pressed it against my belly. Ah, the sensation. I went weak with it.

"It starts with a fire, here," he said, pressing hard. His mouth was against my ear, his voice sending reverberations throughout every sensory receptor I possessed. "And here..." He slipped his hand down, between my legs. I gasped, and the gasp turned into a moan of pleasure as he caressed. "It hurts at first, but only if you resist..." Skillful fingers loosened my muscles, pushed inside. "But if you surrender, if you embrace the sensation..." His fingers stroked, tantalized, found my most sensitive spot and abruptly, powerfully, brought my body to an intense sexual climax that left me sweaty and gasping, trembling in his arms. "It makes this seem like nothing," he whispered. "Like the mere caress of a summer breeze across your skin. Victoria, it is what you were meant to be, it is your right. Shall I take you there, my love? Shall I try?"

Oh, but I was terrified. So many failures, so many expectations dashed, so many voices laughing in my ears. The pleasure he had shown me, the pleasure he had promised me, yes, I hungered for it, I trembled for it, and I dared not take it for my own.

I clung to him, tightening my arms around him, and I whispered, "No...please, don't, I'm so frightened..."

He caressed my back, he kissed my hair. "All right,

love, I won't. It's all right..." He drew me to the bed, wrapping his arms and legs around me, holding me in his embrace. We caressed each other, we loved each other in silent, simple ways, and we fell asleep wrapped in each other's embrace.

When I awoke, I was cold, and he was gone.

CHAPTER ELEVEN

Noel

It was not raining in Seattle, which surprised me. In fact, the pilot informed me, the temperature was in the mid-forties when we touched down that afternoon, and I noticed nothing but a lacework of snow was left on the banks as the limo sped down the highway toward the suburbs where Michael lived.

Suburbs. Michael. Even now I could barely think the two words in one sentence without a shudder. There but for the grace of God go I.

Already I was beginning to regret my foolishness in coming here. What did I really expect to accomplish, after all? Michael had ruined his life, now I was looking to him for advice on mine? What could he tell me that would ease my pain, change my lot, give me more choices? Or perhaps I just wanted to confront him with what he had left me, the life that should have been his.

The little house into which Michael had moved with his human wife Aggie was charming, in its own way. It was situated on a foggy lake, which I didn't like, and surrounded by woods, which I did. It was an elegant brick Georgian design with all the architectural features one might find in a much grander estate, but it was—or at least had been the last time I'd seen it—about half the size of the pool house at Michael's former summer home in Malibu.

The little house had grown by at least one wing and half a story, I noticed as the car pulled into the circular driveway. Construction debris and scaffolding were everywhere, and a crew of three was taking advantage of the fine weather to do something to the roof. The hammering slowed and then ceased as they all turned to stare at the big black car with the bullet-proof windows that stopped before their employer's door.

I was quite sure that my arrival had not gone unnoticed by the occupants of the house, either, although it did occur to me I might have done well to phone ahead. She made me wait through two rings of the bell before she came to the door. Even then, she only opened it partway, leaning against its edge to look me over as though, if she weren't careful, I might try to force a magazine subscription on her.

"Well, if it isn't Noel Duprey," she observed with an inquiring tilt of her head. "If I had only known, I would have been certain to have the red carpet cleaned."

Aggie McDonald St. Clare has never liked me; I can't think why. I've always done my best to be polite to her. Well, most of the time, anyway.

"Mrs. St. Clare," I returned with a dry emphasis on the title. "You are looking lovely as always."

I suppose to some she might be an attractive human female—obviously Michael thought so—but I didn't care for the thin-milk color of her skin or the obscene red of her hair, which she wore far too short, or the wicked tongue that was part of the package. Although I prefer my women taller and more substantial, I will admit she had a certain porcelain-doll charm, particularly dressed as she was today in a big sweater and slim-legged jeans. Disarming, that was what she was, deceptively harmless. As a werewolf, I can appreciate a good deception when I see it, for the last thing Aggie St. Clare could ever be was harmless.

She opened the door wider and stepped back, though with obvious reluctance and a suspicious gaze that never left me. "I suppose you may as well come in."

"You're too kind."

I stepped into the small foyer, glancing around as I removed my coat. Delicious odors emanated from the kitchen—roasting fowl and baking bread and something seasoned with cinnamon. It made me hungry. Beyond that were the scents of fresh paint and turpentine, floor wax and furniture polish, and the wood that burned in the fireplace. An archway with very nice Corinthian molding opened onto the new addition, and before me and to my right was a canvas curtain which, judging from the scents of cedar and outdoor air, concealed the opening to what must once have been a coat closet.

I passed my coat to her, and she hung it unceremoniously on the hook by the door, demanding, "What do you want, Noel?"

I went to examine the archway with its gleaming white paint and expertly carved molding, and inquired, "Did Michael do this?"

"With his own hands."

The room beyond was wide and high-ceilinged, with many windows and graceful curves. It was furnished with sawhorses and canvas drop cloths; I would have gone in to see more but I didn't want to get dust on my shoes. I will admit, though, I was impressed.

"Fine work," I observed. "He's quite good."

"Of course he is," she responded impatiently. "What are you doing here?"

I went into the tiny room with the fireplace. Michael had been here not long ago, his scent was fresh in the room. None of the chairs looked as though they would support me, and I wondered how Michael could stand living here. I would go mad with claustrophobia.

I stood with my back to the fire and my hands linked behind me and I said pleasantly, "I really don't see why you have to be so rude to me, Aggie. What have I ever done to you to deserve such treatment?"

"Oh, well, nothing much at all. You merely kidnapped and drugged me, held me captive a thousand miles from home and forced me to watch you try to kill my husband!"

I made a careless dismissive gesture with my wrist. "Other than that, of course."

She threw up her hands in exasperation and turned away. I grinned. She was entirely too easy to tease.

"Of course, had I not done any of that for which you so unfairly revile me," I reminded her, "your beloved might not have ever regained his memory and his good health and with it the freedom to choose to toss away his life and his career in favor of this deserted little backwater and a human bride. Wouldn't you think for that I might at least deserve a cup of tea?"

She turned back to me with a frown that was almost comical in its ferocity, clearly uncertain whether I had just complimented or insulted her, undecided whether to feed me or throw me out. It was perhaps fortunate for us both that Michael chose that moment to make an appearance.

He smelled of werewolf and sweat, flannel and wood smoke and leather. He wore a plaid workman's jacket over a gray sweatshirt and dusty jeans, leather gloves and a tool belt low on his hips. His hair was braided in a single long rope down his back. I had worried that seeing him again, with my own eyes witnessing the depths to which he had sunk, would be the final cap on my own despair.

I needn't have concerned myself. Michael without a kingdom was still a king. No matter how hard he tried to be human, he was still the most powerful werewolf I would ever know.

I resented this.

He said, slipping his arm around Aggie's shoulders, "Now, Noel, you haven't been in the house five minutes and already you've made her mad. Not the wisest course of action, when you consider she's the cook."

She went all soft at his touch, her frown melting, her shoulders relaxing, her entire body swaying, ever so subtly, toward his. I felt like a voyeur, but I couldn't help it, really: the way their pulses shifted when they came together, blending into the rhythm of each other's, the way their individual scents melted together and created a new scent that was uniquely their own—these were two people who were unmistakably mated, lost forever in the essence of each other. She smiled and lifted her face to his, he bent and kissed her lips lightly. I was fascinated, appalled…and envious.

"Michael," I greeted him cautiously. "You look well."

It was true. Life as a human apparently agreed with him. He was lean and fit and healthy, his skin tanned and firm, his muscles strong in a way that only physical labor can make them. I had for some reason expected him to have deteriorated in the six months since last we met. I was not certain whether I found this, the evidence of his contentment—even prosperity—encouraging or disappointing.

He met my eyes and he said, "I am well."

I decided I was glad.

Aggie said, "I don't think he came all this way to inquire about your health."

"Probably not," Michael agreed easily. He stepped away from her and stripped off his work gloves, then removed his tool belt with a clatter. "Is there any coffee on?"

"I'd prefer tea," I put in.

She gave me a withering look. "I'll put on a pot of coffee," she told Michael. "Are you hungry?"

"Yes," I said, just to annoy her.

Michael grinned. "Don't bother. We'll get something if we want it."

She looked reluctant. "I do have some work to do in my office," she admitted. She glanced at me, then back at Michael. "I don't suppose he'll tell you why he's come until I leave."

"No," I said, growing irritated, "he won't."

She looked at me again and said in a saccharine tone, "Always a pleasure, Noel. Do come again when you can't stay as long."

I resisted a childish impulse to make a face at her retreating back, and Michael's eyes twinkled. "She's really fond of you, you know. Sings your praises when you're not around."

"Yes, well, it does make a refreshing change," I replied. "One gets tired of being treated with civility everywhere one goes."

Michael looked at me for a moment longer, smiling, and, as far as I could tell, he was genuinely glad to see me. I had worried about that, too.

Then he said, gesturing me to be seated, "So, cousin. Troubles already, huh?"

I wanted to ask him how he knew, but that would have been foolish. Of course I was in trouble. Why else would I come to him?

I hesitated before sitting. This was not something I

could talk about confined to a small chair. I wasn't sure
it was something I could talk about at all.

I said, indicating the clatter of hammers coming from
the roof, ''Could we go for a walk?''

A slight inclination of his head signaled both agreement
and curiosity. We went through the French doors and onto
a small patio, then followed a path toward the lake.

I said, ''How do you stand it?''

''The noise? It's the sound of progress. I like it.''

I shook my head. ''The noise, the small spaces, the
humans…the poverty.''

He laughed. Thrusting his hands into his pockets, he
walked with a long easy stride that spoke of confidence
and pride, a man who was absolutely comfortable with
himself. ''Have you ever heard the expression 'to the
manor born,' Noel? That's the difference between us. You
are, I never was.''

This confused me. He, after all, was royalty. I was the
interloper.

The curving lake path took us past the little studio
building where Aggie had her office. Perhaps I mentioned
that she is a writer of some sort for a local paper; nothing
of much consequence, but it keeps her out of trouble, I
suppose. The lights were on inside the office and I could
see her at the window, watching us. I lifted my hand in
greeting and she turned away.

I said, indicating the woods, ''Do you ever run?''

''Of course.'' He seemed surprised by the question.
''The paths are good and the woods are deep. I'll take
you tonight, if you like.''

Now I was surprised. ''She doesn't mind?''

He shot me a look that was puzzled and amused. ''Why
should she mind? She knows what I am, Noel. She loves
me because of it.''

This to me seemed perversely unnatural and not worth the effort it would take to understand, particularly since there were matters of far more personal import on my mind. I said, "But she can't come with you. She can't know what it is you experience when you run or what compels you to do it or what you become in the process. This is a very large and important part of your life that she can never share with you."

Once again he slanted me that odd and probing look. "But she can. She's my wife. She knows what I know, and feels what I feel, just as I do with her."

I simply shook my head, a gesture that indicated, not so much a lack of understanding, as a kind of helplessness. I didn't know how to express myself. I didn't know what to ask. I still wasn't sure why I had come.

"Are you ever sorry?"

"For loving her? God, no."

"For leaving us."

This reply took a second or two longer. "I miss the family," he said. "I'm sorry for hurting them. I miss pack life and I sometimes—not very often—miss the work." A wry twist of his lips softened the words. "But what I've gained is so much more than I lost... No, I can't say that I'm sorry."

Tall grasses, winter brown, grew beside the path, brushing against my legs as we walked. Absently I snapped off the head of one and crushed it between my fingers. "What is this infernal fascination with the human world, anyway?"

If I were Michael, I would have demanded that I come to the point long ago. But Michael has always been the patient one, which is what makes him the superior leader, I suppose.

He said, "Some of us spend as much as half our lives

in human form. The fascination is naturally there. The choice is whether to embrace or despise what we are.''

''You sound like a damn philosophy professor.''

That seemed to amuse him. ''Perhaps that will be my next career.''

At least he had the liberty of choosing.

We were out of sight of the house now, and the sound of hammering was distant, echoing across the lake in muffled pings. The shadows of barren trees stretched in long dark lines across our path. I said, without looking at him, ''How do you have sex with her?''

His half-caught laugh was a mixture of surprise and outrageous amusement. ''The usual way!''

''You mean the human way.''

''Of course. Might I ask what generated this sudden interest? If it's not too personal, of course.''

''And that's enough for you?'' I said, ignoring his question.

His amusement became mingled with exasperation. ''All right, Noel, let's have it. You didn't come all this way to talk about my sex life.''

''Actually…'' I tossed aside the dead blossom I had been shredding and turned to face him. ''I did.''

He looked at me for a long time as though trying to decide whether or not to believe me, and I can't say that I blame him. But I suppose no one could be as miserable as I was and lie about it, because something in my face must have convinced him. He turned and started walking again.

''Tell me,'' he said.

Suddenly it seemed very simple. I said, ''Do you know Victoria St. Clare?''

''I don't think so.''

''She's in the Montreal office.''

"Yes." His voice was thoughtful. "I heard about the troubles there."

Another subject entirely. I determined to stick to the one at hand. "She's an anthromorph."

To his credit, he did not slow his step or reveal his surprise in any way. He merely said, "Ah," in understanding, and let me go on.

The path turned into the woods. I was glad of the deepening shadows. I wasn't sure I could have had this conversation in bright light. "I'm quite obsessed by her, I'm afraid. Emotionally and—physically. I'm aware, of course, that any long-term union between us is impossible. In fact, a mating ceremony has been scheduled for me next month."

I sensed the sharpness of his gaze, but did not meet it.

I went on, "I know, of course, that Victoria is not a possible...candidate, but I can't stop thinking, wondering...wishing..." I faltered as the words that had seemed so effortless moments ago suddenly dried up. There were no words, I realized dispiritedly. There were no words for the torment I was suffering.

"I can't stop thinking about her," I finished at last, and in a tone so low it was barely above a mumble.

We walked a little while longer in silence. Dead leaves crunched under our feet, and occasional patches of ice, hidden in the dark shadows, cracked when we stepped on them.

Michael said, "Does she share your feelings?"

A straightforward question that should have been simple to answer. Like everything else in my life at that moment, it was anything but simple. "It's difficult to say. She guards her emotions closely, which isn't so hard to understand. She's suffered a great deal in her life. I can't

ask her when I have nothing to offer her, but yes, I think
she feels the same.''

"Well now. Isn't this interesting?'' Michael thrust his
fists deeper into the pockets of his jacket, tilting his head
back to catch an errant ray of sun that peeked through a
thicket of evergreens overhead. I could smell his tension,
and the undercurrent of distress he was trying to control.

"So now you'd like me to show you the techniques for
having sexual congress with a female in human form,''
he said. "There's really not much of an art to it, you
know. Perhaps I'll teach a class.''

"Don't be crude.''

The look he shot me was sharp and challenging. "So
that's not what you want?''

"No, it's not.'' I was growing angry now, confused and
irritated and yes, embarrassed. "I'm not like you, I don't
want to be human. I would find no satisfaction in it, even
if I could…restrain myself, which I don't want to.''

His eyes had a rather cruel glitter in the dimness. "Oh,
you could restrain yourself,'' he assured me, "if you
wanted to. And that answers your question, doesn't it?
It's simply a matter of what you want, and what you're
willing to give up to achieve it. Shall I tell you more?''

"I don't want to mate with a human,'' I told him angrily. "That's not why I came here. I know my duty and
I have no intention of neglecting it.''

"But if it weren't for your duty, you would have your
little anthromorph, wouldn't you? You would have her in
any way possible and at whatever cost, isn't that right?
Shall I tell you why you came here?'' He turned on me,
fists clenched in his jacket pockets, his face dark and tight.
"You came to punish me, didn't you?''

"Yes!'' I heard myself shouting at him. "Yes, damn
your dark soul, I did!'' The wind caught my voice and

seemed to magnify it and I was horrified by the sound, by the fury that propelled me, by the carelessness of the words. "I never asked for this, not any of it! I had a good life, a fine life, the life I *chose!* You turn your back on the responsibility that was yours, you shame us all—and you are rewarded with all you ever wanted and I'm left to clean up your mess! I hate you for what you've done, Michael! I hate you for what you've taken from me. And yes, I would punish you if I could."

He looked at me soberly for a long moment. "You won't say it to me, will you?"

I was disoriented, my pulse quick and hot, my breathing fast. The last thing I had expected from him was this calm quiet tone, and a question that made no sense.

I demanded irritably, "What? I've said everything to you I came to say. I'd best go."

I turned to push past him on the trail, but his voice stopped me.

"That you love her." His tone was thoughtful. "I wonder if you have said it to her."

I couldn't go farther. It swept over me, this simple truth: *Love, yes.* That was what I felt. That was what bound me to her, whether or not we were physically mated, and it would continue to do so for the rest of my life.

How could I join with another when the best part of me already belonged to her? All my foolish fantasies of human kings with their multiple wives and even greater numbers of mistresses faded into a bleak and empty future. It was not possible. Where love was involved…it was not possible.

I turned back to Michael, and he must have read it in my eyes because his own eyes grew sad, and touched with compassion. "We pride ourselves on our intellect," he said gently, "but in the end it's emotion that rules our lives, isn't it? I think perhaps your Victoria is not the only one who guards hers too closely."

There was a fallen tree a few yards away. He went over and sat down upon it, resting his elbows on his knees and, in a moment, dropping his head to his hands and pushing back his hair with a long, slow motion. Then he said, "Tell me, Noel, would I be wrong in thinking I still have some small influence over you?"

I answered tiredly, "Of course you do. I wouldn't be here if you didn't."

He dropped his hands between his knees and stared off into the distance. "Then," he said, "you have your revenge." The smile that softened his mouth was wistful and vague. "Now I will spend the rest of my life wondering whether what I've said to you today has caused you to destroy the pack...or destroy yourself."

I came over and sat beside him on the log, yet still several feet away. "Perhaps you don't have as much influence over me as all that."

We sat on the tree trunk for a time, watching the shadows lengthen in the woods and listening to the myriad sounds, far and near, that signaled the ending of the day, tasting the scents that came to us with increasing clarity as the air grew colder. It was good to sit with another werewolf in silence like that. Calming.

After a time, I said, "I couldn't do it, Michael. I couldn't live in exile as you do, apart from others of my own kind." I thought of Victoria and her loneliness, but even she had the company of werewolves, if not the affection of them.

Michael said, "I know that. That's why you're the chosen heir, and I'm building houses for humans."

I looked at him suspiciously, wondering if he was patronizing me. "What are you talking about? I'm the heir because you chose not to be."

He corrected, with every appearance of sincerity, "No, because you are the better man."

I stared at him, murmuring before I could stop myself, "That's what Victoria says."

"You should listen to her."

But I shook my head impatiently. "You've always been the stronger werewolf, everyone knows that. You're the rightful heir and for good reason, I don't pretend otherwise. I'll never be more than a pale imitation of the leader you would have been."

Incredulity slowly filled Michael's eyes. "Is that what you believe? God, you are a bigger fool than I thought!"

But I had no energy for arguing with him further that day, especially on such a hurtful topic. My future was as cold and empty as the dying day and he could have had the entire empire for the asking at that moment. I would have shrugged out of my cloak of responsibility as effortlessly as I shed my human form, and gone off to hide myself in a burrow somewhere until somehow, some day, spring came again.

Michael said, with an odd tight twist to his voice, "Is that what they're saying about me? Is that what you really think? That I would betray the pack, sell out its future for my own selfish gain?"

He got to his feet in sudden agitation and paced a few steps away. Abruptly he swung back to me. "I came prepared to kill for the pack, that day—or die for it. It wasn't just Aggie, don't you know that? I had resigned myself to losing her. What I fought for was the future of those who depended on me. If you had killed me, I wouldn't have blamed you, surely you know that! I was willing to die if that was what it took because *you were the better man.* You were the one who could lead our people into the next century, not me. I was too much a part of the human world and always have been. I've never had your passion for what we are, I've never really understood, the way you do, what it means to be a werewolf. If it had been anyone but you who had challenged me,'' he said, and his eyes were dark and hard with the truth, ''I would be leader today. Believe that.''

Well. I hardly knew what to say, to think. One thing only rang in my mind: *Victoria knew that.* She had seen what I couldn't, believed what I dared not. Michael's words changed everything, and yet... Victoria knew the truth all along.

God, how I needed her. I'm not sure I fully comprehended how much until that moment.

''I'm glad I didn't kill you.''

In a moment he smiled at our private joke, and he said, ''So am I.''

But the amusement faded from his eyes as he continued to look at me, because it was impossible to deny what had finally become so bleakly, desperately clear to me. I had come here expecting to learn something entirely different from Michael—how to cheat, how, perhaps to change the rules to my benefit; how, simply, to love a woman I could never have. What I had discovered was that, for me, there were no compromises. I was not Michael, and the price he had paid for his happiness was far too great.

I said simply, gazing into the dark woods, ''I cannot rule alone. But for me there will never be another queen but Victoria.''

And that was the essence of it, the summation of all my despair. For the love of a woman an empire was lost? Not quite. Only the heart of its ruler. And I was sure this was not the first time in history, human or werewolf, that has happened.

"Your case is very bad, my friend," Michael agreed quietly. "I wish I knew what to tell you."

It was a moment before I could gather the energy to speak. Then I squared my shoulders, lifted my head and got to my feet. I said, "You've already told me what I needed to know."

And then I hesitated. So much lay between us: bad blood, hard words, kinship and rivalry and respect and resentment. Yet in spite of all that, or perhaps because of it, we were bound in brotherhood to each other.

"Michael," I said, "I don't know if it needs to be said…"

"It doesn't," he assured me.

He lifted his arm to me, and we embraced, sure and hard. I felt better for it.

"Stay the night," he said, clapping his hand on my shoulder as we walked back down the path. "Have a meal with us, and we'll run together, or talk, or you can be alone and rest if you like. You can have the little house where Aggie's office is all to yourself."

I wanted to, and the fact that I did surprised me. But already I was shaking my head. "And what will your wife think of that?"

"She's already set a place for you at the table."

I gave a small humorless sniff of laughter. "Unlikely. She doesn't like me, you know."

"But she likes *me*," Michael assured me. "And that's the most peculiar thing about being mated. These things are simply…understood."

And that kind of empathy, I realized with a slow and distant sorrow, was something I would never know, not in all my life.

I couldn't go back to Montreal, not yet. I couldn't face the pain that waited for me there.

"I'd like to run with you again, Michael. Who knows when we'll get the chance to do so again. And there are some other things I'd like to talk to you about, it's true. If you're sure your wife won't mind."

In response, he grinned and looped his arm playfully around my neck, as we had done when we were pups. We walked back to the house together, where Aggie had, indeed, set a place for me at her supper table.

CHAPTER TWELVE

Victoria

How to explain what his coming to me meant? How it made me feel, what it made me think, what it did to my poor, battered heart? The heights of ecstasy, yes, born on the hope that he cared enough to say the things he had said and do the things he had done...and the depths of despair that can only be known by a woman who is desperately, hopelessly in love with the only man in the world she can never have.

Love? It is a pale word, so carelessly bandied about by humans, that has little to do with what I felt for Noel, with what any werewolf feels for the one to whom she or he is destined. I would have given my life for him, yes, but I would have done that before I had ever come to know him, even when he was no more to me than a nebulous ideal of masculine perfection. Now he owned my soul.

This was a difficult thing for me to even acknowledge, much less admit. What had I to do with love? What right did I have to love any werewolf, much less the heir designé of all our people? To fantasize was one thing, to worship from afar quite acceptable, even to share the pleasures he offered...but love? This was a grand and powerful thing, this was beyond anything I had ever prepared for. I was terrified.

There was no hope for it, I knew that. I could never

meet Noel on his own terms, never give him the natural and loving relationship that is the due of any werewolf, the offspring that would be the inevitable, joyous result of such a union. I couldn't even share with him the full understanding of what it meant to be a werewolf.

It wasn't that I didn't want these things. God, how I wanted them. But could I change the way the world turned, the moon, the stars, the coming of the seasons? No more than I could change what I was. I would give him all I had, but all I had would never be enough.

In three weeks he would belong to another, and I would not try to hold on to what I had never had.

In the meantime, there was one thing I could do for him, the only thing really, I had ever known how to do. I could give him my mind, my labor, my dedication. Work. It was my refuge, my salvation. And this time, perhaps, it was the most important gift I would ever give.

I beckoned Sara to follow me as soon as I got off the elevator that morning, and led the way to Noel's office—the only place in the building from which I was certain I could not be overheard. I closed the door on Noel's secretary's outraged look and said to Sara, "I need a log of the e-mail that's been sent out of this office since September of last year. Can I get that?"

Her eyes grew round. "*All* of it?"

"No, just what Greg Stillman sent. Is it possible?"

Sara, bless her, knew I was asking her to do something underhanded, an invasion of privacy at best and illegal at worst. But she never questioned me. She must have known I wouldn't have asked if it wasn't terribly important, and she was right.

She said, still a little skeptical, "Well, that would shorten the list a little. But it would take days—"

"Not every message he sent—just the ones under his personal code."

Her expression cleared. "Ah," she said. "Now *that* I can do."

"Good." I gave a short nod of my head. "I need a list, sorted by destination, as soon as you can get it to me. Get whatever help you need but, Sara, this is top secret."

She nodded, her eyes sparkling. "I gathered that. I hope you fry his butt."

"What?"

"Fire him," she clarified. "He's a pompous bastard and no one likes him."

"Well," I speculated, "I don't know about firing him. But we might just get him transferred to the jungles of East Africa."

She thought about that for a moment. "Fair enough. Anything else?"

"Yes. Is there any way I can read the contents of those messages?"

Now she looked worried. "Oh, gee, Victoria, I don't think so. I mean, that's the point of having network security, isn't it? There may be a way, but it's nothing I would know about, nor would anyone in this building, I would think."

I had been afraid of that.

I crossed my arms over my chest, biting down on my thumbnail. "It's got to be on his computer somewhere," I mused out loud. "If only I had his password."

Sara looked surprised. "You have Stillman's computer?"

I nodded.

Her eyes widened in incredulity and amusement. "Then you have his password, dope! Push F4 on the keyboard. It's a kind of shorthand all the executives use because

they don't want to go to the trouble of typing out their
password every time they enter a program. I can't believe
you didn't know that!''

I stared at her. Could it be that simple? "How would *I*
know what executives do?" I demanded, but already I
was flying out the door, back to my own office, and Sara
was at my heels.

It was that simple. He hadn't disabled the electronic
shortcut; he hadn't changed his code. Why should he? No
one but humans—secretaries, at that—knew about the
shortcut, and no one but I had access to his computer.
Why should he be afraid of us?

And that was how I, the lowliest member of the pack,
ignored, passed over, laughed at and disdained, a woman
acting only for the sake of love, came to discover not only
the identity of the Clare de Lune traitor, but the real secret
of Moonsong.

At three o'clock the next afternoon I was pacing tensely
in the small airport waiting room that was reserved for
arrivals and departures via private plane. Lest you ever
think security for our heir designé is lax, I should point
out that it took far more effort to get this far than I ever
should have thought, and even now the bodyguards did
not take their eyes off me, this despite the fact that they
knew perfectly well who I was and that my business with
him was legitimate. If they hadn't known that, I doubt
very much they would have even let me in the car.

I was calm. I kept telling myself that over and over like
a mantra, and it eventually became more true than not. As
I've said, I tend to retreat in the face of strong emotion,
to grow quieter and more in control, but never had I required more self-discipline to put the technique into prac-
tice than now.

But then again, I wasn't sure I had ever felt quite so strongly about anything before.

I knew when Noel's plane was landing because one of the bodyguards spoke into his radio and the two of them moved into position flanking the waiting-room door. But I knew when Noel himself was approaching because I felt him, like a storm on the wind or the rising of the sun; I felt it in my pulse, in my skin, in the deep aching core of me. *Noel.* His scent, his footsteps, the rustle of his clothing, the sound of his lungs filling with air, the power of his heartbeat—all of it called to me, twisted inside me, caught my breath and snatched it away.

But I was calm. I still had a job to do, and to be otherwise would be counterproductive.

He came through the door with a gust of cold air and a few dry snowflakes. He was wearing an artfully scarred leather bomber jacket and a white silk shirt, pleated dark slacks. His hair was combed by the wind and dotted with melting snow. He carried nothing in his hand but a cellular phone, on which he was just finishing a conversation as he came in. He was not surprised to see me—they would have radioed him I was waiting, of course—but the pleasure that leaped in his eyes when he saw me was almost my undoing.

He folded the phone and handed it to his driver without glancing at him, coming straight to me. He was smiling. "Ms. St. Clare. You didn't have to trouble yourself."

He reached for my hands but I stepped away. He thought it was because I was shy in front of the guards.

"Everything went well in Seattle?"

"Yes, actually. I don't think we have any cause for concern from that quarter."

"Michael is prospering?"

"More or less. It was good to see him."

And so it went, neutral conversation passed back and forth between us for the sake of the guards until we reached the car. It was, fortunately, a short walk.

I settled in the seat opposite Noel in the back of the big limo and the bodyguards took the second car as they always did. Noel activated the privacy screen and the white noise and then before I knew what he was doing, he took both my cold hands in his, holding them still, and leaned forward as though to kiss me. Naturally, I couldn't stop him. But I stiffened, and he didn't kiss me. Instead, he put his face close to my neck and inhaled my scent. Anxiety, distress, excitement, anger, hurt, fear, sorrow, need…it was all there. And when he sat back, his expression was grave.

"What is it?" he demanded quietly.

I had to pull my hands away to extract the papers I carried for him from my big purse. And I dropped my eyes because he knew too much already, and because if I continued to look at him, my calm would break down and I must not allow that, not now.

He looked at the papers I had given him while I explained, still in a very composed businesslike tone, "As you can see, Stillman has been carrying on a very interesting correspondence with Castle St. Clare over the past month. It's all there—every meeting you called, every word you said, my initial design graphics, our magazine mock-ups, the proposal for a television campaign I haven't even showed you yet—everything that has ever taken place in this office regarding Moonsong. As you pointed out before, there's nothing specifically wrong with that. After all, he's a department head reporting in, and if you can't trust headquarters about a top-secret product like Moonsong, then who can you trust? But on the next page, you'll see Greg Stillman was definitely responsible for that press leak about Moonsong."

He turned the page as I added, "And his orders came from Castle St. Clare."

Noel lifted eyes to me that were sharp with disbelief, and then turned his gaze back to the paper. I actually thought I saw color drain from his face as he studied it, reading the words I had transcribed there not once but several times, as though to make certain there was no mistake.

Finally he looked up at me. His face was grim. "So," he said. "I was right. Someone is trying to sabotage me. Do we know who this correspondence has been with?"

I shook my head. "Only that the security code is from someone high up at Castle St. Clare, too high for me to know. I thought you might have access to the codes."

"Yes," he muttered, and dropped his eyes again to the paper in his hand. "I probably do. Damn. I never wanted to believe this. I never expected it, not really."

The distress that backed his words, and the way the truth seemed to age him in a matter of minutes, tugged at me, wrenching my heart. I refused to notice.

I said, "I couldn't find anything on Tango or Cobalt, or any of the other lost formulas. I might be able to if I had more time, or it may be too late. The trail may be cold."

With careful deliberate movements, he folded the evidence I had given him, and tucked it into his pocket. "This is enough for now. Thank you, Victoria." He added quietly, "You did a good job."

"I'm glad you think so," I responded, "because I quit."

His eyes jerked up to me. *"What?"*

"My resignation is on your desk. There's no place for

me at Clare de Lune, I've finally come to understand that. I spoke with Jason and he assures me the job offer was the one thing about him that was sincere, but I don't know that I'll take it. If not the Gauge Group, then some other human firm.'' When I started speaking, my tone was matter-of-fact, my expression composed. Now I started to feel a little shaky, and had to clench my hands tightly in my lap to finish. ''If Michael St. Clare can do it, so can I.''

Noel looked at me with eyes that were so stunned, so weary and bleak and disbelieving, that I had to shift my own gaze from his. In a moment he closed his eyes, rubbing the bridge of his nose with his thumb and forefinger as though the action might clear his vision, and he muttered, ''God. This is a nightmare.''

Then he looked back at me, and he said flatly, ''This is absurd. I don't accept your resignation.'' He pushed a button on the console and spoke to the driver. ''Forget the office. Take me to Ms. St. Clare's apartment. And get us out of this damn traffic.''

My hands tightened another fraction, my grip so hard now that it hurt. I said, ''You can accept it or not, Noel, but it's the truth. I—if it's any comfort, until I met you, I didn't have enough self-respect to do this.'' The catch in my voice was unexpected. It unnerved me. ''Now— I've come too far and learned too much to go back to the way things were. I deserve better.''

A line appeared between his eyebrows, and he leaned forward a little, closer to me. His gaze was intent and piercing with an almost physical impact. With the greatest of efforts, I restrained myself from shrinking back.

''Victoria, what's wrong with you?'' he demanded in a low tone. ''What has happened?''

My nostrils flared with a long slow breath which I intended to be calming. Instead, it brought me his scent—

his power, his compassion, his confusion, his strength. It made my chest hurt. But I had to do this.

I said, "Tell me something." I met his eyes. I *made* myself meet his eyes. "If I were a normal werewolf...if I were a real woman..." God, it was so hard. Why hadn't I expected it to be this hard? "Would you want to mate with me?"

Something leaped in his eyes—a flare of hope, of affirmation, of question. He made as though to reach for me, but this time I did shrink back. "Don't touch me!" I gasped.

He withdrew slowly. His carriage was careful and still, his eyes alert as they flickered over my face and body— alert and concerned. "You're trembling," he said. "What's wrong? Are you ill?"

Trembling? I was coming apart inside, fiber by fiber, thread by thread. My nails left tiny stinging depressions in my skin with the effort it took to hold myself together.

"Please," I said stiffly. "Answer the question."

He released a long warm breath. "You know the answer to that, Victoria," he said. "God help us both, you know. You're the only werewolf I could ever want for a mate."

How I hated him for that—and loved him, and hated myself for loving him, because it was not something I could just turn off no matter what he had done, no matter what he was.

"And if there were a way...a way I could become normal, you would want it for me, wouldn't you? You'd tell me about it?"

"You're as white as a sheet," he said. "I'm stopping the car."

He started to reach for the intercom button but I said, "You're a chemist, Noel. Tell me about kapolin."

He looked at me for a moment as though he was concerned about my sanity, but his hand left the intercom button. "It's a pheromone specific to werewolves," he said. "Some researchers think it may be one of the things that triggers the Change but—"

And he broke off, understanding suddenly dawning on his face.

"It's also the prime ingredient in Moonsong, isn't it, Noel?"

"God, Victoria, how did you—"

I was shaking now, uncontrollably, even my breath coming in ragged little spurts that I had to fight to control. I thrust my hand into my purse and pulled out another paper, the final one. "This is how." My voice was low and cold and I was proud of it; so proud that I barely noticed his reaction as he snatched the paper from my hand.

"It's the product description for Moonsong," I told him unnecessarily. There was a burning behind my eyes and in my chest and it hurt so badly it was all I could do to keep my voice steady, to pronounce the words intelligibly. I wanted to cry but I couldn't cry, not for this, not for him, not now. "The classified version, the one you wrote—the one you wouldn't tell me about."

His voice was a little hoarse, and he didn't raise his eyes from the paper. "You got this off of Stillman's computer? My God, then he knows—"

"*I* know, Noel!" I cried, and the careful bonds of restraint began to fray and break away. "That's what should concern you now—*I* know that you used a werewolf pheromone in a perfume you intend to market to humans! That's illegal and immoral and beyond anything I ever expected of you! God, I believed you, I trusted you, I *worshiped* you…"

Hot salty moisture started to leak from my eyes and I swiped at it with my hand but it wouldn't go away. I was aching inside, broken and tormented, and it took more strength than I had ever known I possessed to continue to drag in breath, to continue to say the words that I knew he had to hear—no, that I *had* to say.

"I know that should be enough to make me hate you," I said thickly, pushing again at the tears that wet my face. "But the worst part is—that's not the worst part! You lied to me. I thought, God, don't you know I wouldn't have cared if all you wanted me for was pleasure? It would have been enough for me! But you made me think you cared for me, that you cared what *happened* to me, and all the time you had the pheromone that could make me normal—you told me, damn you, you told me you had it in its undistilled form and you told me what it could do but you wouldn't tell me what it was, would you? I of all people could never know what the real ingredient in Moonsong was!"

He said, watching me with an odd and careful look on his face, "It's just a theory about kapolin. No one knows for sure—"

"But you could have told me!" I cried. "You could have let me decide for myself, let me try it at least! But you were too concerned with protecting your own illegal research, with proving you were worthy of the job by turning the industry upside down with your revolutionary new product—"

"Is that what you think?" he said hoarsely.

"And all the time you were just using me, mocking me and laughing at me just like everyone else has done all my life—"

"Victoria, stop it! Listen to me." He leaned across the seat and caught my hands in his. I struggled to pull away, but he held firm. He lifted eyes to me that were dark with alarm. "Your skin is on fire," he whispered. He pressed a hand to my wet, hot face, but I slapped it away.

"Leave me alone! Don't touch me, I don't want your hands on me ever again!"

Noel pressed the intercom button. He spoke quietly but his voice seemed suddenly so magnified to me, it hurt my ears. "Find a place to pull over," he told the driver urgently. "Ms. St. Clare is ill. And release the windows back here. We need some air."

He turned back to me. Once again he tried to touch my face but once again I jerked away. Didn't he know how hard this was for me, how desperately I wanted to believe in him, how badly I was hurting now? Hadn't he done enough damage? Why couldn't he just leave me alone?

The back window came down and a rush of icy air whipped my face. I turned toward it gratefully, starving for its healing touch on my scalded skin. I clamped my arms around my waist, holding myself tightly, trying to stop the pain and managing, with the very greatest of efforts, to almost control the hiccuping little sobs that stole my breath.

I said, my voice shaking but otherwise coherent, "Do you know the worst part? Shall I tell you my final humiliation?" And I looked back at him, the tears now dried by the cold wind. "Even now…if you were to offer it to me, if you were to let me try—I'd forgive you everything. That's how badly I want to be with you, even now."

And that was how low I had sunk, my dignity gone, my integrity sacrificed, all for the love of a man who had betrayed me once and would no doubt do so again. But I didn't care. In spite of it all, I loved him still. *That* was the essence of my pain.

His face grew dark with sorrow, his gaze gentle and

ntense. He put his hand behind my neck, holding it
gently, and this time I let him. He said, "Victoria, I have
o tell you something. Take a breath, try to listen."

I turned my face away, because the tenderness in his
voice was destroying me. His fingers tightened on my
neck, making me look back at him.

"Victoria, listen to me," he said slowly, distinctly.
"There is no Moonsong. I made it up. Do you understand
me? *There is no Moonsong.*"

It seemed to take forever before the significance of his
words sank in. I simply stared at him, mesmerized by the
deep dark green of his eyes, the tight grim lines around
his mouth, the sharp angle of his jaw...the firm pressure
of his hand on my neck, the strength of his fingers, the
brush of his breath and the slow hard beating of his heart.
When finally I understood what he was saying, I thought,
*t's over. He's gone, he'll never be mine, the one chance
I had and it's gone, it's over...*

He was saying, "The whole thing, the product descrip-
ion, the campaign, the pheromone, everything—it was a
hoax, a trap designed to catch our traitor, that's all."

And I was thinking, *Everything, from the beginning, a
ie...*

Oh, I know I should have been glad, I should have been
relieved, and if I had been functioning with even a frac-
ion of my customary logic I would have reacted completely differently. But in the past twenty-four hours I had
been assaulted with more extremes of passion than I had
ever known in my life, the heights of ecstasy and the
depths of despair, hope and betrayal, love and loss. Every
thought I'd ever had was tangled and blurred, labored and
twisted. Shock left me feeling light-headed and strange,
hurt and hopelessness burned in my belly like backed-up
tears, too hot for the weeping.

I whispered, "No."

"Victoria, I'm sorry. I never meant—"

And I said, louder, "No!" I tore away from his grip, wild, fearsome fury rising in me, a pain born of loneliness and need and hopes crushed and love denied. I couldn't look at him without knowing what I'd lost, I couldn't hear his voice without the pain of it stabbing through my heart. "No, you're lying, just like you've always lied, and I don't want to hear any more, I won't listen, I won't!"

My breath was coming so quickly and so shallowly that it frightened me. My hand went to my throat and I felt the fast hard beating of the artery there, the pounding of blood in my head that felt as though it was going to explode. Noel's face grew blurred before me, then sharply in focus, so close that I gasped and shrank back from him.

"Victoria, you don't really think I'd do that to you, do you? You can't believe that!"

I cried, "I don't know what to believe!" I pressed my hands to my temples, hard, trying to blot out a sudden throbbing pain. "I only know—I only know that I love you and I'm insane for loving you because there's no chance for us. I always knew that but—but I never expected it to matter and it doesn't, does it? Because there's no chance for us, none at all, ever!"

"Victoria…"

I cried again, "No!" as though the sound of his voice hurt me, and it did; it pelted my skin like small burning stones, and I bent over double with the pain of it, trying not to sob out loud, holding my head.

"Victoria, for God's sake!"

He reached for me but I couldn't bear his touch, couldn't bear the ache that it created inside me when I was already in agony. With a cry, I flung myself at the door, struggling with the door handle.

"Victoria, don't!" he shouted.

I flung out an arm to ward him off; he ducked my blow but parallel slashes appeared in the upholstery overhead. I stared at them in horror, gasping for breath, choking on terror. Fever burned my skin, blurred my vision, twisted in my stomach. I struggled with the door handle, sobbing.

Noel hit the intercom button, shouting, "Stop the car!" He grabbed my shoulders but I screamed at him, twisting away, tearing at the door handle and gasping for air, dying for it.

Suddenly the door fell open and I tumbled out. I hit the ground hard and a stabbing pain went through my hands and knees and sky and earth whirled in a sickening blur; I thought I was going to be sick.

Noel knelt beside me, holding my shoulders. I could hear his breath roaring in my ears, the rhythm of his heart pulling at mine and it hurt. His voice was breathless but loud, something between a whisper and a roar in my ears. "It's all right, love, I'm here. I can help you…"

But a sudden panic ripped through me, an intense, burning need for something I could never have, a hunger like no hunger I had ever known before. I tore myself from his grip, I stumbled to my feet and I ran; I didn't know why. I lost my shoes and the hard cold ground cut my feet, icy wind bit into my lungs.

I was in some kind of field; the highway sounded like a distant ocean to my ears and the sound of my footsteps breaking through crusty snow, crushing brown grasses and small twigs, was like a series of smothered explosions, each one striking my eardrums with shattering force. The wind was arctic but my skin was on fire, I could hardly breathe for the pain of it. I was wearing a thick cable-knit sweater and a blazer over jeans; I tore off the blazer but it wasn't enough; still I was burning up. Gasping for

breath, I clawed at the neck of the sweater, just to loosen
it, just so I could breathe, and the sweater came apart in
my hands. Cold air on my skin. Terror rising to choke
me. I couldn't run anymore. I caught myself against a tree,
then sank to the ground sobbing, afraid I would die with
the pain that was gnawing at me inside, the need I didn't
know how to meet.

I was aware of Noel standing beside the car, watching
me with a kind of helplessness and despair. And then I
was aware of Noel beside me, and it was like magic, he
was so fast, he was so strong. He hauled me to my feet,
me in my tattered sweater and tear-stained face, so
gripped by pain that I could hardly stand straight. He held
my shoulders with a bruising ferocity and he said urgently, "Don't fight it, Victoria, don't!"

And I cried, struggling against him, "I can't! It hurts!"

"It hurts because you're fighting it! Let go!"

But his closeness only made it worse, his touch only
intensified the pain, something about his scent drove
shafts of agonized longing through me and I sobbed out
loud with the intensity of it. "Oh, God, let me go! Please,
I'm so scared!"

"Don't be scared, I'm here, I'll protect you." And now
his mouth was on me, on my face and my neck and my
breasts. He held me tightly and I couldn't break free; he
was so strong, so incredibly strong. "It's all right, Victoria. Let it happen, I'm here. I won't let it hurt, I'll take
care of you—"

And I sobbed, struggling to break free, "No, oh, Noel,
help me, please—"

"I'm trying, love, I'm trying to help you—"

"God, make it stop!"

"No!"

He caught my head hard between his hands and he

covered my mouth with his, forcing his heat and his taste into me, focusing my senses on him and him alone. I felt it rising inside me, that fierce aching need in my womb, the fire in my belly, and it was a wondrous thing, a terrifying, singular and miraculous thing that had at its center one word, one entity, one *raison d'être*: Noel, just Noel.

I grasped him, I drank of him, I clung to him. He tore his mouth from mine and grasped my hand, holding it tight, thrusting it beneath his shirt and against the hard, tight skin that covered his heart. He whispered against my ear, hot and urgent, "Feel my heartbeat, Victoria. Take my strength. Take me inside you. Take me..."

And then he was stripping off my clothes, holding me close, holding me helpless. Already the enchantment had begun to overtake me, his strength and my power blending together and holding me enthralled. His hands caressed my human body, his teeth pressed into my human flesh, until the sensory stimulation became too much to bear, the need swelled beyond the capacity for my fragile form to endure. I broke from him, but not away from him. I cried out for him, but the voice was not my own. Already I was caught in the vortex, control was slipping beyond my grasp. Colors and light and whirling sensation like none I had ever imagined had me in their grip and I couldn't fight it, didn't want to fight it. The last thing I heard with my human ears was Noel's voice: "I love you, Victoria! Come to me!"

I surrendered myself to my nature, and he was waiting for me on the other side.

CHAPTER THIRTEEN

Noel

Shall I describe to you the miracle that happened then, the divine sorcery that caught us up, the magic we created between us and let loose upon the world? I think not. Even if I had the words, which I do not, there are certain things that are sacred between werewolves and to speak of them, even in reverence, is both undignified and blasphemous.

I will tell you this. She was a beautiful wolf. Sleek and jet black with diamond-bright eyes that beckoned me like a siren's call. Could I stop myself from answering that call, from seizing her and claiming the union that was ours by destiny and had been denied us too long? No more than I could stop the wind from blowing or the sun from setting, no more than I could stop my next breath.

And this, then, is the magic of the union of two werewolves, the coming together of not just bodies but souls. This is what humans strive for in their own sad way for all of their short shallow lives but can never know. This is what is called love.

I became Victoria, and she became me. Our thoughts, our experiences, our memories and our essences blended, became so entangled with each other that for a long time after we were separate again, it was difficult to tell what memory belonged to which of us, which feeling was hers and which mine. I knew her loneliness, the hurt and humiliation that had been inflicted upon her by others of our kind and it was a sad and bitter thing, almost more than I could bear. But I also knew the strength that had enabled her to endure, the indomitable spirit that I had so come to admire, her humor, her optimism, her tenderness, her unique view of the world and all that was in it; I knew all of this and I took it inside me.

She knew my most secret fears, my most private needs, for this was part of the sharing, too. She knew things grand and small about me, thoughts and worries, plots and schemes; she knew motives that were pure and those that were not quite so noble. She knew the truth, all the truth, and in all my life she would be the only one who would ever know. Just as I would take her secrets, and only hers, deep into my heart and cherish them forever.

You see now why werewolves take the matter of mating so very seriously.

The moon had long since set before we changed back into our human forms. It was too soon for both of us, but Victoria was young in this way and inexperienced, and there were dangers in staying too long in wolf form the first time. I wrapped her in my leather jacket, for she was too weak to maintain a body temperature high enough to protect her against the elements in human form, and we found a bed of straw and leaves deep in an evergreen tunnel where we lay down together. My own body heat was plentiful, and we were warm in our nakedness as we lay entwined together, stroking each other and murmuring to each other, but mostly just lying silent, wrapped in the essence of each other throughout the short remaining hours of the night.

As the first soft rays of the sun began to creep into the security of our little cave, she tightened her arms around me and pressed her face into my shoulder. "Daylight," she murmured. "It feels so strange."

I brushed back her tangled hair with my hands, and lifted her face so that I could kiss it. Shall I tell you how beautiful she looked to me, my wild and delicate wolf, my love, my mate, my wife? Or perhaps it goes without saying. Only that my heart swelled with such emotion, simply looking at her, that for a time it was difficult to speak.

"I thought I would never know this," I whispered, and I pressed my lips for one intense and rapturous moment against her forehead. "To think, I might never have known this…"

She stretched her arms around my neck, yearning against me, sleek young muscles curving around mine, molding themselves to me. Satin skin, soft shapes, intoxicating scents…I could have stayed like that forever, just holding her, just touching her.

She whispered, "I want…"

I knew what she wanted, my eager young wolf who had only just begun to explore the world that was her legacy. That she would do so with me at her side now and every day for the rest of her life filled me with more delight than I can tell. But this time, regretfully, I silenced her lips with a kiss.

"It's too soon," I told her. "We won't be able to change again for several more hours. And we have to eat."

"I am hungry," she admitted.

I chuckled and once more secured the jacket around her shoulders, settling her against my chest and the warmth I could provide. "I was wondering when you would notice."

Merely changing from one form to another uses up an astonishing amount of calories, and as for the other activities we had pursued that night…suffice it to say, we were both in deep energy deficit. I myself was ravenous. We would start to grow light-headed if we didn't eat soon. But I wasn't quite ready to leave our little honeymoon suite, to bring our private miracle out into the world, even if the only part of the world we need face, at least for the moment, was the driver, who had waited so faithfully with the car throughout the night.

She whispered, deep in awe, "Noel, I never knew, I never could imagine...there is so much more to this world than I ever perceived with my human senses, so much more to love about you than I could even begin to dream—and, oh, I loved you desperately before! But this...this is so powerful, so inexpressible. Words are such clumsy things, aren't they? I keep thinking I'm going to trip over them."

I laughed softly, hugging her, adoring her. "You make my heart sing," I told her, and it was enough. She knew the rest.

But then she looked up at me, a shadow of anxiety deepening her pale wide eyes as she said, "What will become of us now?"

I smiled at her, absently beginning to comb the leaves and twigs from her hair with my fingers. "I think perhaps the South Pacific," I said, "for a month or maybe two. Not Fiji, the beaches are far too crowded there. But we have a private island, did you know that? We can run in the dark of the moon or the full light of day, and there is so much I have to teach you, my love, so much you have yet to see. And I'll be beside you every minute, seeing it all again for the first time through your eyes."

She threaded her fingers through my hair, caressing my face. I loved the sensation. She said with gentle indulgence, "And who will be running the empire while we run on the beaches of your private island?"

I knew what she meant. She knew now the full basis
of my fears about Greg Stillman and his connection with
Castle St. Clare. No one had access to my mock product
description on Moonsong except Sebastian St. Clare himself, who had had to approve every phase of the plan
before it was put into action. If Stillman had a copy, the
only person who could have given it to him was Sebastian
St. Clare.

That meant either that my suspicions about Sebastian's
intentions to sabotage me on this project were correct, or
that our traitor was Sebastian St. Clare himself. Either
way, the situation was grave, for both were crimes against
the pack for which there was no forgiveness—and no re-
course.

I said, "First, we confront Stillman." Ah, how good
that felt. *We.* "He's half cur as it is, it shouldn't be too
hard to get the truth out of him."

"And if the truth is that the plot is deeper than just
him? If it goes all the way back to Castle St. Clare?" This
was difficult for her to say, to even imagine. She was such
a traditionalist. I loved her for it.

"Then," I said, "we will confront Sebastian with it
honorably, and give him a chance to step down quietly.
If he doesn't…"

"War," Victoria whispered.

I nodded gravely. It was not something I could envi-
sion, any more than she could. There had not been a war
among our people in remembered history. But if it
came…

"I don't want to fight, Victoria," I said. "God knows,
it's the last thing I've ever wanted. But for the sake of
the pack…for you…for this…" I placed my hand on her
abdomen, pressing gently against her womb where even

now my seed quickened, and had begun to grow. "For all our children, I will."

She looked at me with eyes that shone with hope and adoration, and she corrected softly, "*We* will."

I looked at her, simply looked at her, for a long and silent moment, drawing courage, giving strength. Then I reached up and removed the St. Clare medallion that I wore around my neck, fastening the chain around the neck of my wife, where it now rightfully belonged.

"We will," I agreed solemnly.

We kissed, and we clung to each other for one last long moment.

Then I helped Victoria to her feet and said, "Come on, let's dress. We have to get back. I can't give you the honeymoon you deserve today, but the sooner this matter is dealt with, the sooner we can start our life together."

She entwined her fingers with mine and replied simply, "We already have."

Simply knowing that gave me the courage to face anything that might lie in store.

We made the driver stop for breakfast, where we gorged ourselves on high-carbohydrate and protein-rich foods. Yes, Victoria even ate meat. She needed it now that she was eating for two.

We could have been wiser, I suppose, knowing what lay ahead of us. But in fairness, neither of us expected trouble so soon. We were soporific with fatigue, drunk on each other and the sugar rush of the huge meal; we walked right into a trap we should have smelled a mile away.

Phillipe met us in the hallway outside his apartment, pacing in an agitated fashion with Victoria's cat in his arms.

She cried, "Socrates!" and ran to Phillipe, snatching the creature from his arms in alarm.

Phillipe poured forth a stream of rapid French that it took my befuddled mind a moment to understand. "Perfectly all right, precious, just frightened to death by those awful men, terrorists, that's what they are, right, kitty? Simply terrorists! I tried to stop them, but what could I do? They were going to break down your door! Then Socrates ran out and it took me forever to catch him, but I knew you'd never forgive me if I let any harm come to your darling pet. I called the police but did the police care? Oh, no, our noble servants of public—"

Victoria cried, "What men?"

And he said, "They're upstairs now, precious, waiting for you. Actually, I don't believe it was you they were interested in so much as your friend—"

"Noel?"

He nodded eagerly. "It was really all terribly exciting—"

Victoria cried, "Noel!"

But I was already bounding up the stairs, propelled by anger and outrage, taking them two at a time and sometimes three. Why, I can't say. Anyone with even a fraction of reasoning power intact would have been running the other way, which was no doubt what Victoria was trying to tell me when she cried out to stop me. But the thought of anyone's breaking into Victoria's apartment and lying in wait for her—or me—infuriated me. Maybe all they had done was frighten her cat, but it was *her* cat.

And so I burst into her apartment ready to knock heads together—and was immediately surrounded by six strong werewolves whose scent and stance told me in no uncertain terms from whence they'd come, and that they meant business. Victoria was right behind me, and I drew her quickly into the circle of my arm when she stopped, with a gasp, at the door.

"What is the meaning of this?" I demanded, but I thought I knew.

One of them spoke, flatly, politely. "You will come with us, please, sir."

"Where?"

"Just come with us. The female, too."

Victoria pressed closer to me, but said nothing. I swept a quick glance around the circle. They didn't touch me, and kept a polite space between us. If I tried to break away, however, I knew they would close that space in an instant.

I said, "Castle St. Clare? Is that where you're taking us?"

Nothing.

Victoria said, "We need to bathe and change our clothes. I'm not going to Alaska looking like this."

I cast her a quick admiring look. It probably wouldn't work, but at least it was an inventive shot.

The spokesperson looked uncertain for a moment, then said, "There are clothes on the plane, miss. And I'm sure you'll be allowed to use the facilities when we arrive at the castle."

So. It was confirmed. I tightened my arm around Victoria. "Are we under arrest?"

The big werewolf replied, blank-faced, "We are authorized to force cooperation if we have to."

Victoria must have felt my tension, because she said smoothly, "That won't be necessary. We're anxious to go, as a matter of fact. Just let me tell my neighbor—"

But as she started to turn toward the door, the circle closed, blocking her exit.

We couldn't change, we couldn't fight, which I suppose

was just as well because I am not at all sure what chance even I would have had against the six of them. We had no choice except to meekly allow them to escort us down the stairs and into the waiting car. As we passed the door, Victoria cried out, "Phillipe! Take care of Socrates!"

And, if you can believe it, the sight of that worried little human's face, peering out from behind his half-opened door with Victoria's cat in his arms, haunted me all the way to Alaska.

They didn't leave us alone for even a moment, to confer or plot between ourselves. Fortunately, it was not necessary. Our minds were synchronous, our confidence in each other unshakable. The clothes on the plane were mine—as of course they would be, since it was my plane—but at least they were clean. En route, Victoria changed into jeans that were too tight and a sweater that was too big for her, and I traded my soiled and wrinkled clothing for fresh ones. We ate again under the silent scrutiny of the guards, and afterward—so strong were we in our trust of each other, so secure in our purpose—Victoria fell asleep in my arms. While she slept, I tugged the gold chain out of the neck of her sweater so that the medallion was displayed on the outside, lest anyone doubt her new status. It gave me peace just to see it resting there between her breasts, and after a time I, too, closed my eyes and slept.

Once inside Castle St. Clare, though, Victoria's nervousness became evident, and I didn't blame her. It was an intimidating place under the best of circumstances, and few people routinely trod the corridors through which we were escorted—the ones that led to the private living quarters of Madame and Monsieur St. Clare.

I didn't like it much myself. Anything could happen to us here in the inner sanctum, and no one need ever know.

I said quietly, "Don't be afraid. We know what we have to do."

She slipped her hand into mine, and tried to smile. "I know," she whispered. "It's just—I've never met him before."

I squeezed her hand, and I wished I could think of something comforting to say…and was glad to know I didn't have to.

They received us in the family sitting room, which disconcerted me. Except for family occasions, even I was never invited here, and I could hardly imagine this was intended to be a social occasion. It was a small—by castle standards, anyway—cozily furnished room, with rugs that were comfortably faded and furniture that bore the marks of pups' teeth. There was a fire on the grate and Earl Grey in the pot, and I was frankly confused.

Grand-mère was doing needlework by the fire, which was another thing that surprised me. I hadn't expected her to be present. Sebastian was reading near the window; he looked up and removed his reading glasses when the guard who had brought us here closed the door behind us. Grand-mère looked up, too, and her face registered surprise—no, astonishment, as she saw the medallion around Victoria's neck.

"Noel, what is this?" she asked, standing slowly.

Sebastian rose, too, and took a step toward Victoria.

Victoria dropped her eyes before his notice and I could sense her preparing to curtsy. I grabbed her elbow hard and kept her upright. My wife bowed her head before no one.

"Perhaps you know Victoria St. Clare. My mate."

Grand-mère exclaimed softly, "Well."

But my eyes were on Sebastian. His only reaction was a slight lift of his eyebrow in acknowledgment.

I said, "I would have liked to have made the announce-
ment in more congenial circumstances."

Sebastian said, "I can't think why you would imagine
these circumstances to be anything less than congenial,
my heir."

The uncertainty was wearing on my nerves, and I was
impatient. "Your thugs broke into Victoria's house and
took us under guard," I said coldly. "They forced us to
come with them against our will. I want to know why."

"Fair enough."

Sebastian accepted the cup of tea Grand-mère brought.
I felt as though I had suddenly wandered onstage during
the third act of a play whose plot made no sense to me.
Victoria's hand in mine was my only anchor to reality.

Sebastian said, "You were brought here because of certain recent unauthorized computer activity in the Montreal
office. Perhaps you can explain it."

I felt the pounding of Victoria's heart, sensed the
warmth go out of her face as she paled. I opened my
mouth to speak but she said, "I can explain it. It was
me."

Sebastian nodded, sipping his tea. "I thought as much.
You used an executive's password to gain access to
e-mail transmissions and certain classified documents?"

"Yes," she said.

Her voice didn't tremble, her gaze didn't waver. I could
have burst with pride.

Sebastian said, "Why?"

I wanted to answer that, to tell him that she had done
it on my orders, but she answered for herself and without
hesitation.

"I did it out of concern for the welfare of the pack, and
loyalty to the pack leader."

God, I loved her. Even Sebastian experienced a flicker

of admiration for her; I saw it in his eyes before he hid it.

He said, "And what did your findings lead you to conclude?"

Now it was my turn to step in. I said, "Greg Stillman has been conducting unauthorized correspondence with someone at Castle St. Clare about Moonsong. He has deliberately released classified information about the project to the press and quite possibly to other industry professionals. We haven't been able to find proof that he was involved in the thefts of the other products but that's only because we haven't had time."

Sebastian nodded thoughtfully, his eyes bold and clear on mine. "So you think Greg Stillman is our traitor?"

"No, sir." A ripple of tension went through Victoria, then relaxed. It had to be done, and this was the moment. She knew that. So did I. "Stillman hasn't the brains or the guts. He's only an operative. He's receiving his orders from Castle St. Clare."

"I see." Sebastian sipped his tea, never taking his eyes from me. "Do you have any thoughts on the identity of this traitor within the heart of Castle St. Clare?"

Our hearts were loud, Victoria's and mine. But they beat together, in that perfect, synchronous rhythm I had noticed in Michael and his wife, in Sebastian and Clarice when I listened for it, in others who were mated as we were. The sound was calming to me, empowering. And I thought, *It's worth it all, then, for this. I lived to hear our hearts beating as one, and I have lived long enough.*

The brief, sweet tightening of Victoria's fingers on mine was as sure as an embrace, reflecting my thoughts back to me. I said, looking him straight in the eye, "Yes, I know who the traitor is. It's you, isn't it, Grand-père?"

His gaze was long and hard and unflinching. It hurt, like arrows in my temples, to hold it. But I did.

He said, "I should kill you for that."

And I said, "No. You won't. And I won't kill you, either, not in battle. No one who's done what you have done deserves such an honorable death."

His eyes narrowed. "So. You have solved the puzzle. You're as clever as I credited you, you and your female. But to come here and accuse me, on penalty of treason, of crimes against our people that are punishable by death—this I did not expect from you, Noel. This is a very, very foolish thing to do."

"You have betrayed the pack," Victoria said clearly. "Did you expect us to ignore that?"

"You might have lived longer if you had."

She answered simply, "But not better."

She was a queen for all time.

Sebastian smiled faintly as he looked at me. "So you think it's worth dying for, this pack that was thrust upon you? Half of them don't even like you, you know. They wouldn't give their lives for you."

"They," I replied, "are not required to."

He looked at me for a long and solemn moment. Then he merely nodded thoughtfully, and turned away, sipping his tea.

"Well, now," Grand-mère said pleasantly. "Now that that's settled, come sit down. We have plans to make. How do you take your tea, child? Noel, I have cinnamon bread for you."

I stared at her, experiencing a quick shaft of alarm that she had lost her mind. The stress had been too much, the certainty of her own fate and her husband's betrayal had snapped her psyche.

Then Victoria said softly, "Wait."

I didn't understand. Most of the time my mind is perfectly in sync with Victoria's, one of us can speak the other's thoughts before they are even formed. But that was my first experience with the indisputable fact that females are—for some reason I still cannot satisfactorily explain—more perceptive about certain matters than males. It seems to have something to do with subtle undercurrents of behavior that men are simply unable to read. She was reading those undercurrents now and coming to conclusions that I had not yet begun to perceive.

She left my side unexpectedly, before I could stop her, and opened the door to the corridor. Sebastian didn't try to prevent her. She looked right and left, then closed the door and turned back to me. "No guards," she said.

I could smell her excitement, hear her quickened breathing, and I began to understand—slowly, uncertainly. We should never have been left alone with them. For the threat we represented, we should be dead by now, or at least under guard. What was going on? What was he plotting?

Grand-mère brought Victoria a cup of tea. "It's mostly cream and sugar," she told her, "but you need the energy—and the calcium."

Victoria reached for the cup but I held out a staying hand. Grand-mère looked at me impatiently, and then at her husband. "For heaven's sake, tell them. This is growing tiresome, and we have matters of real consequence to deal with now."

Victoria said, looking straight at Sebastian St. Clare, "It's not you, is it?"

"No," answered our venerated ruler mildly. "But you did well to get this far. I am impressed…and pleased, I must say."

Sebastian St. Clare had said he was pleased…and he'd looked at me when he'd said it.

And finally I understood. "It's no one at all. It was a setup."

Should I have been infuriated? Outraged, insulted, indignant at having been so ruthlessly manipulated, so shamelessly used? You know nothing about werewolves. I admired the master at work. I *was* clever, I knew that. Damn clever. But he had outsmarted me. How could I despise him for that?

Still, I wished I knew why.

"There was a thief," Sebastian went on, going to the tea table to refresh his cup, "but he was dealt with long before you became involved."

Victoria questioned carefully, "Dealt with?"

"A human," replied Sebastian dismissively. "He was fired."

Victoria and I exchanged a relieved look.

"You have the makings of a strong leader, Noel," Sebastian said, squeezing lemon into his tea. "But you needed a chance to prove it, to yourself, and to me. As far as I'm concerned, you passed every test." And he looked at me. "What do you think?"

Again I looked at Victoria. I said, "Someday, sir, I hope to lead the pack as masterfully as you have done. For now…" She smiled at me and I was strong. I met Sebastian's eyes. "Yes. I think I'm well on my way."

"Good," pronounced Grand-mère, beaming at me. She squeezed her husband's arm affectionately. "Now we can take that tour of the Outback we've promised ourselves for so many years, and after that, the Orient. You know how I love Japan, and I never get to spend enough time there." She looked at Grand-père with sudden alertness.

"Perhaps we'll retire there, do you think? Should we make inquiries?"

Once again I felt reality spinning sideways out of control; I had to anchor myself by reaching for Victoria's hand. How good it was to have someone to reach for. How inexpressibly wonderful to know that she would always be there when I reached.

"What about Stillman?" I asked.

Sebastian glanced at me. "I would keep an eye on him, if I were you. His loyalties were far too easy to purchase, his moral code a little too convenient for my taste. I was thinking he might best serve the common good in another capacity."

"Botanicals," I murmured. "East Africa."

Sebastian lifted an approving eyebrow.

"However," I added, "I've been thinking of making some changes in the way we handle the reassignment of executives. I'd like to discuss my ideas with you."

Sebastian said, "I will be happy to listen, of course. But you don't need my approval. The pack is yours now, to govern as you see fit."

The notion was a little overwhelming. It would take some time to adjust.

I said, because I had to know, "What about Victoria? Was she part of your scheme, too?"

"Well, I certainly didn't expect this!" With a blustering motion, he indicated the two of us in our all-too-obvious newly mated state. "But I was interested to know whether you had the perception—the character, if you will—to see past her physical handicap to the sharp mind beneath, and the courage to exploit that potential to the good of the pack. Obviously..." And he cleared his throat a little. "It worked no hardship on either of you."

I grinned at my mate, my beautiful, brilliant love. I

couldn't help it. And she grinned back. We said in unison, "Obviously."

My *grand-mère* drew us both to the table, forcing tea on us, insisting that Victoria drink every drop of her creamy sweet concoction. "I must confess I'm disappointed in you, Noel," she reprimanded me sternly, and much to my surprise. "Victoria should never have been allowed to experience First Change without other females attendant, and at her age, medics. It could have been dangerous, you know. And then to mate the first time—you were raised to be more responsible. Have you no consideration for the tenderness of her condition? No self-restraint or thought of the consequences? She is but a child in these matters, but I expected better of you."

I said, because it was the only defense I could think of, "It wasn't planned."

She looked at me severely for a moment, until I dropped my eyes. Before one's *grand-mère,* even the strongest of werewolves must eventually bow.

Then she smiled, forgiving me, and reached out to pat my knee. "Well, it all ended well, at any rate."

And she looked at Victoria with a shrewd perceptive eye. "I anticipate an autumn whelping. You'll have your lying-in here, of course, and begin in August I think. We must take no chances with the firstborn. But first we must have the mating ceremony..." And she cast a dry look at me. "A bit redundant, in fact, but necessary in principle. We must of course introduce your new bride to the pack. And then, I think, a separate coronation ceremony—perhaps in midsummer. You won't be too far along to appear by then, and it will take at least that much time to make the arrangements..."

With every word Grand-mère spoke, Victoria's eyes grew wider, her anxiety higher. Finally, I took pity on her

and intervened. "Grand-mère," I said, "this is all very
new to Victoria, and we're both tired. Perhaps another
time would be better?"

But Victoria, barely glancing at me, said to Grand-mère
and Grand-père, "You don't mind? That Noel and I...?
That he chose *me?* That I will mother his children and—
and rule beside him? You don't mind?"

The two elders looked at each other in puzzlement and
surprise. Then Sebastian said, "I think it was a fine
choice, myself. Brilliant." And he cast one of those sly,
males-only glances at me and added, "Considering the
circumstances you started with, damn courageous. The
stuff of legends."

Perhaps it was wrong of me, but I felt ten feet tall.

Then Grand-mère added, in all innocence, "Why
should we object, my dear? You are, after all, a St.
Clare."

Once again Victoria and I shared a grin. My heart was
so filled with her, so complete with her happiness, that I
could have taken flight.

I said, pushing the advantage, "Grand-mère, Grand-
père...I was wondering if, before you go to Japan, you
might consider staying on for a month or two. We haven't
had a honeymoon."

"Oh," replied my *grand-mère,* as though it had just
occurred to her. "Of course you haven't. Certainly something that mustn't be overlooked or postponed. Come, my
dear. We have work to do."

To my astonishment, she took Victoria's hands and
lifted her to her feet. "You need the advice and instruction
of other females of your kind to ease the transition
through this difficult time. No doubt it all seems very
strange and overwhelming now, but—"

Victoria looked back at me in helplessness and confusion as Grand-mère started to lead her from the room, and I got to my feet. "Wait. Where are you going?"

"Noel," instructed Grand-mère with an imperious wave of her hand, "go amuse yourself elsewhere. Leave your bride in the hands of women now, where she belongs."

"No," I heard myself saying. I closed the distance between us and gently pulled Victoria from her grip. I couldn't believe I was defying the most powerful female werewolf of our pack, but for Victoria's sake—for another moment in her presence—I did it without thinking. "She belongs in my hands now."

When I saw the gratitude in my beloved's eyes, I knew I had done the right thing.

"Don't be a foolish boy," said Grand-mère. "She is an infant, an innocent in the ways of werewolves, a stranger to her own nature. For her safety and good health, she needs instruction, guidance, protection. You must surrender her to us now. That's the way it is done."

I said, looking into the eyes I would love for the rest of my life, "I will be her teacher. I'll protect her."

I felt my *grand-mère's* shock and disapproval, but it was a distant thing. I put my arm around Victoria's waist and she leaned into me, softness and contentment, wonder and anticipation.

As we left the room, I heard Grand-mère say, "Such impetuosity. Such passion. It can't be good. This isn't the way it's done."

And then Sebastian's voice, mild and amused, "Apparently it is now." Then, more gently, "It's their turn now, Clarice. Let them have it."

Outside the room, alone and dazed, we walked down the empty corridor. Victoria released a long breath. "Thanks for rescuing me," she said.

"I thought we both could use the air."

We stopped then and looked at each other, wonder and disbelief holding us in its grip. We were awakening from a dream we weren't sure was a dream. We had escaped with our lives when we had been prepared to sacrifice everything. None of it had been real. None of it.

None of it except the woman who walked beside me, the love we had found.

She said, "Noel…"

And I said, "I know. It will be a while before I can even put it into words."

Her voice, dazed and soft, reflected my own cautious amazement. "Yes."

Looping our arms together, we started walking again. "I never thought it was him," she said musingly after a moment. "Intellectually, I knew the evidence was there, but I never believed it in my heart."

"I must learn to listen to your heart," I said.

She pressed her cheek to my shoulder in a brief embrace then tilted her head to me, smiling. "And I'll learn to listen to yours. Between us, then, we'll always know the right thing to do."

What a beautiful promise. And all the more so because it was true.

I said, kissing her tenderly, "I know now why no one has ever ruled alone."

I walked with the woman I love through the corridors of my home, the great rooms and long halls, grand staircases and deep balconies. I felt her awe, I saw her wonder. And then, as we came at last to the ground floor and the wide glass doors that opened onto the snow-covered park, she stopped and looked back, and said with only a little concern, "Will we live here now?"

I hesitated. "I'm afraid we must, most of the time.

There are other houses, of course, that we can visit. You can keep your apartment." I smiled. "Maybe we'll buy the whole building, and give it to your friend Phillipe to manage."

But her anxiety didn't entirely dissipate. "What about Socrates?" she inquired.

"The cat?"

She nodded. "What will become of him? Where will he live?"

I hesitated only a moment, then I sighed. "Here, I suppose. He'll live here."

She laughed and flung her arms around my neck, and how could I resist her pleasure, how could I remain invulnerable to her charm? I swept her off her feet and into my arms and carried her, my queen and my love, into the bright light of day.

* * * * *

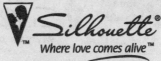

LONE STAR
LSCC
COUNTRY CLUB
EST. 1923

Where Texas society reigns supreme—and appearances are *everything.*

On sale...

June 2002
Stroke of Fortune
Christine Rimmer

July 2002
Texas Rose
Marie Ferrarella

August 2002
The Rebel's Return
Beverly Barton

September 2002
Heartbreaker
Laurie Paige

October 2002
Promised to a Sheik
Carla Cassidy

November 2002
The Quiet Seduction
Dixie Browning

December 2002
An Arranged Marriage
Peggy Moreland

January 2003
The Mercenary
Allison Leigh

February 2003
The Last Bachelor
Judy Christenberry

March 2003
Lone Wolf
Sheri WhiteFeather

April 2003
The Marriage Profile
Metsy Hingle

May 2003
Texas...Now and Forever
Merline Lovelace

Only from

Silhouette®
Where love comes alive™

Available wherever
Silhouette books are sold.

Visit us at www.lonestarcountryclub.com   PSLSCCLIST